ChangelingPress.com

Grizzly/Wolf Duet

Harley Wylde

Grizzly/Wolf Duet

Harley Wylde

ISBN: 978-1-60521-801-4

Publisher:
Changeling Press LLC
315 N. Centre St.
Martinsburg, WV 25404
ChangelingPress.com

Printed in the U.S.A.

Editor: Crystal Esau
Cover Artist: Bryan Keller

The individual stories in this anthology have been previously released in E-Book format.

Table of Contents

Grizzly (Devil's Fury MC 8)

The Beginning

Harley Wylde

May -- I know what everyone sees when they look at him. A rough biker from the wrong side of town. But they don't know John the way I do. He's kind, protective, and there's no one I'd rather be with. Unfortunately, he's keeping me in the friend zone. He's saved me multiple times, but when he finds me being attacked by the town's golden boy, I see the Grizzly his club has named him for... but even at his most vicious I'm not scared of him. I don't care that he's a little older than me, or that people whisper when he walks past. I love him, and I know I'll keep loving him until the day I die.

Grizzly -- She's too sweet, too good. Too perfect. May deserves the best life can offer, a respectable guy. That isn't me. She might see me as some cuddly teddy bear, but there's blood on my hands. I earned the name the Devil's Fury gave me, and I wear it proudly. So I push her away, keep her at arm's length, and make sure she thinks I don't desire her even a little.

It's a lie. Biggest one I've ever told. There's only one thing I want more than my club -- more than my next breath -- and that's May.

Prologue

Grizzly
Summer, 1982

I ran my hand over my cut, proud as hell that I'd earned my patch. As the newest member of the Devil's Fury MC, I should have been at the clubhouse enjoying the party. Instead, I found myself hiding in the shadows by the pond on the outskirts of town. If anyone owned the property, they were long gone. The land had grown wild with weeds. The tall grass around the pond blocked it from view of anyone driving past.

I heard May giggle and a splash. Jealousy ate at me. I had no right to feel any sort of emotion about her at all. She wasn't mine. Never would be. May was a good girl. Sweet. Angelic. Not at all for the likes of me. I'd noticed her in school, even though I'd kept my distance. Until I'd discovered she liked to come swim here. The first time I saw her in her two-piece swimsuit, I'd had to pick my tongue up off the ground. Who'd have thought little May had curves like that? She'd only been fifteen at the time, and I'd had no business looking.

"Stop it, Mike." I heard another splash. "I said no!"

My heartrate kicked up and I crept closer, quietly shifting the tall weeds aside for a better look. The dumbass jock she'd come with seemed to be copping a feel. The way May squirmed and shoved at him, I knew she wasn't just playing around. When she'd told him to stop, she'd meant it. Dickweed didn't seem to understand.

When he tried to work his hand down into her swimsuit bottoms, I knew I had to do something. I wasn't about to let him molest her while I stood idly by. Even if I did belong to a club that didn't exactly walk on the right side of the law, there were lines I'd never cross. Hurting a woman was one of those.

I stepped out of my hiding spot. The moment May saw me, hope sparked in her eyes. Yeah, I wasn't walking away. Not without making sure she was safe.

"I think she said no."

He turned to look at me, a sneer on his lips as he eyed my cut. I knew all about Mike Malone. Star forward for the basketball team. Just the sort of guy May should be with, if he weren't such a douche.

"Let her go, Malone."

"Or what?" he asked.

"Or I'll make you, and then you'll have to run crying home to your mommy. She said she wasn't interested, but you must have too much wax in your ears." I folded my arms. "Or maybe you got hit in the head with one too many basketballs. You should catch those passes with your hands and not your face."

I honestly had no idea how well he played, or what the fuck his position on the team even did. I'd never been into basketball, and I sure as hell hadn't been to any of the games at school.

He backed away from May and made his way toward me. He slogged through the water and onto the shore, slicking his hair back from his face. We were nearly the same height, but I had a bit of muscle on him. And I knew how to fight. Prissy boy here didn't stand a chance.

"You lay one finger on me and my parents will sue your ass."

"And what exactly do you think they'll get? I don't have a house. My bike is a piece of shit. Even I can admit that, but one day it won't be. I don't have a damn thing you'd want, Malone." I held my hand out to May. "Come on, angel. I'll make sure you get home safe."

May hurried out of the pond and grabbed her towel, wrapping it around her. She came straight for me, giving the jock a wide berth. Couldn't blame her. He didn't seem like the type to lose gracefully. Now that he'd decided May should give him what he wanted, he wouldn't back down. Not until he was forced to.

If he kept bothering her, I'd have to pay him a special visit. Make sure he got the message loud and clear. May wasn't for him to play with. Or anyone else for that matter.

"This isn't over," Mike said. "I'll ruin you!"

"You can try." I smirked. "Your parents might be well-off, and maybe this town thinks rainbows shine out your ass, but you don't scare me. You're just a little boy pretending to be a man. Men don't hurt women, numbnuts."

I backed up, keeping my eyes on him until we were far enough away I felt safe turning away. I wouldn't put it past him to try and stab a man in the back. Seemed like the chickenshit sort of thing he'd do. I led May away from the pond and stopped next to my bike. She only had on flip-flops. There was no way she could ride on back like that.

I straddled my bike and motioned for her to come closer. I lifted her, making her squeal, and settled her sidesaddle across my thighs. It wasn't perfect, and I'd have to go really fucking slow, but at least I wouldn't worry about her burning her legs or feet on the pipes. I didn't even give a shit that her suit and towel were soaking the thighs of my jeans and my shirt.

"I live in the Willow Brook Apartments," she said.

"I know." I winked at her. "I make it a point to know where the pretty girls are."

Her cheeks turned pink, but she smiled. I started up my bike and slowly pulled out onto the road. I crept along, not wanting to take any chances with the precious cargo in my lap. When we reached her building, I parked my bike and walked her up to her apartment. I didn't trust Mike not to have followed us and wanted to make sure she got inside and locked the door.

"Thank you," she said. "I don't know how you happened to be in the right place at the right time, but I'm glad you were. I don't think he'd have stopped."

I reached out and traced her nose with my finger. "Anytime, angel. Glad to have been of service. Now, lock up. I'm not leaving until I hear that deadbolt."

She gave me another smile, then shut the door. Once I heard all the locks click into place, I finally pulled myself away. If she'd known why I was there, she wouldn't have been thanking me. She'd probably have been terrified she had a stalker. I'd never hurt May, but it seemed I needed to keep an eye on her. Whether she liked it or not, she'd just gained a bodyguard. No one would put out the light I saw in her. I wouldn't let them.

It just never occurred to me that sweet little May would be such a magnet for trouble, or that she'd need my services several more times.

Chapter One

I flipped my hair out of my face and glanced at the boy lying in bed next to me. My parents were out of town so he'd spent the night. Even though he'd pushed for more, I hadn't given in. Something felt off. We'd been talking for a few months, but Seth got more and more aggressive with each day that passed. It was time to break up with him, but I wasn't sure how. The few bursts of temper I'd witnessed worried me.

I quietly slipped from the bed and grabbed some clothes from the dresser, then went to shower. I'd thought he was different from the others, but I'd been wrong. He'd put on a good show, but his façade was starting to crack. Not trusting him, I locked the door before I undressed. I should have listened. My friends told me he was bad news, even if I'd thought he'd seemed so sweet. If anyone should know better than to believe the lies people told, it was me. My father was a professional liar.

Saturday should mean a fun day for a high school girl like me. Instead, I had to figure out how to ditch the boy in my room. There was a lake party tonight, one I'd been invited to. If Seth was going, I wasn't sure I should. He'd been bad enough last night. Adding in alcohol seemed like a recipe for disaster.

I finished my shower and pulled on my clothes. After braiding my hair and brushing my teeth, I slipped out of the bathroom and tiptoed through the bedroom. My stomach rumbled. I wasn't the greatest cook in the world, but breakfast I could easily handle. When I got to the kitchen, I pulled out eggs, milk, bacon, and the bread.

I'd just started the eggs when a throat cleared behind me and I whirled, spatula in hand. Seth leaned against the doorframe, a smirk gracing his lips. At one time, I'd found him sexy. Even now, the girls in school squealed when he walked by. If they wanted him, they could have him. I'd give them my blessing.

"Nothing prettier than a girl in the kitchen," he said.

I tried hard to hold back the sneer. Right. He'd be the type to want me barefoot in the kitchen. Maybe with the right guy, I wouldn't mind it so much. I'd always wanted kids. A big family. Just not with a guy like Seth. And I sure as hell didn't want to start that family my senior year of high school.

"You should probably head out," I said. "I have some stuff to handle today and a project to work on."

Anger flashed in his eyes as he pushed off and came toward me. "You're kicking me out?"

"Yeah, I am." I lifted my chin, hoping he didn't notice my hands were trembling. If he came after me, I wouldn't be able to defend myself. Not for long. "Besides, I'm meeting a friend for lunch."

"Friend?" Seth pressed in closer. "You don't mean that filthy biker scum, do you?"

"John isn't scum." My hand tightened on the spatula. I knew what everyone thought of him. The boy from the wrong side of town. The troublemaker. The kid who'd already patched into the Devil's Fury MC. I saw a different side of him.

Seth laughed in my face and pressed his lips to mine. I backed up, but he reached out, wrapping his arm around my waist, refusing to let me go. He forced his tongue into my mouth, and I swung as hard as I could, hitting his head with the spatula. It was enough to make him release me. He stumbled back.

"Stupid bitch! Do you know who I am?"

"Yeah. A dick."

He snarled and advanced on me. "I'm Seth Cartwright! My father owns this fucking town, and by association, so do I. Which means I own *you*."

"No one owns me," I said. I backed up until I hit the counter. I could smell the eggs burning, but I didn't dare turn even long enough to shut off the stove.

Seth gripped my hair and shoved me to my knees. "I do. I fucking own you, May, and I'm tired of waiting. You want to run your mouth? Fine. How about I give you a better way to use those lips and tongue?"

I screamed and beat at his legs, thrashed in his grip. I heard a roar like a damn bear and the wood door splintered. One minute, Seth was reaching for the zipper on his pants, and the next he crashed into a wall. I looked up, tears blurring my vision, as John went after him. He landed blow after blow, not stopping until Seth fell to the floor. I stood, my legs barely holding me, as I went to my savior.

I placed a hand on John's arm. "Stop. He's done."

John's chest heaved. Even at nineteen, he was a force to be reckoned with. I couldn't really call him a boy, not at six and a half feet tall and a wall of solid muscle. He'd grown up. Become a man. We'd been friends since last summer, and he'd become my protector. My confidant. My best friend.

"You so much as fucking look at her again and I will end you," John said, then spat on Seth. "I'm getting May out of here. I want you gone. Immediately. Understood?"

Seth groaned but nodded.

John herded me toward my room and shut the door behind us. "Shoes, May. Now."

"You're going to get into trouble. You know his family is powerful. They'll come after you."

He took two steps, closing the distance between us, then reached up and cupped my cheek. His touch was gentle for such a large guy. "May, he was going to rape you. If I'd gotten here any later…"

He took a ragged breath and I wrapped my arms around him. John hugged me, and I felt his heart pounding. Until he'd graduated, he'd gone to our school, but I hadn't taken much notice of him. That changed when he'd saved me this past summer. He seemed to be making a point of it. I didn't know how he kept turning up exactly when I needed him to, but I wouldn't question it. This actually made the fourth time he'd been my knight in shining armor.

I drew back and scanned the leather cut over his shoulders. He'd earned it in the last six months and wore it with pride. I traced the name *Grizzly* stitched on one of the patches. It made me smile, since he did sound a lot like a pissed-off bear when he got angry. John made me feel safe. Cared for. But I'd already made the mistake of trying to get a kiss from him. It hadn't gone well, so I'd backed off, and decided to accept his friendship. I couldn't blame him for not wanting more. I'd heard about the women at the clubhouse. Why would he want an inexperienced virgin like me?

I'd given up all hope after seeing the women one night. I'd been out with friends and we'd driven past the clubhouse. A group of scantily clad women were going in, their hair and makeup done, their nails painted. I'd known then I couldn't ever dare hope to hold his attention, not compared to women like them. Not plain little May.

"Come on, May. Get your shoes and whatever else you need, but take your backpack. We're leaving on my bike and I don't have room for a bunch of crap."

"Okay. Just give me a minute."

He ran his fingers over my cheek, then stepped back. "I'll make sure Seth is gone and turn off the stove."

He left, and I sank onto the edge of the mattress. Why couldn't a guy like him want me? No, I attracted the assholes like Seth instead. I knew John would come back if I didn't hurry. I got up and grabbed an empty backpack from my closet. I put the notes I needed for my project in there, in case I had a chance to work on stuff for school, as well as my favorite paperback. Maybe it was optimistic of me, but I also threw in a change of clothes and a pair of pajamas. The sexiest ones I owned.

I zipped it up and put on my shoes, then hurried from the room. John had shut off the stove and cleaned up the mess. Seth was absent. The front door to my apartment stood open, the frame splintered. I wondered if I should stay here. What if someone stole everything while I was gone?

"I borrowed your phone. I've got a Prospect coming to watch the place," John said, as if he'd read my mind. I glanced at him, and he winked. "Your face is expressive as hell, May. Can't keep any secrets from me."

I hoped he was wrong about that, or it meant he knew exactly how I felt about him. It would hurt too much if he knew I was falling in love with him and still wanted me only as a friend. I didn't think my heart could handle it.

"Come on, angel. We can go to my place for a bit."

"Your place? I thought the clubhouse was off-limits."

He rubbed the back of his neck. "Well, it is, but I thought we could hang out in my room. As long as you're not around the other guys, I don't see it being an issue."

His room. At the clubhouse. Where all those women went to party. Did he take them to his room too? Was that where he... I quickly shut off that train of thought. Even though some part of me wanted to know, I also didn't. It was too painful. And yet my mouth and brain obviously weren't connected.

"Are you taking me to a place where you hook up with the... whatever you call them?" I cringed and couldn't believe I'd just asked him that.

He folded his arms over his chest, making his biceps bulge in a way that had my mouth watering. It was really unfair. He shouldn't look so amazing. Not when he didn't want me the way I wanted him. It sucked.

"Are you asking me if I fuck women in the room where I'm taking you?" he asked.

I hadn't expected him to be quite so direct. My cheeks burned hot. "Y-yes. That's what I'm asking."

His lips twitched, as if he struggled not to smile. "You're so damn cute, May. No, angel. I haven't taken any women to that room."

My shoulders slumped. He hadn't taken anyone *there*, but he'd been with women. He was nineteen. Nearly twenty. Single. And one of the best-looking guys I'd ever seen. I couldn't blame the women for wanting him. With his neatly trimmed beard, the power and cockiness he exuded, I didn't doubt he had girls and women falling at his feet. I could never compete.

I heard his heavy tread, then his boots came into view. He tipped my chin up. "May, what's going on?"

"Nothing." I forced a smile. "It's fine. Thanks for stopping Seth earlier. I'd hate for my first time to --"

His grip on my chin tightened and my gaze flashed to his. "Your *first* time?"

"Y-yeah. I thought you knew. Wasn't that why you only wanted to be friends?" My cheeks burned hotter. "I mean, unless you're just not attracted to me at all, which I guess I can understand considering the women you're around all the time. They're more... curvy."

The day my friends had driven past, I eagerly looked out the window. Secretly, I'd hoped for a peek at John. Instead, I'd felt like my heart was breaking even more because I knew I'd never be as sexy as those women.

"May."

I snapped my mouth shut.

"You're a fucking idiot."

My eyes went wide. He said *what*? "Excuse me?"

"An idiot. You think I pushed you away because I don't want you? Jesus. I want you *too* much, angel. Good girl like you deserves so much better than me."

"John, you've saved me several times now. You're not some monster. I know what the people around here say about you and your club, but I know different. You'd never hurt someone, unless they deserved it."

He shook his head. "You're something else. You know that? One of a kind."

"Am I still invited to go with you? Now that I've embarrassed myself. Again."

"You have no reason to be embarrassed. You're beautiful, May. Smart. Sweet." He rubbed his thumb across my lip. "Innocent."

"I've made out with guys before. Just because I'm a virgin doesn't mean I haven't done anything at all."

He growled and his eyes darkened. "Fair warning, angel. You won't be doing those things anymore. Not unless it's with me. Another guy so much as puts his hands on you, and I'll tear him apart."

I smiled and reached up to run my fingers over his beard. "You say the sweetest things."

He snorted and took my hand. "Come on. Time to go. Just remember, at the compound, you call me Grizzly."

I followed him out my busted front door. He gave a nod to a man in the hall wearing a cut like his, except it said *Prospect* on it. If I'd have known babbling about my insecurities where he was concerned would get me anywhere, I'd have done it long ago. Since last summer, John was the only one I'd wanted.

Chapter Two

Grizzly

Holy hell! My little May was a virgin? I'd known she was too good, too sweet for a bastard like me. My dad was an abusive asshole, and my mother was just a junkie looking for her next fix. I hadn't wanted the filth in my life to touch May, but it seemed she attracted her own monsters. If being with me kept her safe from guys like Seth, then I wasn't going to let her out of my sight.

May pressed against my back, her hands clutched at my waist. Having her plastered to me as my bike roared through town felt more right than anything else in my life. I'd seen the way she reacted when she thought I was fucking the girls at the club. I may have gotten my dick wet a time or two -- or more, but since saving May, she'd been the one on my mind. The disappointment I'd seen in her eyes had nearly gutted me.

I'd pushed her away, thinking it was for her own good, but I was damn well lying to myself and knew it. I wanted her, and it seemed she wanted me too. I'd tried to tell myself she had a crush and it would pass, but maybe I was wrong. If I thought her parents wouldn't flip the fuck out, I'd claim her here and now. Didn't matter to me she was only seventeen and still in high school. There was only two years between us.

I pulled up to the clubhouse and parked my bike at the end. I tapped May's leg and she got off. Moment of truth. She'd never been to the clubhouse, and for good reason, but if I was going to keep her in my life, I needed to see if she could handle it. The bitches inside could be catty, and I'd need a strong woman beside me, someone who could stand up to them. Even though I'd just patched in less than a year ago, I hoped one day to have a shot at an officer's position. I'd just have to work my ass off until then.

I shut off the bike and took May's hand, leading her inside.

Smoke filled the air and music blasted from an old jukebox in the corner. Several of my brothers were sprawled in various spots around the room, some with their pants open. A few of the club whores were already here, willing and ready, and barely dressed. I felt May tense and could only imagine what she thought of all this.

I led her through the room to the back hall and up the stairs. I unlocked the door to my room, shoving it open to let her in, following close behind. The second the door clicked shut and I twisted the lock the tension in the room went up. May glanced around the small space and I tried to see it through her eyes.

"I know it's not much," I said, rubbing the back of my neck. Her apartment might not be in the ritziest part of town, but it was nicer than this place. I hadn't paid much attention to her bedroom, but I imagined it was filled with pretty things. I'd been too focused on May at the time and trying not to rip Seth apart with my bare hands.

My bed was a queen but the comforter was just plain navy. I'd gotten it at the discount store, along with the gray sheets. The dresser was old and scarred. One of the drawers wouldn't close all the way, and I didn't have a closet so I always left my boots on the floor.

"Bathroom is through there," I said, pointing to the closed door across the room. "It's clean."

Damn well better be. I'd scrubbed it myself. I'd learned the hard way not to let the club whores in here, not even if they claimed to just want to help clean. My brothers might trust them, but I sure the fuck didn't. May went over to peer inside. It was just a small room with a sink, toilet, and a shower I barely fit into, but it was mine.

"Not as nice as your place," I said, shoving my hands into my pockets.

"Are you kidding?" she asked. "It's yours, John."

I winced and glanced behind me at the closed door, hoping no one lurked outside and heard the slip-up. I'd told her to call me Grizzly while we were here, but maybe she'd thought I meant only in the presence of others. I hadn't been overly clear about it and probably should have been. It wasn't like she'd been around the club before. In my private room, it didn't matter much what she called me. I just didn't want any of my brothers, or the club whores, overhearing her use my actual name and think she meant something to me.

She did. She meant the world to me. I just didn't want them to know it. Not yet.

"Bet your room is pretty," I said. "I didn't pay much attention earlier."

"Those pretty things come with a price," she said. I'd wondered about her home life. She hadn't talked much about her parents, except to say they went out of town a lot. From what I'd seen, they didn't seem to care what she did.

I nodded to the little TV on the end of the dresser. It was small, but I had cable. I even had a VCR and some movies, thanks to the club. Some of my brothers had hit a warehouse a few months back, and while most everything had been sold, we'd been given the option to keep some of the stuff.

"We can pick out a movie to watch."

May's cheeks flushed as she eyed the bed. I didn't exactly have chairs in here. She toed off her shoes and sat on the bed, then swung her legs up onto the mattress. If she hadn't knotted her hands in her lap, I might have believed she was comfortable, but it was clear it made her anxious to be here. I didn't know if it was the clubhouse, or me. Might have been both.

"I shouldn't have brought you here," I said.

Her gaze shot to mine. "What? Why?"

"You're fidgeting. Uncomfortable." I shook my head. "This is my world, May. Not yours. It's why I tried to keep my distance. You don't belong here."

She got off the bed and came closer, not stopping until she placed her hands on my chest. "John, where I belong is with you. I can get used to this place. I don't care where we are as long as we're together."

I reached up to cup her cheek. Her skin was so damn soft. The way she looked at me, the innocence in her eyes, nearly took me to my knees. The world didn't have nearly enough people like her, and I worried life would chew her up and spit her out. Another reason I'd held off was her age. At only seventeen, I had no right to put my hands on her. It wasn't illegal for us to be together, but it didn't mean people wouldn't take exception to a sweet high school girl dating someone like me.

The people in town would talk, and I knew it was May who'd bear the brunt of the censure. I didn't want her to suffer through something like that. She deserved to have the world at her feet.

"I should take you home and stay far the fuck away from you." I sighed. "But I don't think I can. They'll test you. The club and those women out there. I can't be here to protect you all the time, May, and they won't let me. I don't want this life to harden you.

You're my angel and I want you to always stay this sweet. I'm worried being here will change you."

"If I can't handle it, I'll let you know," she said. "I admit what I saw when we walked in wasn't at all what I'd pictured. It shocked me, and I certainly don't want to strip down out there like those women."

My hold on her tightened. "You won't have to."

Well, fuck me sideways. She might. They could very well ask her to show her loyalty in ways I'd never allow. I hadn't thought everything through and might have just dug a hole neither of us could escape from. The club had rules, and if May wanted to be part of my life, she'd have to abide by them too.

"May, there's something you need to know. Leaving this room isn't safe. Not even if you're with me. There are certain rules to follow while you're here. When it comes to women, they're fair game. Even if they knew I wanted to make you mine, they'd push you. Test you. And I don't mean mine as in the sort of relationship you have at school. It's more. A lot more."

"Like we have to get married?" she asked, her head tipped to the side.

"No. The club doesn't do marriage. They need a chance to get to know you. After some time has passed, I can ask them to vote on whether or not you can be my old lady. You'd get a cut kind of like mine but it would say *Property of Grizzly* on the back."

She moved in closer, the heat of her body pressing against me. Fuck if my dick didn't get hard. I wouldn't act on it. Not right now.

"Are there other old ladies?" she asked.

"Just one. Magda is the Pres's old lady."

A fist pounded on my door, rattling it on the hinges.

"Open the door right fucking now, kid," King bellowed.

I pushed May behind me and unlocked the door, letting it swing open. King, the club's Treasurer, looked pissed as hell, his gaze zeroing in on May. The look he shot me was full of fury, but I refused to back down. Besides, he wasn't much older than me.

"Why the fuck am I getting a call from Don Cartwright about you running off with his son's girlfriend? Not to mention he says you beat the little shit and left him black and blue."

I heard May hiss like a pissed-off kitten. "I'm *not* that asshole's girlfriend."

I closed my eyes briefly and shook my head. Now wasn't the time for her to decide she was all tough and shit. Yeah, she'd have to prove she was worthy of being part of the club as my old lady, but this wasn't the first impression I'd hoped for.

"Not his girlfriend?" King asked. "Then just who the fuck do you belong to?"

I saw her step out from behind me and point in my direction. "Him."

I straightened to my full height, which put me a good three inches taller than King. I should have gone over more shit with May before I brought her here. She had no idea what she'd just done. He rubbed a hand over his eyes and muttered something that sounded like *Jesus H Christ*. "All the women you have at your disposal, and you pick one who's going to cause the most trouble. The Pres is going to be pissed."

"Magda will love her," I said, hoping it was true. She'd taken on the role of mother to all of us, and if anyone needed mothering, it was May. I was counting on the two of them bonding and smoothing my girl's way with the club.

"You know we need to run this by Bullseye," he said.

"I know. She needed me, and a safe place, King. I wasn't going to leave her there with a busted door." Never mind I was the one who'd torn through it. I'd do it again too if meant keeping May safe.

His eyebrows went up. "Is that where Isaiah went?"

"He's watching the door until it can be repaired or replaced. I hadn't had a chance to call anyone yet. Had to bust it down when I heard what was happening."

King's shoulders sagged. "I don't want to know, do I?"

"He was going to rape her, King. I know this club isn't exactly squeaky clean, but if I find out anyone is hurting a woman that way, I'll gut the bastard. Brother or not, Cartwright's kid had her on her knees and was trying to unfasten his pants." Fury rolled through me again just remembering the scene I'd walked in on. The fucker was lucky he was still breathing, although it seemed I shouldn't have been so lenient.

"The Cartwrights are going to rain down hell on us if we keep her here," he said. "But you were right to protect her. She says she belongs to you, but you know damn well how things work around here."

"I know." Didn't mean I liked it. If I ever got into a position to make a difference, there were a bunch of things I'd change. The first being how the club would try to treat May. I didn't think I could keep my cool. "Anyone touches her…"

He looked over at her again and nodded. "Right. Got it."

"So how do we do this?" I asked.

"Head into Church and take her with you. I know it's not done, but we're not bringing in the full club. Just Magda, Bullseye, the three of us, and Killer. We'll start small."

I took May's hand and followed King down the back stairs. He motioned for us to enter the club's sacred space and presumably went to get the others. Magda arrived first, clucking her tongue at us.

"You starting trouble, Grizzly?" she asked.

"No, ma'am. Just finishing it."

She smiled and pulled May into a hug. "Welcome to the Devil's Fury. The big growly men will be here in a minute. I'd say their bark is worse than their bite, but I'd be lying. Don't worry. If this one here wants to keep you, I'll give you my support. He's a good one, which means you must be too. Doubt he'd want to hang onto a girl who wasn't a sweetheart."

"She's an angel, Magda."

"You know anything about this club, girl?" Magda asked May.

My girl shook her head. "Only that Grizzly is part of it. And I know people around town don't think much of any of you, which is stupid. I've never met anyone better than Grizzly."

Magda studied May, staring into her eyes for so long I wondered if she was trying to hypnotize her. "All right. You let me handle Bullseye. Once he falls in line, Killer will too. But be warned. You'll have to fight to keep him, May. There are women here who'd love to get their hooks into Grizzly, and they'll see you as competition."

May lifted her chin. "They can't have him."

"I'm afraid you'll need more than words. You ever fight?"

May's eyes went wide. "N-no."

Magda sighed and focused on me. "Boy, I hope you know what you're doing. Those jackals out there will chew her up and spit her out."

"No, they won't. They'll have to go through me," I said. And I meant it. Never again would someone hurt May. Not on my watch.

Chapter Three

May

When the man John had called King came into the room, he brought two others with him. I assumed it was the Bullseye and Killer mentioned before. All of them seemed big, rough, and a little scary. Even with Grizzly and Magda at my side, I'd have been a fool not to worry. What if they didn't want me here? And what had King's cryptic words meant? What exactly was expected of me in order to be with Grizzly?

I noticed their names were on their cuts, just like Grizzly's. I knew I needed to keep thinking of him that way, or I'd slip up and call him John at the wrong time. I didn't want to embarrass him, or make him angry. He'd stressed the importance of using his club name, and I'd make sure that's what I did.

Bullseye looked me over, making me feel a little like I was on display. "How old is she?"

"Seventeen," Grizzly said. "She's still in high school, but I don't care, Pres. I've tried to stay away and I can't. She means too much to me. Besides, it's not illegal for us to be together so if you're worried about extra heat from the cops there's no need."

"You know how things work around here," Killer said. "She understand what's expected?"

Grizzly tensed and shook his head. The other three men stared me down, making me want to hide behind him. Only Magda's silent presence at my side kept in me place. She'd said she'd talk to Bullseye. So far, she was only observing. Was this a test? What if I failed it?

"Our young Grizzly here wants to make you his," Bullseye said. He looked at Grizzly again. "I'm assuming you want a property cut for her."

"Yeah, I do," Grizzly said.

"Thing is, we don't know you, girl. We don't trust you. To be part of this club, you have to earn your place. In this case, you have to prove to us you can be what Grizzly needs. What we need," Bullseye said.

"How do I do that?" I asked.

Killer smiled. "Women here are fair game. For anyone. Unless you're wearing a property cut. Which you aren't."

My stomach flipped. "Wh-what's that mean?"

"It means you give every brother in this club what they want, when they want it, and prove you're loyal to us." Killer's smile turned cold. "And if you survive with your mind intact, and the club whores don't kill you, then we'll take your old lady status to a vote."

Horror filled me and I stared up at Grizzly. Had he known what they'd want me to do? How were they any better than Seth Cartwright? Or Mike Malone for that matter? I couldn't, *wouldn't*, be used like that.

"If anyone touches May, you'd better be prepared to put me down," Grizzly said. "I will kill anyone who hurts her."

Magda took a step forward, folding her arms under her breasts. "Bullseye, you damn well didn't make me go through all that when you made me your old lady. This sweet, innocent girl isn't a whore, and I refuse to let you turn her into one."

Bullseye snarled. "You refuse? Is that what you said to me?"

Magda inched forward, her steps slow and measured. She didn't stop until she stood toe to toe with him. Even though she'd dropped her voice low, I could still hear her. "You'd best sleep with one eye open, old man. You hurt that girl, or make Grizzly watch the club abuse her, and I will cut off your balls, then shove them down your throat and watch you choke and die."

Grizzly rocked back on his heels, but the room had gone completely silent. I had to assume her confronting him like that wasn't the norm. At the same time, I was a little in awe of her. I'd never met a woman so fierce. It was at that moment I realized what Grizzly needed from me. Not meek, shy May. The girl I'd been all my life. He needed someone like Magda who would fight back. I wasn't sure I had quite as much backbone as her, but for Grizzly I'd try.

"I won't be used like that," I said. "I've never been with anyone before. The only man I want is Grizzly. Anyone else touches me and they'll have to force me. Is that what all of you are? Rapists? Is the town right about you?"

Killer's head went back like he'd been physically hit. "No! Of course, we aren't rapists. Women beg us to be with them. They'll do whatever we want, and like it."

"Well, I won't," I said. "You can never make me want you. I'll never want your hands on me, or any other part of you. I'm with Grizzly, or I'm with no one."

Grizzly reached down and took my hand, giving it a squeeze. I smiled up at him, hoping I wasn't making a mess of things. I'd meant every word, though. What I didn't understand was why he'd want to be part of a club like this. He seemed so good and kind, at least with me. Did he have another side? A darker one? The way he'd rescued me three times from the unwanted attention of boys in my class, and once when I'd been stranded in the rain, I'd thought he was a hero. I didn't like the idea of him being like these men and using women just because he could.

Time to blink the stars from your eyes, May. He's just a guy like all the others.

I hoped he'd prove me wrong. I wanted him to be the Grizzly I'd put on a pedestal, the one who rushed in to save the day. To be fair, he'd told these men he wouldn't accept them using me that way. Still, I'd realized he'd been aware of what they'd demand, which meant they'd done it before. Since Magda was the only old lady, had the rule been a deterrent for anyone else wanting to have someone special in their life? Or did it mean the others had failed?

Magda's words about not having to go through something so horrific to become Bullseye's made me think no one else had attempted it. I studied the men across from me and it became rather clear. For whatever reason, they didn't *want* anyone else to have an old lady. I wondered if Grizzly had realized their intent. As I watched them, and saw the way Bullseye's gaze softened on Magda, I knew I was right. It was clear he adored her, and he'd have never asked her to do something like offer herself up to the entire club. For whatever reason, they wanted the others to remain single. Even Killer looked at her with a certain fondness.

My curiosity was piqued, which wasn't always a good thing. I couldn't wait to be alone with Grizzly again and ask a few questions. I only hoped he'd know the answers, or it would make him question things enough that he'd find out what was really going on with the Devil's Fury. He was so proud to be part of them. I'd hate for him to leave. Would he even be able to? I had no idea how places like this worked. Once he'd patched in was that it? He could never walk away?

Bullseye looked at Grizzly, dragging his gaze away from Magda. "You know if we put it to a vote, no one will let her in. They don't know her, Grizzly. She'd have to hang out around the club, prove her worth, but with the way things stand now, she wouldn't be safe from their attentions. Not even if they knew you wanted her."

Magda made a *hmpf* sound. "I'll say she's mine."

Bullseye rolled his eyes to the ceiling and looked as if he were mentally counting, or possibly praying for patience. "And you don't think the club will find it odd you have a kid who isn't mine, one who's never been around before?"

Magda turned to me. "Where are your parents?"

"Somewhere. They go out of town a lot. It's okay. I'd rather be alone than have them home anyway." I'd never told a soul why I didn't like my parents being home, and I didn't plan to start now. I hoped they didn't push for more information. There was only so much I was comfortable telling them.

"What's your full name?" Magda asked.

"Angelica May Ross, but I go by May. And before you ask, my parents are Sam and Laura Ross. I don't know what they do for a living to travel so much. I asked once and they got weird looks on their faces and changed the subject."

"And that didn't seem unusual to you?" Killer asked.

"Of course, it was! But pressing for an answer might not have been a good idea. My dad can be volatile when he gets angry. I try to keep the peace when they're home and enjoy my freedom when they're gone."

I felt Grizzly tense. "Exactly how volatile?"

Crap. I shouldn't have said anything. He turned me to face him, forcing my chin up so I'd have to look at him. The way his jaw tensed, the flare in his eyes, told me I'd said too much but I couldn't take it back now. He'd push until I told him everything.

"My dad isn't a nice man," I said. "Sometimes, if things don't go his way or you disagree with him, then he'll talk with his fists."

Grizzly growled and the snarl on his lips would have had me taking a step back, if I could have. The way he gripped me, I wasn't going anywhere unless he permitted it.

Chapter Four

Grizzly

Despite the fury I felt over May's confession, and hearing her dad had been abusing her, I hadn't missed the look on Killer's face when she'd mentioned the names of her parents. The club knew something about Sam and Laura Ross, and I wanted to know what the fuck it was. First, I needed to take care of May. The fact Magda had stood up for her was a start, but Killer and Bullseye were right. She'd need to prove herself to the club, and I had no doubt they'd do what they could to test her. And I fucking hated it.

I left her in Magda's care so I could get to the bottom of things. Killer and Bullseye would have appeared relaxed to anyone else, but I knew better. There was a tightness around Killer's mouth and Bullseye's fingers twitched every now and then. They were hiding something.

"So who are Sam and Laura Ross... to the club?" I asked.

"You're not an officer, kid. You only get to know what we permit," Bullseye said.

"Maybe, but right now whatever you know could put my woman in danger. I wasn't kidding. I want a property cut for May. And I want to know why you've made it so damn difficult for anyone here to have an old lady." I folded my arms and watched them. It hadn't occurred to me until now something was up, but Magda was right. If they hadn't made her jump through those hoops, why set up that shit now? "If May being mine is going to put her in more danger than she seems to be in already, I have a right to know about it. I'm not trying to be disrespectful. You know I'm honored to be a member of this club, and I have your backs, but right now I need you to have May's back too. Tell me what I need to know so I can keep her safe."

Bullseye sighed, shared a look with Killer, then they both took a seat. They motioned for me to grab a chair and I did, waiting to see what they had to say. Something told me I wasn't going to like it. Not even a little.

"Laura and Sam Ross don't have a direct connection to the club," Bullseye said.

"No, but an indirect one, right?" I asked.

Killer nodded.

I was missing something. And I wasn't sure if it was a connection to May herself, her parents, or all of them. I had a feeling it was more than just one thing. The club was keeping me in the dark, which meant my other brothers probably didn't know about this shit either. Why keep the info from all of us? It put a target on anyone who didn't know what the hell was going on, made us vulnerable.

"No offense, Pres, but this shit needs to stop. I don't know what you're keeping from the rest of us, but I don't like not knowing who my enemies are."

"The less you know the better off you'll be," Killer said.

"Why not let me be the judge of that? Especially if May is in the middle of this, and likely doesn't even realize it?"

Bullseye gave him a nod.

"Cartwright is running drugs and women. He's using the Ross couple as mules. The mom is getting drugs out of Mexico, and the dad is finding young girls for Cartwright's stable. He has three underground brothels in this state, as well as some in four other states." Killer leaned forward, bracing his arms on the table. "I'm betting if your girl isn't dating Cartwright's boy, then he's been planted in her life to keep an eye on her. Maybe as leverage against her parents, or for some other fucked-up reason."

"I told you I stopped him from trying to rape her," I said. "Wouldn't matter if she'd been dating him or not. She's not now."

"If he knew she was a virgin, he might have been testing the merchandise so to speak. Perhaps her parents have sold her to Cartwright, or maybe the man just plans to take her out from under their noses. If her parents raise a fuss about her being here, it's going to cause the club some issues," Killer said. "It may be legal for you to date your girl, but her parents could still go to the cops and have them come look for her."

"Are we in Cartwright's pocket?" I asked. I'd worry about May's parents later. Right now, I needed to find out what I could about Cartwright. He was at the heart of all this shit.

"We have some deals going with him," Killer said, his tone careful.

"I know our club isn't exactly law-abiding, but are we now into selling women? Because I didn't sign up for that. Maybe some of these other fuckers wouldn't care, but I do."

Bullseye cracked his neck. "We need Cartwright to drop his guard. We've spent a damn year trying to get into his good graces, earn his trust, and make sure he doesn't suspect why we're really there. Before him, it was Dean Foster. He ran things in this town for damn near a decade before Cartwright took him out."

"And that's why you don't want anyone to have an old lady?" I asked.

Killer shifted in his seat. "Who said we don't want anyone to have an old lady? Bullseye has Magda."

"Right, and only Bullseye has one. You've made sure the rest of us don't want to even attempt to have a serious relationship with someone. I want to know why," I said.

The two shared a look and communicated silently. At first, I thought they might not answer my question. After all, I was just a patched member. If I poked the bear too much, I'd find myself busted up or in a shallow grave. If it weren't for May, I'd back down, but I couldn't risk it. I needed to find out everything I could to ensure she stayed safe.

"Women make us weak," Bullseye said. "Cartwright knows all he has to do to get to me is threaten Magda. Same shit Foster used to pull. If we have a bunch of old ladies around here, it gives him even more leverage over us. How did you know we were trying to persuade everyone to stay single?"

"Magda said she didn't have to do what you're asking of May. It means those rules weren't always in place. Something changed and I wanted to know what."

Bullseye sighed and ran a hand through his hair. It was clear my questions were agitating him, which wasn't a good thing.

"Now you know," Killer said. "We didn't think things through before Magda was voted in. It was only afterward we discovered we'd given our enemies the perfect leverage over us. We can't make an exception for May or the club will want to know why you don't have to play by the rules, boy. I know you want to keep her, but it's not in her best interest right now."

"Look, you said yourself her parents are up to their eyeballs in crap with Cartwright. Sending her home isn't going to keep her safe. She's already on his radar, and now that she's not allowed his little bitch of a boy to have his way with her, they'll be after her." I leaned back. "Maybe let the club know she's here under my protection? It will make her hands off while giving them a chance to get to know her and keeping her out of Cartwright's hands."

Killer smirked at Bullseye. "He's thinking like an officer. Knew we made the right choice patching him in."

Pride swelled at his words. I'd love nothing more than to earn my spot as an officer in the club. We didn't have any openings right now and wouldn't unless someone decided to step down or ended up dead.

"Does that mean you agree? May can stay with me?" I asked.

"Your girl can stay," Bullseye said. "We'll let the others know why she's here and that she's off-limits. Doesn't mean those club whores won't try to sink their claws into her. She'll need to be tough to make it in this world, Grizzly. If you want to keep her, see that she learns the rules."

I nodded and stood.

"Keep thinking the way you do, and proving yourself, you might just be an officer one day," Killer said. He jabbed his finger in Bullseye's direction. "This fucker can't live forever."

The Pres flipped him off. "You just want me six feet under so you can console my old lady."

Killer grinned at him but didn't deny the claim. I walked out shaking my head at their antics. Now that I knew May wouldn't be tossed out, it felt like a weight had been lifted off my shoulders. I'd have to tell her the good news and figure out how to either get her things from her apartment or buy her some new clothes. Either way, she wouldn't be going back there alone, and I damn sure wasn't letting her stay with her parents again. It was clear they couldn't be trusted.

I found her with Magda in the kitchen, making cookies of all things. My girl had her hands in a bowl of dough while Magda prepped the baking sheets. I brushed a kiss against May's cheek, settling my hands at her waist. She smiled up at me, happiness shining in her eyes.

"I didn't know this could be so much fun," she said. "I've never baked cookies from scratch before. Or any kind for that matter. My mom isn't exactly the domestic type."

"I'm no gourmet chef, but I can teach you the basics," Magda said before sprinkling chocolate chips over the dough. "Knead those in and we'll add a bit more. Then I want you to roll them into small balls before you put them onto the baking sheets."

May nodded, her brow furrowed in concentration.

"You're going to need some clothes, May." I leaned over her shoulder to watch her roll the dough into balls. "Want the stuff from your apartment or want me to go grab some new things from the store?"

She tensed a moment. "You don't need to spend money on me."

"The club will handle it," Magda said. "Neither of you needs to worry about the cost. Just leave Bullseye to me."

I ran my nose over the shell of May's ear, making her shiver. "Need your sizes. All of them."

I heard her breath catch and watched as her cheeks flushed a pretty pink.

I'd thought to send out a Prospect to pick up a few things, but that look on her face? Yep, I would be shopping for May myself. In fact, I'd be buying her a few sexy things. Even if I didn't get to see them yet, I'd know what she had on under her clothes. I breathed in her scent, then stepped back, leaning against the kitchen wall as I watched her and Magda.

The glances she cast my way, the flush to her cheeks, and the sparkle in her eyes were enough to make me realize I'd made the right choice. Not just in bringing her here, but in keeping her. May was mine, and I was never letting her go.

Chapter Five

May

My face had felt like it was on fire when I'd opened the bags Grizzly had left for me. He'd showered and changed before stepping out of the room, claiming he needed to talk to King about something. The bras and panties were lacy and far sexier than anything I'd ever worn before. The thought of him buying them for me made me squeeze my thighs together as a shock of awareness went through me.

The roughness of the lace scraped across my nipples, making them even harder, and the panties were damp within minutes of putting them on. I stared at my reflection, head cocked, trying to compare this new May with the old one. I'd dried my hair, then used the curling iron Grizzly had purchased. He'd bought some mascara and a pot of lip gloss, but no other makeup, which was fine. I seldom wore any. I could have used some hairspray, but he hadn't picked up any.

I worked the mascara into my lashes, watching as they darkened and seemed thicker and longer. Using the tip of my finger, I smoothed the gloss over my lips. With the tousled curls and new underthings, I looked… not like me. I liked the changes, though. I still couldn't compete with the women I'd seen here before, but I no longer looked like sweet little May either. I was walking a line somewhere between the two.

The door opened and I spun, eyes wide and arms crossing over my chest as Grizzly tromped back into the room. The second he saw me, he froze. The man blinked twice, growled like the bear he'd been named after, and slammed the door shut. My chest heaved with every breath as I watched him, feeling like a mouse about to be pounced on.

"You're fucking gorgeous, May." His gaze skimmed over me before rising again to linger on my breasts. He came closer, reaching out and prying my arms loose. "You have no idea the things I'd like to do to you right now."

The deep rasp of his voice and the hunger in his eyes made me shiver. I stepped closer, my breasts pressing against his chest. I felt the hard length of his cock through his jeans and my cheeks warmed. "No one's ever seen me like this before."

Oh, they'd seen me in my two-piece swimsuit, but this was different. I knew the lacy material didn't exactly hide much.

"Killing me, Princess. Fucking killing me."

"Thank you for the clothes and other stuff." I licked my lips, trying to be seductive but I probably looked like an idiot. A seventeen-year-old virgin and a biker. We were as different as night and day. I looked up at him from beneath my lashes.

He lowered his head, his lips by my ear. "If I didn't know how innocent you are, I'd tell you exactly how you could thank me. I'm going to lose my damn mind tonight, knowing you have this on under your clothes. I want to kiss you. Mark you. Make sure every damn brother down there knows you're mine."

I swallowed hard, my breath catching. I wanted that, so much, but I didn't know how to ask him for it.

His voice dropped lower. Got deeper. "I can see your nipples, May. How hard they are. Makes me want to pull down the cups of your bra, suck those hard little buds into my mouth, and see just how wet I can make you."

"Oh, God," I murmured, barely holding back a whimper.

"You ever let a guy suck your nipples, May?"

"N-no."

He placed his hands on my hips, squeezing. "Just how far have you gone, Princess?"

I wanted the ground to open up and swallow me. I knew Grizzly was experienced. What would he think of just how little I had? "I've kissed before, and…"

He growled. "And what, May?"

"They've touched me. My breasts. Under my shirt. A-and one… one of them put his hand down my pants. Over my panties." I wasn't going to count the touches a few had taken without permission.

His hold on me tightened until I knew he'd leave bruises. "You're mine now, May. You understand? Your breasts? Mine. Those pretty nipples? Mine. And your pussy is damn sure mine. Anyone touches you and I will cut off their fucking hand and shove it up their ass."

His words should have frightened me, but they didn't. If anything, I burned even hotter for him. Was something wrong with me? Violence shouldn't turn me on, should it? Or was it only because it was Grizzly making the threats?

"Then maybe you should touch me." I sucked in a breath the moment the words left my mouth. I hadn't intended to say them.

His eyes turned darker, his expression fiercer. A little shiver ran through me as I watched him struggle for control. I wanted him to let go, to do whatever it was he wanted. I needed to know what it would feel like for him to kiss me, really kiss me. To touch me.

"You don't know what you're asking for, May."

I looked up at him. "I'm seventeen. Nearly eighteen. I know you're older, but I'm still legal. More than. Or is it because I'm a virgin?"

He closed his eyes and drew in a deep breath. "Sweetheart, you have no idea what it does to me, knowing you've never been with anyone before. I don't like that others have touched you, but they didn't get all of you."

I reached up and tugged on his beard. "They wouldn't have had that much if someone hadn't been so stubborn."

His eyes flashed a moment, going even darker. "What are you saying, May?"

I pressed even closer to him. "I was waiting for you. You're the only one I've ever wanted, John. You keep saying I'm yours. Prove it."

I didn't know where those words had come from, or why I'd gotten so bold. I was more the type to stick my nose in a book and hide in a corner than go after what I wanted. Until now.

His jaw tightened. "It may not be illegal for us to be together, but people around town aren't going to look too favorably on a relationship between us. Not just because of who I am either. You might be legal, but you're still in high school."

"I didn't know you cared what other people thought." I hesitated a moment. "Or is it more that you're embarrassed to be seen with someone in high school?"

"It's not me I'm worried about, May."

In other words, he was holding back for me. To protect me. I couldn't be angry with him. As badly as I wanted his lips on mine, his hands on my body, I wouldn't push him.

I felt a bit of my spark die. "So you won't kiss me?"

He reached up, gripping my hair in his hand. "Oh, I'm going to kiss you. I'll even do a little more. But the big finale? That we're saving for your birthday. My club may not care, but I won't have the people in this town looking down on you."

I couldn't hold back my smile, and then he was kissing me. His lips devoured mine and he thrust his tongue into my mouth. The way he held me, tasted me, made every part of me want to beg for more. It felt like fire licked along my skin and burned me on the inside. My panties weren't just damp. They were soaked.

John groaned and the hand still at my hip slid around and down to grab my ass. I squeaked in surprise when he gave it a squeeze. Without breaking our kiss, he managed to topple us to the bed, the weight of his body settling over mine. He moved his hand from my ass up my ribs, his thumb brushing the underside of my breast.

"John." His name was little more than a whisper between kisses. "Please. Please touch me."

He drew back and gazed down at me, his eyes holding mine as he tugged down my bra. When he cupped my breast, stroking my nipple, my clit throbbed. He held my gaze as he lowered his head and took the hard peak into his mouth. He sucked, licked, and even nipped it before switching to the other side. I ran my fingers through his hair, holding him to me. Nothing had ever felt so amazing.

If this was what sex was supposed to feel like, I could understand why the girls in my class were so eager to sleep with the guys at school. No one's touch had ever made me want more. I'd endured the others because I thought there was just something wrong with me. Now I knew different.

"John. I-I…"

He pulled back. "So fucking beautiful, May. I'll be jerking off later, remembering the way you look right now. These beautiful tits on display, your cheeks flushed."

I squirmed beneath him trying to ease the ache that was building.

"Ever had an orgasm?" he asked.

I shook my head.

He leaned down and kissed me again. "Goin' to make you come, May. Give me that first orgasm. Let me see how pretty you are when you're falling apart."

He slid his hand into my panties and his fingers stroked my pussy. I moaned and spread my legs farther. I'd always thought I'd feel embarrassed if I was laid out like this, but I wasn't. Not with Grizzly. He rubbed my clit with his thumb, and I felt his finger slide inside me.

"So tight. So wet." He peppered my lips with kisses before moving to my breasts again. "Come for me, angel."

The sensations rolled over me, stealing the breath from my lungs. When I didn't think I could take any more, he pressed on my clit a little harder and it felt like the earth fell away. My body tensed and my thighs trembled. A keening sound escaped my lips before I could hold it back as wave after wave of pleasure crashed over me. When it abated and I was able to focus again, I saw him smiling down at me.

He pulled his hand from my panties, then stuck his finger in his mouth. My cheeks burned as I watched.

"You taste good, angel. Makes me want to drink it from the source."

I gasped and clutched at the bedding.

"But right now, you need to get dressed so we can head downstairs. Just remember who you belong to." He nipped my neck, biting a little harder before releasing me. "And now the others will know too."

My hand went to my neck and I knew he'd left a mark. The possessiveness in his eyes made me want to stay right where I was, and finish what we'd started. I understood why he wanted to wait, but it didn't mean I had to like it.

I finished dressing, tugging on the low-cut black tank and skintight jeans. The boots he'd picked out for me laced up and had decorative buckles on the sides. Thankfully, they had a modest heel. If he'd gotten me spiked heels, I'd have ended up on my face. I'd never figured out how to walk in them.

Grizzly helped me tuck in my shirt, his fingers lightly stroking my belly. He pressed another kiss to my lips before picking up a belt off the dresser. He slipped it through the loops on my jeans and fastened it. It had small silver studs dotting the length of it and was definitely meant for someone more badass than me.

"Let's go show them what you've got," he said. "And, May, no matter what happens, don't back down. You show them fear, and they'll tear you to shreds."

I swallowed hard and nodded. Good to know. I was determined not to embarrass him. I didn't think I was nearly as tough as Magda, but maybe one day I would be.

I followed him to the main area. Smoke hung heavy in the air and music blasted from a jukebox in the corner. The party couldn't have been going for very long, and yet the room was packed. My eyes went wide when I noticed a few women were already topless and one had stripped all the way down to the skimpiest pair of panties I'd ever seen. The lace ones Grizzly had bought for me seemed like granny panties in comparison.

I tightened my hold on his hand. One of the topless women homed in on him, a smile stretching across her bright red lips as she sauntered over on sky-high heels. The way her hips moved mesmerized more than one man as she drew nearer. If I'd tried to walk like that, I'd have probably fallen.

"Grizzly! I've been waiting for you." She pouted and ran a long fingernail down his chest. "I thought you'd never show up."

He gripped her hand and shoved it away. "Not now, Donna."

Her gaze slid over to me, her eyes narrowing. "Who's this little bitch?"

Grizzly let out a growl and he snarled at the woman. He really did sound more animal than man most of the time. The fact my panties got wetter every time he rumbled at someone like a damn bear should have probably concerned me. I'd always been taught good girls didn't end up with guys like Grizzly. But he was all I wanted.

"She's none of your concern," Grizzly said. "Move the fuck away, Donna. I'm not dealing with your petty bullshit tonight."

The look she cast my way was enough to make the hair on the back of my neck stand up. She wasn't done, not by a long shot. I had a feeling I needed to watch my back around her. For whatever reason, she seemed to feel like she had some sort of claim on Grizzly, and she didn't like me encroaching on her territory. Had they slept together? Did I even want to know?

One of the other Devil's Fury members came over, eyeing me like a piece of meat. "Fresh blood? Isn't she a little overdressed?"

"This is May," Grizzly said.

The guy blinked and straightened before backing up a step. "Shit, sorry. Bullseye told us about her, but he didn't mention she was a damn knockout. I'll spread the word so you don't have brothers trying to get in her pants all night."

"What exactly did the Pres say?" Grizzly asked. "He excused me from Church so I could buy a few things for May."

"She's under club protection. More specifically, under yours." He glanced at me again. "You have shitty parents. I have no idea why they'd work for a bastard like Cartwright, but we'll keep you safe. Name's Beacon. You need anything, just ask."

I gave him a smile of thanks and noticed his patches said he was the club Secretary. As we moved through the crowd, I met a few more of the members, including the Treasurer, King. Even though I'd seen him earlier, we hadn't been formally introduced. I had to wonder about Beacon's words. What did he mean my parents worked for Cartwright? And so what if they did? The man was well-known around town, and no one seemed to look down on him. I had a feeling there was something I didn't know, something important.

Grizzly stopped at a table along the wall and sat, tugging me onto his lap. He gave a nod to the man on his left. "This is Blades. He's fairly new to this chapter. On the other side of him is Freckles."

I waved at the two redheaded men. I wasn't about to ask why Blades had been given such a tough name while Freckles had the name of some cute pet. I didn't think I wanted to hear the answer.

"I'm Yeti," the tall blond next to me said, holding out his hand. I gave it a quick shake, thinking he seemed familiar. He smirked. "We went to school together. Dropped out last year and patched into the club."

That's right. Now I remembered him. We'd had a few classes together, even though he'd kept to himself. William Brown. I'd wondered why he'd dropped out. It wasn't all that uncommon. More than one girl I'd gone to school with had gotten married and dropped out, and several of the guys had gotten full-time jobs. I'd stuck it out, even though I didn't know what I'd do next with my life. My parents had never discussed my plans for after I graduated.

"Don't you worry, little girl." Blades smiled at me. "We'll keep you safe. The way this one here is holding onto you, I have a feeling he wouldn't mind you sticking around even after your parents have been handled."

My cheeks warmed as I glanced at Grizzly. I wouldn't mind either. I'd love nothing more than to be his and stay with him. Although, I hadn't imagined everyone would be so accepting of my presence. The guys were treating me like a little sister, but the way Bullseye and Killer had spoken before, I'd expected them to demand I strip down and service them or something. Whatever he'd said to them, it must have had a very big impact.

"I wouldn't mind if he wanted to keep me," I said, my cheeks getting hotter by the minute.

Yeti flicked the spot on my neck where Grizzly had bitten me. "Seems he'd like that, seeing as how he marked you and all."

"Surprised you didn't tell the Pres you wanted a property cut for her," Blades said, eyeing Grizzly.

"I did, but I won't put her through the shit the club requires for her to prove herself. There wouldn't be a brother left breathing afterward. Any fucker who touched her would die a bloody and painful death."

Blades studied him quietly. "I understand. If I had a sweet thing like her, I'd want her all to myself too."

One of the mostly naked women sauntered over and ran her fingers over Grizzly's shoulder. She gave me a malicious grin as she leaned forward, putting her bare breasts in his face.

"Want to have some fun?" she asked him. "You know I'll give you anything you want."

Grizzly eyed her breasts before looking up at her face. I tensed on his lap, wondering if he'd take her up on the offer. Even though he'd said I was his, I didn't remember him saying he was mine. Did it work that way? What happened if he wanted one of these women? Would I have to sit back and just pretend it didn't happen?

"Did I give you permission to touch me?" he asked.

Her smile faltered and she removed her hand. "You haven't complained before."

He motioned to me. "Does it look like I'm here to party with the likes of you? Show some fucking respect for me and my woman."

She frowned, her gaze flicking from him to me and back again. "She's not wearing a property cut like Bullseye's old lady."

I saw Magda making a beeline for us. I didn't know where she'd come from, but the fierce look on her face warmed me. My parents had never stood up for me, but it looked like Magda was about to come put this woman in her place. Which made me realize I shouldn't let other people fight my battles. If I wanted Grizzly's club to accept me, I needed to prove I belonged her.

Standing up, I turned to face the woman who still hadn't backed off. I folded my arms and lifted my chin, hoping I looked far braver than I felt.

"Are you deaf?" I asked her.

The woman snarled. "Stay out of this, bitch."

I straightened to my full height, which was still barely five feet. When she put her claws on Grizzly again, I knew I had to do something or risk these women running roughshod over me. I let out a breath and reached out, grabbing a handful of her hair. I yanked, tumbling her to the floor at our feet. When she tried to stand, I tightened my hold on her hair and shoved my booted foot down onto her chest.

"I'll fucking kill you!" She screeched and beat at my leg, but I didn't let go. I felt Magda stop at my side, her presence bolstering me.

"No, you won't." I leaned forward, putting more weight on her until she gasped, and her eyes went wide. "But if you come after Grizzly again, I *will* kick your ass. Keep your filthy hands off him."

Magda patted my shoulder and I released the woman. "That's my girl. Come on. Let the whore go and we'll go to the kitchen. We can snack on the cookies we made earlier."

"Y-you made *cookies*? With the Pres's old lady?" The woman on the floor rubbed at her chest. "Who the hell are you?"

Magda put her arm around my shoulders. "She's my adopted daughter and Grizzly's woman. Next time you fuck with her, remember that. What she did was mild. You know damn well what will happen if I get my hands on you."

With that, she steered me away. I felt everyone watching as we walked out of the main room and down the short hallway to the kitchen. Magda already had a plate of cookies in the center of the table and she'd pulled out two ice-cold sodas.

"You told her I was your adopted daughter," I said as I took a seat.

"I did, and as far as I'm concerned, you are. Bullseye already knows how I feel. I've made it quite clear to him that I'm going to claim you as ours, and if he doesn't like it, he can go suck rotten eggs."

I snorted my drink and coughed, trying to catch my breath. "You told him that?"

Magda smiled. "We've been together a long time. Since I was sixteen. Well, unofficially. It took him a while to make me his old lady. We wanted kids when we were younger, but it just never happened. Then Bullseye became the club President and we knew the timing was just all wrong."

I reached over and placed my hand over hers. "I'd be honored to be your daughter."

The warmth in her eyes as she smiled at me made me feel happier than I had been in a long time. Magda would have been an amazing mother, unlike the woman who'd given birth to me. If anyone proved that being able to have children didn't necessarily mean you should have them, it was Laura Ross.

Chapter Six

Grizzly

I'd been so fucking proud of May tonight. She'd impressed my brothers not only sitting at our table, but those who'd been close enough to pay attention to what was going on. The way she'd put the club whore on her ass was sexy as hell. I hadn't realized May had it in her, but she'd proved me wrong. I knew I was a long way from getting to make her mine in the eyes of the club, and give her a property cut, but it was a step in the right direction.

She lay curled against me, her head on my shoulder as she slept. I'd enjoyed a few beers with my brothers before I'd found her in the kitchen, laughing with Magda as if they were old friends. Or mother and daughter in truth. I couldn't believe she'd claimed May in front of everyone. I wondered if Bullseye knew.

I hated that I couldn't make her mine. I hoped like hell if we settled the issues with Cartwright it would mean things could change around here. I couldn't be the only one who wanted an old lady. The way Blades had talked tonight, I had a feeling he wouldn't mind finding a woman to call his own. Yeti was a little younger than me and I knew he was still happy to screw around with the club whores, but some of the other guys seemed to be getting tired of the casual pussy.

Maybe it made me less of a man, but I wanted to hold a woman at night, watch her sleep peacefully in my arms. Like I was doing right now with May, except I wanted it every fucking night. The taste of her was still on my tongue and I knew she was the woman I wanted to keep for the rest of my life. I just had to make sure it was safe first.

"You're thinking too hard," she murmured.

I stroked her arm and kissed her forehead. "Go back to sleep, May."

"Can't. My pillow is too tense."

I chuckled and gave her a slight squeeze. "So now I'm just your pillow?"

"Mmm. I want you to be more, but you said we had to wait." She snuggled closer. "I'm just trying to follow your rules."

I snorted. "Yeah, right. You didn't dress in as little as possible, then practically crawl on top of me because you were following anything except your own desires. You want me as much as I want you, and it's a big fucking turn-on, May. It's just not safe right now. Not only because of the rules of the club. It's not safe outside the Devil's Fury. There are people who would hurt you just because you're mine."

I ran my fingers over the patch of exposed skin above her panties. She'd put on a clean tank and changed into another pair of the panties I'd picked up earlier, and that's all she'd decided to wear to bed. The little temptress!

"Is that why the ridiculous rules were put into place? So none of you would want to claim a woman?" she asked.

"You're too perceptive. And yes, that's why." I sighed. "I hate to say it, baby girl, but your parents are in the thick of it. Beacon shouldn't have opened his mouth earlier. He didn't know you have no idea what your parents are up to. It's not safe for you to go home, but you aren't entirely safe here either. If Cartwright's men were to attack, you could be captured or killed. Since I put his son on his ass for touching you, it makes you even more vulnerable. It won't just be the senior

Cartwright trying to use you to get to the club, or even your parents. The younger one will want payback."

She traced a pattern on my chest before pressing a kiss to the side of my neck. The heat of her breath as it fanned across my skin had my dick even harder. She wasn't making it easy to keep my hands in respectable places. I wanted nothing more than to strip her down and claim her innocence. Make her mine in the most basic of ways.

"I was in danger before you brought me here, John. At least I have a chance as long as I'm by your side, and there's honestly nowhere else I'd rather be. As for my parents, I don't delude myself into thinking they care. If I were to die tomorrow, you and Magda are the only ones who'd even notice. I might not know what they do for Mr. Cartwright, but I have a feeling it isn't something legal."

I turned, rolling her underneath me. Stroking her hair back from her face, I studied her in the moonlight. I'd never seen anyone as beautiful as May. It wasn't just her physical beauty, but her inner beauty. She was sweet, but it seemed she was strong as well. There was no woman more perfect for me than my angel.

"How many days until your birthday?" I asked.

She chewed on her lower lip and something flashed in her eyes. It almost seemed as if she had a confession to make. Had she already turned eighteen and had just been fucking with me?

"Does it really matter? If we're down to counting days, what's the difference?" she asked. "If anyone asks, we can say I'm eighteen. It's not like I have a driver's license for them to check, and who's going to ask to see my birth certificate?"

"I want to do right by you, May. I've fucked up enough things in my life. It's bad enough just being mine could damn well ruin you. This town isn't going to look at you the same way once our names are linked."

She reached up and cupped my cheek. "John, my parents aren't nice people. Once the truth comes out, do you think anyone is going to see me as sweet, innocent May? Because they won't. They'll wonder if I was part of it all. I may not know everything they're up to, but don't think I didn't notice the look on Killer's face when I said their names. And the way Beacon mentioned their connection to the Cartwrights only confirms that. Your club knows something about them, which means my parents are into some illegal stuff. I don't know how bad it is, and I don't care."

"You're an angel, May. *My* angel. Anyone who sees you any different isn't worth your time. As for your parents, they don't just work for Cartwright. They play an integral role in his business, but I don't want to tell you more than that."

She bit her lip, giving my beard a slight tug. "I think I'm falling for you, John. Don't break my heart. I don't think I'd survive it."

I kissed her soft and slow. She might be falling for me, but I damn well knew I was already ass over head in love with her. I'd never met her equal and knew I never would. She was amazing, and she'd be mine one way or another.

The window rattled and the bed under us vibrated. I heard shouts and a stampede of booted feet. My heart hammered in my chest as I stared at May. I didn't want to leave her behind if it wasn't safe in the building, but taking her with me could be bad too.

"Put some clothes on. Quickly," I said, rolling out of bed. I drew on my jeans, a black tee and my cut before shoving my feet into my boots. I wasn't about to take time for a damn belt or socks when I didn't know what the fuck was going on out there.

Once May was ready, I grabbed her hand and led her to the door. I picked up my Glock 17 off the dresser and cracked the door open just enough for me to view the hall. May squeezed my hand as I stepped out of the room. One of my brothers ran past, shrugging on his cut and his pants still undone.

"What the fuck is going on?" I asked.

"Someone set off explosives."

I had a feeling all this was connected to Cartwright. Sure, the club had other enemies, but they weren't the type to try and blow up the clubhouse. Assuming that's what happened. Until I got my orders, I wouldn't know for sure what was going on. When I ran across Magda, I left May with her, pressing a quick kiss to her lips.

"Stay safe, sweet girl. Do what Magda says. I'll come get you as soon as I can."

Magda wrapped her arm around May. "We're going into the cellar."

I gave her a nod, some of the tension easing from me. What Magda called a cellar was actually a trapdoor that led to an underground room and a hidden passage that would carry them about a mile from the clubhouse. It would hopefully get them far enough to be safe from whatever was going on here.

I rushed to the main room where Bullseye was barking orders. The club's VP, Sandman, was standing by his side, which drew me to a quick halt. Last I'd seen him he'd been full of holes and dying. What the hell was going on?

The emptiness in his gaze chilled me as Sandman scanned the room, seeming blind to the chaos around him. No one else found it strange he just happened to reappear when someone set off explosives? Where had he been the last few months? The way Bullseye glanced his way a few times told me the President didn't trust him right now either. Not completely.

Killer approached. "Cartwright's men set off some small explosives along the perimeter. Not anywhere near close enough to take out the building, which makes me wonder why he bothered. If he wanted our attention, he's got it."

"You think it was more of a distraction?"

Killer leaned in closer, his voice dropping. "You mean because our VP suddenly appeared after not hearing from him in months? The very man we believed had died on our last run?"

"Something like that," I said, not wanting to mention my distrust out loud. Not being an officer, I wasn't about to say I was suspicious of our VP.

"Bullseye isn't too accepting of Sandman's return right now either. But he could have walked in here without all the extra shit. So I don't think he's the reason for the explosives."

"Then who…" Every muscle in my body froze. May. Cartwright had called to demand we return May to his son, and we'd refused. This wasn't about the club at all. It was about my woman.

I rushed back the way I'd come and tried to lift the cellar door. Magda must have locked it from the inside. The door didn't budge, and I heard the rattle of the bolt on the other side as I yanked on the handle several times. Backing away from the trapdoor, I raced through the clubhouse and went out to my bike. By the time I had the engine going, Killer and Yeti were beside me mounting their bikes as well. They followed as I drove away from the clubhouse. I knew exactly where the hidden tunnel would let out. I only hoped I wasn't too late.

The wind whipped through my hair and my headlight cut through the darkness. The back roads behind the clubhouse were rough, nothing more than dirt. The bikes kicked up dust as we made our way toward the back half of the Devil's Fury property. A small form lay on the ground at the entrance to the tunnel and it felt like all the air had been sucked from my lungs. I brought my bike to a skidding halt, barely pausing long enough to put down the kickstand before I rushed toward the woman.

Magda. I brushed her hair back and saw the blood trickling from a wound on her head. From the swelling and bruising, it looked like someone had bashed her over the head.

"Jesus," Killer muttered, kneeling next to me. He took Magda into his arms and cradled her close. "Magda, can you hear me? Wake up."

She moaned and her lashes fluttered before she opened her eyes all the way.

"Good girl," Killer murmured. "I'm going to take you to Bullseye, but first I need to know what happened. The kid here is about to lose his shit."

He wasn't wrong. It felt like I was unraveling at the seams. May was gone. I knew in my gut Cartwright had her, and I worried he'd let his son finish what he'd started.

"They took her," Magda said, her words slurring. "Her parents and two others."

"Her parents?" I asked. "Are you sure?"

"She recognized them," Magda said. "Tried to stop them, but I couldn't. They hit me and snatched her from my arms."

Killer pressed a kiss to her brow. I wondered exactly how close the two of them were since she was Bullseye's old lady, but now wasn't the time. "You did good. Let's get you to your old man."

She groaned as he stood, lifting her into his arms.

"I'll go with Grizzly," Yeti said. "You know he's going after May and he shouldn't go in alone."

"Stop by the clubhouse first. You need more men with you. Take Blades and Beacon. When I can, I'll see you get more reinforcements. You know where they're taking her?" Killer asked.

"No. I'll check her apartment first, in case her parents just took her home. If she's not there, I'll go to Cartwright's place. I won't go in guns blazing. I'll sit and watch, see if I can figure out if she's there or not," I said.

"Keep your cool," Killer said. "We'll do whatever we can to get her back. Just don't go in half-cocked and do something stupid or you'll both end up dead."

I nodded and went to my bike. Yeti followed. When we stopped at the clubhouse, Killer filled in Blades and Beacon after handing Magda off to a furious Bullseye. I knew if I didn't tear Cartwright apart for stealing May, the Pres would go after him for harming his old lady. Couldn't blame him.

Chapter Seven

May

Knowing your parents don't care if you live or die and being present when they actually hand you over to a monster are two different things. I had to wonder why they'd even had me. It had always been clear they didn't love me. My heart ached as I thought of Magda. They'd hit her so hard! If they'd killed her... No! I wouldn't even think it. She had to be okay. Someone would find her and get her the help she needed. As for me, once Grizzly knew I was missing, he'd track me down. I didn't doubt it for a second. I just hoped when he got here, he wasn't falling into a trap that would get him killed.

Don Cartwright circled me, his hands behind his back as he eyed me up and down. I felt like a horse being auctioned off. He reached out to touch my hair, testing the texture. Squeezed my breasts and my ass. Fear and revulsion rolled through me, but I forced myself to hold still and take it. There would be a time to fight back, but standing in a room with four armed men wasn't it. I'd end up shot or worse.

"And she's seventeen?" Mr. Cartwright asked.

"Yes," my mother said.

"No," I said, then glanced at the clock on the wall, seeing it was after midnight. "Not anymore. It's my birthday."

"It would have been better if you'd brought her here several years ago. I can always find buyers for the younger girls. Girls, and even boys, thirteen to fifteen years old do really well. Even younger. But by this age... Well, I'm sure I can get a decent price for her." He stopped in front of me, gripping my chin tight. "How experienced are you?"

"W-what?"

"Are you a virgin? And don't fucking lie. I'll have you examined to make sure you're telling the truth."

My stomach knotted and I fought back the bile rising in my throat. Examined? And buyers... like he'd done this countless times. What exactly did my parents do for this man? The thought of them helping him sell kids made my stomach knot even more. How could they do such a thing? Were they completely heartless? Did they not have a conscience at all?

His hold on my chin tightened and tears stung my eyes. "Yes, I'm a virgin."

He hmm'd and stepped back, releasing me. "Then I may be able to find someone after all."

Seth strolled into the room. He seemed as if he hadn't a care in the world, despite the bruises on his face and his split lip. The moment he noticed me, his lips tipped up in a smirk. As much as I didn't want to be sold to some stranger, I didn't exactly want his hands on me either. I didn't know how I'd get out of this, but I needed to figure something out. Or say a prayer Grizzly found me in time.

"Well, if it isn't my girlfriend," Seth said.

"I'm not your girlfriend," I said. "I tolerated you because I couldn't have who I wanted. Things are different now."

"Not so different if you're still a virgin." He sneered at me. "What? The nasty biker wouldn't even touch you? Or were you a frigid bitch with him too?"

My fingers twitched as I fought the urge to smack him. I wanted to say something to put him in his place, but I didn't dare. The last thing I wanted to do was let anyone here know exactly how far I'd gone with Grizzly. Although, right now, I was wishing he hadn't held back. What if he didn't make it in time and I ended up with some strange man?

Not helping! Don't think about it.

"Show her to her quarters. She'll need to be bathed and properly attired," Mr. Cartwright said.

"It would be my pleasure," Seth said, taking a step closer. His dad held up a hand.

"Not you. I need her to still be a virgin, if she's telling the truth. If you go down there, you'll do something stupid and her value will drop."

Right. Because I wasn't worth anything more than a sale to these people, including my parents who hadn't said a damn word since bringing me here, except a one-word response to Cartwright. They didn't have a flicker of sympathy or regret in their eyes as one of the armed men grabbed me.

"Come on, girl," he said, yanking on my arm and dragging me down a hall. When we reached a door, he shoved me through, and I nearly fell down a flight of stairs. As I descended into the dark, keeping one hand on the wall, I worried I'd never see Grizzly again. Even if he did figure out where I was, how would he ever get in here to save me?

I'd noticed the wrought-iron fence, and the guards when we'd arrived. It would be suicide for him to even try getting into this place. As much as I wanted to go back to the clubhouse, I didn't want Grizzly to risk his life for me. I cared too much about him. I had no doubt if Mr. Cartwright got his hands on any member of the club, he'd kill them. Watching Grizzly die would be worse than whatever was in store for me. I could get through this as long as I knew he was still alive and out there somewhere, hopefully trying to find a way to rescue me.

You couldn't have taken some self-defense classes? Or learned something useful?

No, but then I hadn't exactly thought I'd ever end up in a situation like this one either. Whoever contemplated their parents selling them? Your parents were supposed to love you and care for you. Granted, mine hadn't ever seemed to care. I still hadn't ever thought they'd be so cold as to sell me to the highest bidder.

At the bottom of the stairs, the man flipped on a switch and the room lit up. I wished he'd just left the lights off. Chills skated down my spine as I looked at my surroundings. Whimpers drew my attention to the cage in the corner. Three girls were inside. They'd been stripped, and had bruises covering their skin. If they were being sold, I couldn't think of why anyone would pay for them in this condition.

"Unless you want to join our little toys, you'll do as you're told," the guard behind me said, giving me a shove toward a room on the right.

Toys? I wasn't sure I wanted to know. Still, maybe there was a way I could help them if I knew more about why they were here. If I did get a chance to escape, I could try to take them with me. "Why do you call them that?"

"Because they're here for us to play with," he said.

I glanced their way again. Two of them looked younger than me and the other girl was a little familiar. They'd hurt those girls for sport. Would the same thing happen to me when I got to whoever was going to buy me? Could I survive?

The man shoved me into a small room. A twin bed sat against one wall. The rest of the space was empty except for a door. He nudged me toward it, and

I discovered a bathroom. It was just a small shower, a toilet, and a sink hung on the wall.

"You need to get clean," the man said.

I waited, thinking he'd leave. Except he didn't. He folded his arms and stared. I turned, giving him my back and wondered if I could go through with it. Could I undress in front of him and wash? It didn't look like he was going to give me a choice. My hands shook as I removed my shirt and jeans. I was wishing for my non-sexy underthings as I stood in front of the stranger. Instead, I had on one of the lacy sets Grizzly had bought for me.

I reached behind me to unlatch the bra and let it fall to the ground. Before I got a chance to take off the panties, gunfire sounded from somewhere above. The man in the doorway cursed and I heard him stomp away. I didn't know how much time I'd have, so I quickly put on my clothes again and peered into the bedroom. He'd left, but it didn't mean he'd gone back upstairs. I tiptoed to the bedroom door and tried to see out into the main area without getting caught.

The girls were subdued and huddled together. I crept closer, not seeing the man anywhere down here. As I neared the cage, I tried to figure out how to open it. I didn't have a key. Scanning the area, I saw a line of hooks and keys. It couldn't really be that easy, could it?

I grabbed all of them and ran back to the cage. I tried every key, until one worked. The door swung open on squeaky hinges.

"Come on. Let's find a way out." I held my hand out to them, but they just cowered farther back into the cage. "Don't you want out of here?"

"They'll kill us, like they did Daisy," one of them said.

"Daisy?" I asked.

"She tried to run. They made an example of her. Strapped her to a table in the middle of the room and forced us to watch as they tortured and raped her, before they finally slit her throat." The older girl pressed closer to the other two. "We aren't ever leaving this place. Not unless we're dead."

I couldn't fault them for being scared. I was terrified, but I refused to give up. I left their cage open, in hopes they would change their minds and try to get out of this place. Making my way up the stairs, I noticed the gunfire seemed to be farther away now. I wasn't sure if that was a good thing or bad thing. Would the guard come back? Or had we gotten lucky and someone had shot him?

At the top, I peered through the doorway and breathed a sigh of relief. I saw several men in Devil's Fury cuts fighting with Cartwright's men. I recognized Yeti and hoped if he was here, then Grizzly would be too. I ran from my hiding place and sprinted toward the front of the house. Maybe if I could get outside, I'd have a chance of getting away from this madness.

A strong arm wrapped around my waist from behind and hauled me back against a broad chest. I thrashed, slamming my heels back into the man's shins. There was no way I'd go back down to that room!

"Hey! Easy, angel."

The fight drained from me. "Grizzly?"

He released me and I turned to face him. Tears welled in my eyes and I threw myself into his arms. He'd found me!

"Did you think I wouldn't come for you?" he asked.

"I didn't know how you'd get into this place."

"No one takes my woman and gets away with it," he said. "Heard your parents were there."

I nodded. "They hurt Magda."

"She'll be okay. Did they hurt you?" he asked.

"Not exactly."

He tensed. "What the hell does that mean?"

"I have some bumps and bruises, and they embarrassed me. Mr. Cartwright felt me up, testing the merchandise, I guess. Said he might have a buyer for me. One of the guards made me strip and was going to watch me shower, but... I guess you guys broke into this place. I heard guns going off and the man left."

"Which man?" Grizzly asked, scanning the area.

"It doesn't matter. Please. Can we leave? I want to get out of this place."

"If your parents and Cartwright aren't handled, they'll just come for you again," he said. "I'm not walking out of here until I know they're dead."

I could tell he wouldn't budge on the matter. He'd meant every word. Which meant I needed to find my parents in all this chaos. It looked like nearly the entire club was here. Grizzly held tight to my hand. We went room by room. It wasn't long before we found my mother. She lay in a pool of blood, her throat slit and her sightless eyes staring up at the ceiling.

By the time we reached the back of the house, we'd also passed my father and Seth. Both had been shot multiple times. Which only left Mr. Cartwright. We found him in the backyard, along with Killer and Bullseye. The President of the Devil's Fury looked like the thing of nightmares. If I hadn't known we were on the same side, I might have peed myself right then.

"Grizzly, get your woman out of here," Killer said, not taking his gaze off Cartwright. "She doesn't need to see this."

"He touched her," Grizzly said.

Killer took a step back and waved at Cartwright. "Then get a few hits in. But don't kill him. The Pres gets that honor."

Grizzly released me and stalked toward Cartwright. He slammed his fist into the man's face twice. When he hauled back his arm to do it again, Bullseye grabbed his fist and yanked him back.

"That's it, kid. Get your girl out of here." Bullseye shoved him toward me. "Take her to see her mom. She's worried sick."

"My mom?" I asked.

"My woman adopted you, remember? Makes you our kid. Now do as you're told. Go see your mom and take this hothead with you," Bullseye said.

Warmth filled me at his words, and I tugged on Grizzly's arm. "Come on. Take me to the clubhouse."

Grizzly gave a low growl but swung me up into his arms. Before he carried me off, I remembered the poor girls in the basement. If they hadn't been found yet, someone needed to save them. I looked over at Bullseye.

"There's a few girls in the basement. They've been badly abused, and they're terrified."

Killer flashed me a smile. "We'll handle it. Go see your mom and don't think about this place anymore."

Grizzly moved quickly around the side of the house and out to his motorcycle. I clung to him, eager to leave this place behind.

Chapter Eight

Grizzly

May had insisted on taking a shower and changing before she saw Magda. After what she'd been through, I could understand. I'd helped her undress and wash. Held her while she cried. Now she sat in a chair by the Pres's bed, holding Magda's hand. The woman had tears in her eyes as she stared at May.

"I failed you," Magda said. "But you're my strong girl and you came home."

"You didn't fail me. You've been the best mom ever." May licked her lips and her knee bounced up and down as she fidgeted. "Would it... I mean, could I..."

"She wants to call you Mom," I said.

Magda lit up, the biggest smile spreading across her lips. "I'd love nothing more. My sweet girl. You're the best gift I could have ever received."

"And you know damn well you didn't fail her. Sandman betrayed us all. Then he took the coward's way out and put a bullet in his own head before any of us had the chance."

After May had been taken, Bullseye had lit into Sandman, questioning where he'd been, how he'd survived. The VP had broken down and admitted to joining Cartwright's crew after we'd left him behind. Didn't matter the club had thought he was dead. He'd decided to get even by switching sides.

May openly cried as she hugged Magda. I decided to leave them alone for a few minutes, but I wouldn't be far. As it was, Bullseye had left two Prospects to guard Magda, and a few brothers were in the main area and standing guard outside. He hadn't taken any chances with his woman. Hopefully, he'd finish off Cartwright and things would settle down. It would put an end to the human trafficking in this area, at least for now. The club would take over the drug business for this region, and who knew what else. I had a feeling Cartwright was into more than selling girls and drugs.

I went to the bar to get a cold beer and kicked back at one of the tables. I'd give my woman a few more minutes with Magda before I decided to steal her away. It was my hope, when the dust settled a bit more, the club would vote her in as my old lady. With Magda and Bullseye claiming her as their kid now, I didn't see why anyone would stand in my way. Unless the Pres didn't think I was worthy of his new daughter.

May might have lost her birth parents, and her entire life might be changing, but I had a feeling things would be looking up for her. She had the love and support of this club now. And she had me. I'd do anything for her. Hell, I could admit I loved her. Maybe I needed to tell her. Was she ready for something like that?

"You going to sit here and second-guess yourself or go get your woman?" Blades asked, kicking my chair.

"When did you get back?" I asked.

He nodded toward the door. "We're all back. Bullseye took care of Cartwright. The cleaners have been called, and now… now it's time to party."

I eyed the blood spattering his clothes. "Might want to shower first."

He threw his head back and laughed. "You may be right there. I plan to indulge in as much pussy as I can tonight. Wouldn't want to scare the ladies off."

I snorted. "Ladies. That's a good one."

He smacked the back of my head. "Don't go disrespecting them. Just because they spread their legs easier than most doesn't mean you can look down on them."

"Tell me that again after they've tried to start shit with the woman you want to claim. Right now, I hope they all give me a wide berth. I'm not up for their games."

"Go get May. Bullseye will be wanting to spend some time with Magda. Besides, your woman may want a quiet night in your room after all she's been through. Better take some drinks up there. You can get a Prospect to bring you some food when you're ready. Whether it's a snack or later on for breakfast."

"Good idea." I stood and slapped Blades on the back before heading to the Pres's room to get May. She and Magda were quietly talking when I stepped into the room and both stopped immediately. A pretty blush spread across May's cheeks.

"Tell him," Magda said.

"Tell me what?"

May stood and came toward me. "My birthday is today. I'm eighteen. And... when I was with Cartwright, and he... Well, I was wishing you hadn't waited. That you'd claimed me. Made me yours. If he'd succeeded in selling me and my first time had been with some strange man, I think I'd have died inside."

Oh, hell. I gathered her close and glared at Magda. "What kind of mother encourages her kid to have sex?"

Magda gave a weak laugh. "The kind who knows love when she sees it. You love my girl and she worships you. Waiting was foolish. It's not like it's illegal for the two of you to be a couple. The two of you belong together. Don't waste another minute, Grizzly. Life is too fleeting."

"She's right," May said. "We don't know how many tomorrows we'll have. I want to enjoy every last one we have together. I love you, John. You're the only one I've ever wanted, and I'll love you until the day I die."

I cupped her cheek and stared into her eyes. "Love you too, May. You're it for me. I did my best to stay away, thinking you deserved better. I was an idiot and I'm sorry. But why the hell didn't you tell me your birthday was so close? I was thinking it was days or weeks away, if not longer."

"I guess it just bothered me you were so hung up on me turning eighteen. It didn't matter. It wasn't illegal for you to be with me when I was seventeen, and it wasn't like you were going to force me. I wanted to be with you. Still do."

"Get out of here. Let an old woman rest," Magda said, her voice getting weaker as sleep tugged at her.

I led May from the room and to what would now be *our* room. I didn't know how the Pres lived here with Magda. As loud as this place could get, and as crazy, I'd have preferred to take May to a nice cozy house. A place that was just our own. Maybe someday we could have a home. For now, the room at the clubhouse would have to do.

"Why don't you change into something comfortable," I said. "Want me to grab you a soda from the kitchen? The guys are going to party in celebration of Cartwright being gone. It's going to be loud, and I'm not sure you're up for that scene."

She sank onto the foot of the bed. "Definitely not up for a party."

"I'll be back in a few minutes."

I stepped out into the hall and went for the drinks I'd promised her. While I was in the kitchen, I grabbed a plate of the leftover cookies. By the time I got back to the room, May was under the covers. I set the drinks and cookies on the dresser, then locked the door so we wouldn't be disturbed. Unless the place was on fire, or we were under attack, I didn't want anyone barging in.

"Ready for bed?" I asked as I shrugged out of my cut and set it on the dresser. I toed off my boots and pulled my shirt over my head. When I reached for the button of my jeans, I noticed her cheeks were flushed. "Or is my angel ready for something else?"

She gripped the covers tight a moment, then flung them off, leaving her bare to my gaze. I stared, thinking I must have died and gone to heaven. May was... perfection. I'd seen her mostly naked before, but this... this was different. She'd stripped down completely and crawled into our bed.

"Fuck, May. Never seen anything so beautiful in my life."

Her cheeks flushed a darker shade of pink and she gave me a shy smile. "Hurry up and finish undressing. I'm not sure how long I'll feel this bold."

"You have nothing to be ashamed of. Besides, you're mine, right? That means I get to look whenever I want. I also get to touch you. Kiss you." I finished removing my clothes and crawled onto the bed beside her. "Fuck you. God, May. You have no idea how bad I've wanted you. Since long before I should have."

"Then take me, John. I'm yours."

I kissed her, ravaging her mouth as I traced her curves with my fingers. As much as I wanted the moment to last forever, I didn't think I could hold on that long. Still, it was her first time and I wanted to make it memorable for her. If I'd planned tonight, I could have bought some candles or something. Women liked that shit, didn't they?

I trailed my lips down her neck, across her collarbone, and down to her breast. Taking my time, I tasted her. Teased her nipples until they were hard little buds. Sucked on the tips until she made the sweetest sounds and clung to me. I traced her slit with my fingers and found her already wet and ready. I knew I wasn't exactly small and didn't want to hurt her.

I worked her pussy with one finger, then two, bringing her close to the edge again and again, yet never letting her fall. Sweat slicked her skin and she clawed at the bedding.

"Please, John! Please. I need... need..."

"Does my angel need to come?" I asked.

"Yes! Stop teasing me!"

I smiled and kissed her again as I drove my fingers into her faster and harder. I rubbed her clit with my thumb, and she detonated, crying out as her body tightened and her back bowed. I felt the hot gush of her release and groaned, wanting to feel her do that while my cock was inside her. Before she came down her from her high, I settled over her.

I nudged her entrance with the head of my cock and slowly pushed inside. She was so damn tight! I worried it would be too much for her and tried not to rush, even if I did want to thrust into her hard and deep. Her nails bit into my shoulders and she gazed up at me with complete trust in her eyes.

"Do it," she said. "I know it might hurt, but I don't care. I need this, John. Need you. All of you."

I flexed my hips and slid in farther. She gasped and her eyes dilated. I worked my cock into her, making her take a little more with every stroke. When I was fully seated, my dick twitched inside her.

"Ready?" I asked. "Think you can handle more?"

She nodded and I started a slow and steady rhythm. I shifted my angle so I'd press against her clit. It didn't take much to make her come again. The feel of her squeezing my cock made me see stars. I couldn't hold back anymore. Our hips slammed together as I rode her hard and fast, taking what I wanted. When I came, I roared out my release, pumping my cum into her.

She lay under me, panting for breath, wisps of her hair clinging to her face and neck. She reached up, running her fingers through my beard. She and Magda had been right. Waiting had been foolish. May was the same now as she'd been yesterday. There was only two years between us. I'd be twenty in another few weeks. But our ages were just numbers. I loved her, and she loved me. That's all that mattered.

"You're my everything, May." I smoothed her hair back. "I'm sorry I waited so long to make you mine."

"You can make it up to me."

"How's that?" I asked.

She smiled. "Give me more orgasms. We have a lot of time to make up for. Think you can go again?"

I pressed deeper inside her so she could feel I was still hard as a damn rock. "Yeah, I can. But I don't want to make you sore. There isn't exactly a tub here where you can soak."

"Don't need one. I just need you." She leaned up to press her lips to mine. "You're all I ever needed. My knight in shining armor. My protector. My heart and the other half of my soul."

"Shit, May. I'll never be that eloquent. And I'm damn sure no one's idea of a hero."

"You're mine."

I felt like I grew two sizes, and I didn't mean my dick. I was her hero? She really saw me like that? For her, I'd strive to be a better man. I wanted her to be proud of me. Whatever it took, I'd make sure she never regretted coming here with me. Being mine.

I'd love her for an eternity, no matter what came our way. As long as we were together, I knew everything would be okay.

I spent the next few hours making up for lost time, until she fell asleep in my arms.

"Love you, angel. With all my heart."

I kissed her brow and watched over her until sleep claimed me as well.

Epilogue

May
One Year Later

The clubhouse was packed. Not only were all the Devil's Fury present, along with me and Mom, but the club whores were already stripped down and having fun. At least, I assumed it was fun for them. I couldn't imagine being with all these men willingly if they didn't enjoy it at least a little.

Mom and Dad were in the corner keeping an eye on things. Grizzly hadn't appeared yet. He'd left for an errand an hour ago and still hadn't returned. Dad swore it wasn't club business, so I wasn't too worried. Whatever it was must have just taken longer than he'd anticipated.

I grabbed a cold soda and went to join my parents. Mom hugged me and then sat on Dad's lap so I could take her chair. Killer was in the spot on the other side of Dad and King sat across from them. I knew Grizzly kept trying to puzzle out the relationship between my parents and Killer. It wasn't my secret to tell, but I might have accidently walked in on something I shouldn't have a few months back. Like my mom sandwiched between the Pres and Sergeant-at-Arms. I wasn't about to judge. For whatever reason, they didn't want the club to know so I'd kept quiet.

"Your old man is back," Killer said with a nod toward the doorway.

Grizzly pushed his way through the crowd and stopped to kneel next to my chair. I started to get up so he could sit, but he placed a hand on my thigh, holding me in place.

"Grizzly, what's going on?" I asked.

He reached into his pocket and pulled out a small jewelry box. He flipped open the lid and my jaw dropped.

"May, you already wear my property cut, and you know I love you more than my next breath. Will you be my wife? I want everyone to know you're mine. Not just here in the club, but out there too."

"Oh, Grizzly," I murmured and reached out to tug on his beard. "I'd be honored to be your wife."

He slid the ring onto my finger, then kissed me until I was gasping for air. He lifted me, took my seat, and settled me on his lap. I blinked at up him, then glanced at my parents and Killer, who were all smiling but didn't seem to be the least bit surprised.

"You knew!" I accused.

"Maybe," Mom said. "I picked up some magazines the other day that had articles about weddings in them. Thought we could get a few ideas about your dress and what sort of ceremony you want. And don't worry about the cost. Your dad and I are covering it."

Dad winked at me. "Only kid we'll ever have. You can have the biggest wedding you want, anywhere you want."

My heart warmed. I might not have been born into their family, but they'd welcomed me with open arms. Bullseye and Magda were the best parents. I'd gotten lucky when Grizzly had brought me here a year ago. I owed him my life, and so much more. And now he wanted to marry me!

Since I'd graduated ten months ago, I'd been a bit lost. I helped around the club as much as I could, but I'd wanted more. We'd been trying for two months now to have a baby, but every time my period came disappointment hit me really hard. A knot formed in my throat and my eyes burned as I looked at the man who meant everything to me.

"What if I can't have kids? I know you made me your old lady, but marriage... I don't want you to wake up one day and regret your decision to be with me. We've been trying, but it's not working. Maybe I'm defective."

He rubbed my nose with his. "Angel, I don't care if we have kids or not. Do I want them? Sure. But if we can't have one of our own, it won't be the end of the world. The only thing I can't live without is you."

A tear slipped down my cheek and he wiped it away. I didn't know what I'd ever done to deserve someone like him. People saw a rough biker, a scary man who broke the law.

To me, Grizzly was honorable, protective, had the biggest heart of anyone I'd ever met, and he was the most loving man. I felt lucky every single day that I got to be part of his world, stand by his side, and fall asleep in his arms. And now this...

"As long as I have you, I don't need children," I said. "I want them, but we'll just have to keep trying and see what happens. If you're sure you'd be okay if we can't have any, then I won't bring it up again. You're all I've ever wanted."

"You're all I need, May." He kissed me soft and slow. "Don't ever leave me, angel. If you do, you'll be taking away my sunlight and all the warmth in my life. Because *you're* my life, May. My everything. I will love you for now and always, and that's not just a promise. It's my solemn vow."

I melted against him. He always claimed he didn't have the right words to say, and yet he always seemed to find them. I looked forward to our future, whatever it might bring. I'd been existing until a year ago. Now I was living, and I was going to make the most of every second of every day.

He leaned in to whisper in my ear. "Come on. Let's go celebrate you agreeing to be my wife. And maybe we'll practice a little more and work on expanding our family. But, May, I meant what I said. You're all I need."

I smiled at him. "Then take me to bed. We can make some more memories together. One day we'll be old and feeble. We can look back on days like this one with a smile and remember what it was like to be young and in love."

"I'll always be in love."

I sighed as he carried me into our room. "So will I. I've loved you since you swooped in and saved me from Mike Malone at the pond. Nothing will ever change that."

He set me down. "Strip, woman. Let's see how many times I can make you scream tonight."

With a smile, I did as he commanded and hoped it would always be like this. Even a year later, I felt like I was burning from the inside out from a simple touch. And his kisses? They still made my knees go weak. If anything, I fell more in love with him with every day that passed.

There were times I was so happy it felt like my heart might burst. He'd given me a family, and his love. As long as I had both of those, I didn't need anything else. Never would. And soon I'd be Mrs. John Moore.

If life got any more perfect, I'd probably float away on a cloud of bliss. We had a once-in-a-lifetime type of love, the sort fairy tales were based on.

"You've given me what I dreamed of as a little girl," I murmured between kisses. "A happily-ever-after."

"No. Happily-ever-after implies our story is over, and ours is just beginning."

Wolf (Devil's Fury MC 9)

Harley Wylde

Glory -- Who up and moves to another state where they don't know anyone and don't have a job or a place to live? Me, that's who. When I heard Devil's Fury was running an underground clinic for women like me -- victims of boys pretending to be men -- I knew I had to be a part of it. What I didn't count on was falling for an alpha biker with a heart of gold or turning to mush every time he holds my daughter. There's more to Wolf than most people realize, and now that he's decided I'm his and he's mine, I'm holding on and never letting go. I won't even let a killer stand in the way of my happily-ever-after.

Wolf -- When my ex left for greener pastures, I should have been broken-hearted. So why wasn't I? One look at the angel who walks into Church and I know... Glory's meant to be mine, and so is her adorable little girl. Just one problem. Well, two. She's skittish -- she's been badly hurt by men before, and I'm not exactly a prize. I came back from the war broken physically and mentally. I know Glory can do better. But I always get what I want, and I want Glory. When someone tries to destroy my new family, I know I'll do whatever it takes to keep them safe... even if it means letting Glory see the darkness inside me.

Prologue

Glory

I'd lost my mind. What sane person picked up and moved to another state without having a job lined up, all because they wanted to volunteer for an underground clinic, which could lead to imprisonment? Me, that's who. Although, I now questioned exactly how sane I was. My daughter, Sienna, wasn't quite a year old, so she didn't understand what was happening. As long as I fed her on time, and maintained her routine, she didn't much care where we lived. She did need a roof over her head and I didn't have housing figured out.

My hands trembled as I followed Tank through the Devil's Fury clubhouse. Until the second trimester of my pregnancy, I hadn't even known him, or his wife. Emmie had become a good friend since then, and when I'd heard what the Devil's Fury wanted to accomplish, I knew I needed to be a part of it.

"Let me do the talking," Tank said. "You'll know when you need to speak up."

"All right. I won't get in trouble for being here?" I asked, looking around.

"No. You're with me, and that's enough. Only my brother is expecting me, so we may not get a warm reception when we first walk in. Their bark is worse than their bite, at least where women are concerned. Just don't fuck up and you won't have anything to worry about."

Right. Because that didn't make chills skate down my spine. Exactly what would they do to me if I did fuck up? I wasn't sure I wanted to know.

Tank pushed open some double doors and strolled inside with me on his heels.

"Don't start the party without me," Tank said, a smile in his voice.

A man stood at the head of the table, and I assumed he was the club President. I didn't know much about the way a place like this worked, but Tank's wife had gone over the basics. I eyed the man's cut. *Badger -- President.* Yep, I'd been right. I tried to hide the way my hands trembled and hoped no one realized I was out of my depth right now.

"Motherfucker," Badger muttered. "I should gut you for barging into Church uninvited."

My stomach clenched and I gave Tank the side-eye. I hoped he was right about these men not getting angry and taking it out on me. I'd defend myself, but I doubted I was much of a match for the guys in the room. And gut him? Did he mean literally?

"Technically, I had an invitation from your VP, and I come bearing gifts." He reached over and yanked me from where I'd stood partially behind him. I winced and wanted to rub my arm. "Meet Glory."

"We don't allow club whores in Church," one of them said. I eyed his cut. *Demon -- Sgt. at Arms.* Same rank as Tank. Which meant I needed to toe the line, according to Emmie. However, I've never been good at doing what I should.

Tank winced and I felt my face flush. A club whore? That's what they thought? I wanted to scan my clothes, thinking maybe I'd dressed wrong. No. Jeans and a heather gray tee. Nothing overtly sexy about what I had on. In fact, my shirt was even on the loose side.

Anger sparked inside me. Emmie had explained what the club whores were, and how these men didn't respect them, not even a little. They used them and tossed them aside. And this asshole thought I was a club whore?

I jabbed a finger in Demon's direction and snarled. "I'm not a fucking club whore. You try to put your dick anywhere near me, I'll rip it off."

Badger sat and leaned back in his chair, apparently settling for the show. I hoped like hell there wouldn't be one. I'd been warned not to let these men push me around and at the same time, I had to act respectful. It was a fine line, and I hoped I didn't cross it. Even though being around men still scared the crap out of me at times, I didn't want them to think I was too soft. They needed to know I could handle myself in this world. If I couldn't prove myself to them, I could be asked to leave.

Demon stared down his nose at me.

"First off, I have a woman so I wouldn't *want* my dick anywhere near you. Second, you point at me again, and I'll --"

Badger cleared his throat and shook his head, giving Demon a look that clearly said *shut up*. The Sergeant-at-Arms clamped his lips shut and glared at me. I folded my arms and stared back, faking way more bravery than I actually had. I hoped no one noticed I was shaking.

"Introduce Glory, Tank," someone else said.

"Glory has a four-year degree in biology and was accepted into medical school. She only attended for one semester before she had to quit and stay home," Tank said.

"Why did you have to quit?" another man asked. *Blades* was stitched on his cut.

"Fuck that. She doesn't even look old enough to be out of high school." The man partway down the table leaned forward, a ghost of a smile crossing his lips. "No offense."

I looked up at Tank, knowing this was the moment he'd mentioned. The time I'd knew I needed to speak. They needed to hear my story, understand why I was here and why I needed to help in any way I could. I faced the table of men.

"I graduated high school when I was fourteen, then finished my four-year degree in three years. I was seventeen when I was accepted into medical school. The reason I dropped out is personal, but considering why I'm here, I'll share it with you. I was walking across campus one night when two guys dragged me off into the bushes. They hit me several times, nearly knocking me out, then took turns raping me."

I scanned the room, stopping on each brother for a few seconds before moving on to the next. I dared for one single man to utter anything about me deserving it, or any other bullshit I'd already heard a million times since the incident. Several gazed back at me with sympathy. Others looked furious, but I didn't think it was at me. No, I thought they wanted to track down the two men who'd hurt me, and if I had names for them, I'd gladly let them do their worst. I doubted I was their first, or their last, victim.

"I have a daughter as a consequence of that night. No one found me for thirty-six hours, and by the time I was treated, it was too late for the morning-after pill to be as effective. They treated me for STDs and sent me on my way." I took a breath and my fingers clenched and unclenched at my sides. "My parents threw me out when I refused to have an abortion. Sienna, my daughter, is developmentally delayed but she's an angel. No matter how she was conceived, I'm lucky to be her mom."

"You dropped out to take care of your kid or because you were scared to be on campus?" another man asked. I checked for a name, needing to make sure I could recognize these men later. *Ripper*.

"A little of both," I admitted. "I'm eighteen, in case anyone wondered. Almost nineteen. Tank heard about your project to help rape victims and thought of me. We met at the OB-GYN when I was there for a check-up during my pregnancy, and I spilled my story to his wife."

The VP, Slash, narrowed his gaze at Tank. "Anything I need to know, brother?"

Tank shook his head. "Got a vasectomy when the girls were about two years old. Those three are more than enough. We were just there for a routine thing. Emmie didn't want to go alone."

"You want to help as what? Medical staff?" Badger asked me.

"After having been the victim of two rapists, I can understand where these women are emotionally and mentally," I said. "I have enough training to help with the basics, but you'd still need a licensed doctor or nurse practitioner. I'm CPR certified, and I've been taking some online nursing classes. I just haven't been able to do the hands-on part because of Sienna."

"She'll need a place to stay," Tank said. "Any objections to letting her use one of the apartments?"

"They only have one bedroom," Ripper said. "She needs more space if she has a daughter."

I wanted to smile. These men had no idea the conditions I'd been dealing with since finding out I was pregnant. A one bedroom behind a fence? Seemed more like paradise to me. Having two bedrooms was a luxury, and not one I necessarily needed. As long as I had a roof over our heads, could keep Sienna cool in the summer or warm in the winter, and keep us both fed nothing else mattered.

"Sienna isn't quite a year old," I said. "She's small enough we can easily share a room. We don't want to be any trouble."

Voices outside the door had Tank turning to peer into the hallway. He stepped out of the room a moment and returned with a pink bundle in his arms. He handed my daughter over, and I cradled her in my arms.

"She's so small," Ripper said, "She's like a little doll."

I smiled. "She's my angel."

Maybe some wouldn't have felt the same way. Yes, she'd been conceived in a horrible way, and her father was a monster, but I could have never gotten rid of her. I didn't begrudge anyone who felt the need to get an abortion or give their baby up for adoption. Those options just weren't right for me. Sienna was a part of me, and even though we struggled, I'd wanted to keep her. She was my bright spot from a horrible moment.

"You can use my house," Ripper said. "I'll stay at the clubhouse."

His offer took me by surprise, and I blinked at him a moment. He couldn't be serious, could he? The way he stared me down said yes, he was very serious.

The VP and President shared a look. To say they seemed surprised was an understatement, which made me wonder... exactly why had Ripper offered his house? Did he expect something in return? He'd said he'd sleep at the clubhouse, but...

"I'm not throwing you out of your house," I said. I didn't mind the one bedroom someone had mentioned. It would be preferable to staying in a stranger's house. At the least the other place seemed to be something they kept vacant for guests.

"Fine. It's three bedrooms. You can have one and Sienna can have the other. We can be roommates until you get on your feet." Ripper smiled, and the flash of his eyes said he had me over a barrel. If I refused his offer, I'd seem like a bitch. Agreeing put me under the roof of a strange man. Still, Tank wouldn't have brought me here if he didn't trust these men.

I opened my mouth to protest, but Tank leaned down and whispered in my ear. "He won't do anything you don't want him to. But I can promise he'll do his best to *convince* you to want the same thing he does. Might even end up with a daddy for sweet little Sienna."

My cheeks burned and I nodded. I had no intention of taking on Ripper or any other man, but I wouldn't say no to sharing the house with him. If he wanted more, he'd be sorely disappointed.

"She accepts," Tank said.

"Anything else?" Badger asked. "Any other surprises I need to know about? No. Good. Everyone get the fuck out. Ripper, help Glory get set up at your place and let me know if they need anything."

I eyed Ripper, wondering if he had an ulterior motive to sharing his house with me. Tank seemed to think the guy might push my boundaries, but was it possible he was just being nice? Wouldn't matter. Even though he seemed harmless enough and was good-looking, he wasn't my type. I had once been attracted to the flirty types of guys. Since meeting the Dixie Reapers, I'd discovered bikers tended to be big flirts. Since having Sienna, things had changed. I didn't date anymore. Even if I did, I would go for someone a bit more... somber. Reliable. Serious. Yes, serious was a good word. I didn't want to raise two kids. At least, not when one was supposed to be a grown man.

Tank nodded to the door and I followed him out of the room, with Slash right behind us. We didn't stop until we'd stepped outside and walked over to the truck Tank had loaded down with my things. Sienna's crib and a few boxes were in the bed. It wasn't much, but it was all we owned, other than the one bag I'd packed with our essentials we'd need immediately, and of course Sienna's baby seat and diaper bag. I smiled, remembering Tank called it her "go bag." Emmie had rolled her eyes when she'd heard her other half say those words, and I'd decided I didn't want to know. It sounded like something a secret agent would have, or a criminal.

"Ripper's house is that way," Slash said, pointing to the right of the gate. "It's about half a mile down the road. Has some sort of flowering tree out front. Think Shella called it a dogwood. The old ladies had it planted there when Ripper patched in and got the keys to the house. Just look for a tree with white flowers."

Tank punched his brother in the arm. "I know what a dogwood is, fucker."

Slash's eye twitched and I bit my lip so I wouldn't laugh. I had no doubt he'd have a bruise where Tank had given him a love tap. The man was like a walking mountain, and his fists were the size of a bear's paw. And yet, when he held his girls, he had a gentle touch.

"Stop by the house when you're done. Too bad Emmie and the girls couldn't come with you." Slash gave him a little salute and started walking to his bike.

"Next time," Tank called after him. "Or better yet, bring your ass to Alabama more often. The girls miss their Uncle Slash, and now you've given them an aunt. When I told them you'd gotten married, they squealed and nearly busted my eardrums."

I could easily imagine Harlow, Westlyn, and Kasen bouncing as they gave off high-pitched squeals in their excitement. I'd come to love those girls, and I'd miss them. Maybe if Slash did go to Alabama he'd let me and Sienna tag along. It would be nice to visit the friends I'd made at the Dixie Reapers. Emmie and Ridley had even tried setting me up with one of the men there. Warden wasn't much older than me, and while he'd been nice, I knew he wasn't ready to settle down. If I'd given in and gone on a few dates with him, he'd have lost interest when I wouldn't sleep with him.

Tank leaned down, lowering his voice so only I could hear him. "You okay living with Ripper?"

I nodded. "You wouldn't have brought me here if you didn't trust these men. Although he may change his mind pretty quick. Sienna isn't always the easiest baby in the world."

Tank winked. "It will either be good practice for the future, or excellent birth control."

I snorted, then laughed outright. He wasn't wrong. Since having a baby, I'd decided the best way to guarantee kids didn't do stupid shit was to give them a fake baby that cried at all hours and couldn't be easily soothed. After a few days, they'd decide they didn't want kids anytime soon. Then again, most teens thought they were invincible and probably figured all those teen parent statistics could never happen to them.

"I'll drive your stuff over to Ripper's house and help you get settled. I'll be here overnight if you need anything, but I'm heading out first thing tomorrow. If you change your mind and want to go back, let me know."

I squeezed his arm in gratitude. "I'll be fine, Tank, but thank you."

I secured Sienna in her seat and climbed into the passenger seat of the truck. Tank stared me down and I realized he was waiting for me to fasten my seatbelt. Even though we weren't going far, it seemed he took our safety seriously. Tank drove down the winding road through the compound and stopped at a house with a pretty dogwood tree in the front yard. It didn't look like the sort of place a single biker would live, but what did I know? The Dixie Reapers all had homes similar to this one. Then again, they were more family-oriented these days. The handful of single men wouldn't stay that way long, not if the old ladies had any say in the matter. Ridley, Darian, Emmie, and Isabella had fun making the younger guys uncomfortable by trying to set them up.

I eyed Ripper's house again. It was charming. And rather perfect for a small family. Too bad we weren't going to *be* a family. Not if I had any say in the matter.

It took about an hour to unload everything and set up Sienna's room. Ripper and Tank worked well together, and once the big Dixie Reaper had left, I was alone with a strange man in a strange place.

"My offer still stands to let you have the house," he said.

And now I felt like shit. He had to feel the tension radiating off me. It wasn't his fault, and I refused to blame all men for the actions of two assholes. Maybe if they'd caught the men responsible, I'd feel a little less jumpy. Part of me didn't feel safe knowing they were still out there, all because I hadn't recognized them. Supposedly none of the cameras in that area of campus were working that night. I personally called bullshit. Not being able to afford a lawyer, I couldn't fight the school on the issue. To keep me quiet, they'd waved my tuition for that semester, and given me an additional five thousand dollars to help during my "difficult time." I'd known they were paying me off. I'd taken the money, knowing without a name, or a way to point out my rapists, the police wouldn't do anything.

I shook off the memories and tried to smile at Ripper. "Not necessary. I appreciate you giving us a place to crash while I figure something out. I know the clinic will be run by volunteers so I'll need to find a way to pay the bills while I finish my degree. I'll just have to find something that will work around the hands-on training I'll be doing." Assuming I could get anything set up at a local clinic or a nearby hospital. There was a chance I wouldn't be able to get the clinical portion of my program done as long as I lived in Blackwood Falls, but I felt like I needed to be here.

"Blackwood Falls is on the small side. Might not be too many employment opportunities." Ripper shrugged. "You can stay as long as you need to."

Right. It felt a little like he was undressing me with his eyes. He hadn't done or said anything inappropriate, yet being alone with him, especially with him standing so close, made my skin crawl. I needed to make things as clear as possible. The last thing we needed was to have a misunderstanding, in particular when it came to where I'd sleep. Not just tonight but any night.

"You seem like a nice guy, Ripper, but just to be clear, I don't want to date. Ever."

His eyebrows lifted. "That's a long time to be alone."

"I won't be. I'll have Sienna." I folded my arms and rubbed my hands up and down my biceps. "Look, I know it's been over a year since I was raped, but I still don't do well around men. Being here with you is going to be a challenge for me. If you move too fast or get too close, there's a chance I'll flinch. It's nothing personal."

A sober expression crossed his face and understanding lit his eyes. "More than one woman here has been assaulted, Glory. You aren't alone, and not one damn man here will do anything you don't want us to. You don't want to date, or fool around, you don't have to. Just make sure you're up front with everyone."

"You're not pissed?" I asked.

A smile ghosted his lips. "No. Disappointed, maybe. You need to do what's right for you and Sienna. If that means we can only be roommates, or maybe friends, then I'll abide by your wishes. I might be an asshole sometimes, but I'm not a monster. Besides, I was hoping we could have a good time, but I'm not ready to be a daddy."

"Thanks, Ripper."

Being here just might work after all… assuming he didn't run screaming into the night when Sienna decided sleep was overrated and the entire house should be up with her.

Chapter One

Glory

When Ripper had said finding work in this town wouldn't be easy, he hadn't been joking. I'd been in Blackwood Falls a week and had applied at every restaurant, bar, and shop in town. Either they weren't hiring, or they just weren't calling me back. I didn't want to stay with Ripper any longer than I had to, but if I couldn't support my daughter I didn't have a choice. As it was, my money was running out and soon I wouldn't even be able to pay for my own groceries. The money from the college was nearly gone. I'd used most of it on medical bills, and what little was left wouldn't get me by for much longer.

The club had loaned me a vehicle so I could get around town. I hated relying on the Devil's Fury so much. Badger had insisted I use one of the club trucks, and even made sure someone put gas in it. It didn't feel right taking advantage. I liked paying my own way, but if I couldn't find a job, I didn't know what more I could do.

As it was, I could tell Ripper didn't care much for having Sienna around. He'd been nice enough, and I couldn't blame him for not wanting a crying baby under his roof. He wasn't her father, and he shouldn't have to put up with sleepless nights. Even though he'd offered to stay at the clubhouse, I didn't want to boot him from his own space. I'd mentioned it to Badger and asked about the one-bedroom apartment. He'd stalled and put me off. If something didn't change soon, I'd have to press the issue.

I almost wondered if Badger wasn't trying to play matchmaker. If he was -- I hated to tell him, but he was doomed to fail. Ripper and I weren't compatible in the slightest. We wanted different things from life. For one, he went to the clubhouse every night to party and came home drunk and smelling like cheap perfume. I didn't own him, and he could certainly go where he wanted or be with whomever he wanted, but the way he stumbled into the house late at night didn't exactly endear him to me.

I parked the truck at the clubhouse and got Sienna from the back seat. Since it was the middle of the day, and I didn't see any other cars in the lot, I hoped it was safe to go inside. The last thing I wanted to do was carry Sienna inside and find half-dressed women, or worse. The women of the Devil's Fury had been very clear about what to expect if I ever stepped foot in the clubhouse when I hadn't been invited.

"Come on, baby," I murmured to Sienna as I pushed open the door. "Let's see if Badger is in his office."

I hated asking for help. There wasn't anything wrong with letting people give you a hand up when you needed it, but I'd fallen so far it felt like all I did was ask others to bail me out. Ripper let me stay in his house, the club let me use one of their trucks, and now I was going to ask for more. I felt horrible about it.

The interior of the clubhouse seemed brighter than it had the other day. I scanned the room and noticed a few bikers at a table playing cards, a lone guy stood at the bar, and someone was behind it wiping the space down. Taking a breath, I gathered my courage and started across the room.

"Badger's not back there," the man at the bar said, his voice deep and husky. It skated across me and I held back a shiver. Didn't stop my nipples from getting hard.

What the hell?

I'd never reacted this way to someone speaking before. Or from anything else for that matter. I shifted Sienna so she'd hide my reaction to his voice before I turned to face him. He stared at my daughter, a look of longing crossing his face for a brief moment, before he held my gaze.

"What do you need, Glory?" he asked.

"You know my name, but I don't know yours."

His lips kicked up on one corner. "Wolf."

Of course, his name would be Wolf. The guy had predator written all over him. I had no doubt he huffed and puffed and threatened to blow up the skirts of every woman in town. Although, with a voice like his, not to mention his looks, I figured most would just spread their legs before he even had to ask.

"Do you know when Badger will be back?" I asked.

"You could always stop by his house if it's an emergency," Wolf said.

By his house? My nose wrinkled and I shook my head. No, there was no freakin' way I was going to bother the guy at home. I knew he had a wife and kid, and I'd heard the woman was pregnant again. If our roles were reversed, I wouldn't want some strange person dropping by my home unannounced.

Wolf stood and came closer. Whatever woodsy scent he wore wafted toward me, and I couldn't stop myself from taking a deep breath. *Not helping*! I wondered if I could hold my breath, so I wouldn't be tempted to do something stupid… like rub up against him. I didn't know what the matter with me was, but I needed to fix it.

"What's wrong, Glory? Maybe I can help."

Wrong? Other than me desiring a man for the first time in my life? "There's nothing wrong, exactly."

He reached for my arm, giving my elbow a gentle tug toward the bar. He kicked out a stool and motioned for me to sit. It left him towering over me until he reclaimed his own stool.

"Sweetheart, you haven't come to the clubhouse since that first day. You wouldn't be here tracking down Badger if you didn't need something. I promise, I don't bite," Wolf said.

My cheeks burned as I thought about him nibbling on me. *Stop it, Glory!*

I sucked in a breath and decided to just be honest. Well, minus the part where he was sending my hormones into overdrive. That was for me to know and... well, *only* for me to know.

"Ripper has been super nice, but I feel like Sienna and I are cramping his style. I thought I'd ask Badger about the one-bedroom place someone mentioned the day I got here. It's not right to ask Ripper to give us a place to stay indefinitely."

Wolf leaned against the bar. "Thought it was only temporary."

"It would be, except I can't find a job. I've applied everywhere. And without a job, I don't have money coming in, which means I can't afford a place to stay. Once my savings is gone, I can't even buy diapers for Sienna." I left out the part about being down to my last few hundred.

Wolf rubbed at the whiskers on his jaw. He didn't have a full beard like a lot of the guys here, but he definitely hadn't shaved in a few days. Why did I find it so sexy?

"You did a brave thing, coming all this way to help other people. The clinic is important to Shella. There isn't much the club won't do to see it succeed,"

Wolf said. "And that includes paying you for your time."

I opened my mouth to protest, but he held up a hand to silence me. I snapped my jaw shut and waited to see what he'd say.

"I don't know how much we'd be able to pay you. For now, you can use the truck as long as you need it, and we'll cover the gas for it. If the club doesn't want to cover it, come see me. If you don't like living with Ripper..." Wolf tapped his fingers on the bar. "I can understand wanting and needing your own space. I'll talk to Badger and Slash. Maybe we can have something ready for you in a day or three."

"I don't want to be a bunch of trouble for the club," I said.

Wolf gazed around the clubhouse. "I know we don't seem like the type, but we like helping. Especially women like yourself. I don't know what's going on with you and Ripper, and I don't need to. If you want your own place, we'll make it happen. Need diapers or anything else? Just tell us."

I reached over and placed my hand on his forearm, trying not to react to the heat coming off his skin, or the funny feeling in my stomach from being so close to him.

"Thank you, Wolf. I didn't mean to imply anything. I'm not used to accepting help. As for Ripper, he hasn't said anything, but I know Sienna is keeping him up, and honestly, the way he comes through the house smelling like cheap perfume makes me a little uneasy." I released his arm, realizing I still held on. "I know the women who come here aren't forced. And Ripper hasn't tried anything with me. Still... I think it would be best if I found somewhere else to live."

His hand clenched into a fist and his jaw went tight. "He comes home smelling like perfume?"

I nodded slowly. "He's usually a bit drunk and I've seen lipstick smears on him. There's no reason he can't keep living his life the way he always has. I'm just not comfortable being around him like that, or having my daughter see him that way. I know Sienna is just a baby, and she won't remember anything happening right now. I'm just... uncomfortable."

Wolf shook his head, muttering something about insensitive idiots and showers. I didn't quite understand it all.

"Badger can rip me a new one later if he wants, but we're getting you moved. Now." Wolf stood and winced. I noticed he favored his right leg. He walked off with a slight limp, yanking his phone from his pocket. "Come on, beautiful. Let's get you settled into your own place."

I hurried after him, my cheeks burning. Beautiful? Hardly.

By the time we reached Ripper's house, there were two other trucks out front. Wolf opened the door and reached for Sienna, then hesitated. "Okay if I get her?"

I nodded, my heart taking off at a gallop when he cradled my sweet girl against his chest. She cooed at him and grabbed onto his cut with her wet fingers. He didn't seem to mind the slobber and smiled down at her. *Crap*. If he kept doing things like that, I'd be in big trouble. My hormones were already all over the place where Wolf was concerned.

It didn't take long to pack my things and haul them over to a duplex toward the back of the property. Wolf set up Sienna's bed first. I fed her some baby food and laid her in her crib when she started to yawn. The place came with furniture. There was a full-size bed in the bedroom and a small dresser. Wolf had placed Sienna's crib between my bed and the wall, away from the windows.

He checked the kitchen and muttered something under his breath.

"Everything all right?" I asked.

"You have basic dishes and pans, but there's nothing stocked in the fridge or cabinets. Make a list of stuff you need for Sienna and anything else you'd want from the store. Since she's sleeping, I'll leave the two of you here and go grab what you need."

I started to tell him it wasn't necessary, but I stopped myself. Even if I didn't want him to pay for everything, I knew I didn't have enough to stock a completely empty kitchen. Instead, I'd be grateful and accept his help.

"Thank you, Wolf."

He gave me a slight smile and eased down onto a kitchen chair, rubbing at his leg partway down his right calf. I chewed on my lip a minute. I might not be able to pay him back with money. It didn't mean I had nothing of value to offer.

"Want me to take a look?" I asked. "Maybe I can help."

Something flashed in his eyes. Embarrassment?

"Wolf, everyone gets hurt. Even big, strong guys like you."

"It's an old injury and it's far from pretty. Nothing can be done for the pain right now. I'll soak in some hot water later."

I knelt at his feet and placed my hand on his knee. "Please? You're doing so much for me. I need to repay your kindness. I know I'm a burden on the club right now, unable to even pay for my own groceries. I need to do something to give back."

"You don't owe me anything," he muttered.

"Wolf."

He growled and yanked up his pants leg. I blinked as I realized why he'd been rubbing at his leg. It was missing from partway below his knee. The prosthetic he wore had a boot attached, but I could see the angry skin where it attached to his leg, despite the sleeve.

"IED," he said and tried to pull his pants leg down. I stopped him and lightly ran my fingers over the angry-looking skin.

"When you get back, make sure you have a change of clothes with you."

"What?" His brow furrowed.

"You're going to soak in the tub here and, then I'm going to rub some ointment into your leg. The skin is irritated."

"Putting the leg back on to go home would ruin whatever good you were able to do. I'll be fine, Glory. Been taking care of myself for a while now."

I sucked at guessing ages, but Wolf appeared to be somewhere between late twenties and late thirties. I didn't know when he'd been in the military, but if he'd been injured by an IED he must have served at some point. From what I'd learned, quite a few of the men here had been in the military.

"Then let me drive Sienna over to your house after you get back. I'll bring the ointment with me and treat your leg after you soak a little." I gripped his knee. "I can make dinner, so you won't have to worry about cooking tonight."

He watched me, his eyes giving nothing away. "My leg doesn't disgust you?"

I ran my hand down his calf and over the top of his prosthetic. "No. I'm sorry you lost part of your leg, Wolf, but it doesn't make you any less of a man. If anyone's told you otherwise, they were idiots."

"You're not what I expected," he murmured.

I smiled. "Ditto."

He sighed and ran a hand through his hair. "Fine. I'll bring your groceries back here, help you put everything away, then I'll head home and soak my leg. I'll leave the front door unlocked for you."

I had a feeling this wasn't my best idea ever, but I refused to back down. Seeing this side of Wolf, the vulnerability, did something to me. Getting close to a man right now was the last thing I needed. I had a degree to finish, a baby to care for, and needed to get my life together. Adding a man to the mix was a recipe for disaster.

You're just repaying his kindness, Glory. I nearly snorted. Yeah, I didn't believe it even when I just said it in my head. No, Wolf was a temptation, and no matter how badly I'd get burned, I wanted to move even closer to him.

This wouldn't end well.

Chapter Two

Wolf
Three Months Later

Glory worked too fucking hard. I leaned against the wall, my ankles and arms crossed, as I kept an eye on her. Technically, I was here to make sure no one busted into the clinic while the latest patient was here. At least, those were the orders I'd been given by the VP. Worked out well, since I liked making sure Glory was doing okay.

The day she'd arrived, I'd kept my mouth shut. I'd noticed the way she stood in Tank's shadow, a slight tremor making her hands shake. Then he'd dragged her forward and she'd found her courage, or faked it really well. The way she'd mouthed off to Demon still made me smile. Fucker needed to be put in his place every now and then.

Since then, I'd been her silent shadow, never letting her know I was keeping watch. I'd stayed close as she applied for jobs in town. It had broken my damn heart each time she'd come out looking dejected. The first time she'd come in late from doing a ride-along on an ambulance, I'd been the only one anxious. The others had just shrugged and said she'd be back when she'd finished. They might have been right, but I hadn't been able to shake the *what if something happened* feeling. Knowing her past, I'd decided to err on the side of caution, and I'd ridden over to the hospital. I'd arrived just as the ambulance returned and Glory had stepped out. Then I'd hung around and followed her home.

If she'd known I was there, she never let on. Hell, I'd followed her multiple times since then. It wasn't that Blackwood Falls was dangerous, but any town had a bad element. Too much shit had gone wrong over the years for me not to worry when she didn't come home on time. Now I made sure she got where she was going, and back to her place without any issues.

And if I remembered her gentle touch the night she'd helped with my leg, I kept that shit to myself. No one had ever wanted to take care of me before. Most women saw my leg and either pitied me or were revolted by my stump. Not Glory. I should have known she'd be different. If she were like all the others, I'd have been able to keep away. Instead, I tended to lie in bed at night and imagine she was lying beside me.

Griz had noticed my preoccupation with Glory and gave me shit about it. Of course, he'd been smiling at the time so I knew he wasn't worried. I hadn't turned into a stalker. Except when it came to Glory. I didn't like letting her out of my sight. Grizzly had asked if I was compensating for Franny deciding to up and move, and maybe at first, I had been. Glory had shown up the day Franny had given me the news. She'd known I wouldn't leave my club, so moving to another state had meant us saying goodbye. I'd toyed with the idea of making her my old lady, but something had always held me back. Now I knew what it was... she wasn't the right one. That and she'd never been able to look at my leg. The times we'd been intimate, I'd either kept my pants on or she'd looked everywhere but at the stump below my knee.

Sienna fussed from the playpen in the corner. The club had set it up so Glory could bring her along when she needed to work in the clinic. The little girl's cheeks flushed a deep pink and crocodile tears slipped down her face. Yeah, she was gearing up for a doozy of a fuss. I pushed off the wall and approached, kneeling down beside the playpen.

"Hey there, beautiful," I murmured in a low voice. "You tired of being locked up?"

She snuffled and hiccupped as she reached for me. Glory might have my head all kinds of fucked-up, but this little cutie? She had me wrapped around her finger. Or possibly her entire hand. I smiled and reached into the playpen, picking her up.

"Come on, gorgeous. Your mom isn't finished working yet." I cradled her to my chest, my hand splayed across her small back. At fourteen months, she wasn't quite as far along as other kids her age. Sienna had only started crawling shortly after they'd come to live here. I didn't know when she'd walk, or talk for that matter. Glory didn't seem worried, and anyone could see Sienna was a happy baby.

Glory walked past on her way into the exam room, letting her fingers trail along her daughter's arm. She winked at me. "I see she has her favorite guy."

I smiled and nodded. "The little princess here will be just fine. You do whatever you've got to do."

"Thanks, Wolf," she said softly, pausing to give me a smile before she hurried into the room.

Yeah, it wasn't just Sienna who had me whipped. I'd wanted a family for a while now, and some might say Glory and Sienna were convenient, but it was more than that. I'd been drawn to the two of them. I'd taken more notice of Glory than I should have. Franny and I had technically still been together when Glory had arrived at the Devil's Fury. It didn't matter she'd broken things off later that day, after she'd decided she would definitely be leaving town. I'd never been a cheater, and I never would be. There were times I felt guilty for taking notice of Glory when she'd burst into Church with Tank, even if Franny did seem to be happy where she'd moved. Last we'd spoken, she'd started dating someone. A nice, decent, law-abiding sort. Sounded boring as hell to me, but it was probably better for Franny.

Sienna babbled at me as she grabbed for the patches on my cut. I pried her fingers loose, then twirled our joined hands through the air, making her giggle. I'd learned the hard way she was stronger than she seemed, when she'd torn one of my patches off last month. Glory had been horrified, but I'd rolled with it. Yeah, I'd had to ask someone to stitch it back on, seeing as how I couldn't sew for shit. It had been worth it though to see the triumphant look on Sienna's face as she'd waved her prize around. The guys gave me shit about it, and I'd flipped them off.

I danced around the waiting room with Sienna, smiling as she giggled. God, but I loved this little girl. She'd had my heart almost from the start. The poofy pink tutu she had on hung over my arm, and the sparkles on her top caught the light. She really did look like a princess. Acted like one too. Sweet one minute and demanding the next.

She grinned at me, showing off her new teeth, and a bit of drool slid down her chin. I walked over to her bag and grabbed a cloth, wiping the spit from her face. She babbled, reaching for the bag and I wondered when she'd last eaten. I knew Glory kept some baby food in the bag and I dug through it until I found the small jar of squash and a spoon. I set them on the reception counter and pulled a bib from the bag.

"All right, little princess. Ready to eat something?"

She reached for the jar of food, yammering nonsense and kicking her feet. Yep, my girl was hungry. And yeah, I thought of her as mine. Even if Glory and Sienna didn't seem to want a man in their lives -- or at least Glory didn't -- I still wanted these two to be mine. I sat in Glory's chair, put the bib on Sienna, then opened the jar of food. I anchored Sienna with one arm while I used my other hand to feed her. Between bites, I set the spoon aside and cleaned her face of any excess food. Pretty as a princess, but messy like a boy. I smiled and kissed her temple before giving her another bite.

The door opened and a woman darted inside. She looked around the room before focusing on me and coming toward the counter. Shadows bruised the skin under her eyes, and she shifted from foot to foot. The way she twitched and jumped at every sound told me one of two things. She was going into withdrawal, or she'd been assaulted and needed our help. She blinked at Sienna and some of the tension eased from her body.

"Your daughter is cute," she said.

Warmth spread through me. "Thanks."

I felt a presence next to me and saw Glory with a soft smile on her face. Oh. Right. Maybe the woman had been speaking to Glory and not me. Although, the thought of this little one being mine felt all kinds of right.

Glory placed a hand on my shoulder and moved in closer. Her scent teased my nose, and my cock went semi-hard. It wasn't the first time it had happened, and I doubted it would be the last. I hadn't seen her in anything sexier than a T-shirt and jeans, or the scrubs she had on right now. Not knowing what was hiding under those clothes was more of a turn-on than all the skin the club whores showed off.

Since I'd been with Franny until three months ago, I hadn't touched a club whore in a while. And after... Well, I'd been too fascinated by Glory to even look at the easy women at the clubhouse. Other than stopping by to socialize with my brothers and get a cold beer, I avoided the parties. No reason to be there if I didn't want the easy pussy. I'd grown tired of it long ago, to be honest, but I'd kept up appearances. Until Franny.

"Do you have an appointment?" Glory asked.

"No. I heard about this place from a friend. She said…" The woman looked around again and lowered her voice. "She said if I needed help and needed to avoid the hospital I could come here."

I felt Glory tense and reached up to place my hand over hers. It seemed to work, and I felt her ease up again.

"It depends on the sort of help you need," Glory said. "Were you assaulted?"

The woman nodded only to hesitate a moment. "Not exactly."

"Which is it?" Glory asked.

"I had unprotected sex. The guy got rough, and I think he may have torn something. I'm bleeding and it's not that time of the month."

Something seemed off about the woman's story, and her behavior. She stated everything like she'd memorized it, with no emotion. The way she jumped at every little thing made me question her motives, but I knew Glory would help if she could. She couldn't stand for anyone to be in pain. I wasn't convinced there was anything wrong with this woman. Other than being a liar. An exam would let us know if she was telling the truth.

"We only have one doctor on staff tonight and she's helping someone right now. Are you able to wait?" Glory asked.

The woman seemed twitchy as she backed up. "No. It's okay. Maybe I was mistaken and it's not so bad."

Before either of us could say anything, she bolted from the room and out into the alley. Someone had told her about this place, but who? And why? Had she given the sob story to another woman, one who'd believed her? I didn't like the thought of this place being talked about all over town. If the cops raided us, Glory would be in a world of trouble. She wouldn't only face prison time, but she'd lose Sienna. I couldn't let that happen.

I handed the baby to her mom. "Hold her for me, sweetheart. I'll be right back."

She clutched Sienna to her chest and stared at the door. "You felt it too?"

I nodded. "Yeah, something's off with that woman. Lock the door behind me, and don't let anyone leave until I return."

I left the clinic and waited until I heard the lock click into place. Then I went down the alley in search of the woman. I heard her voice, low and not too far away. I crept closer, sticking near the building. The way her voice echoed, it sounded like she was on the side of the dumpster facing the brick wall across from me.

"I told you I couldn't get in," the woman said. "Look, S. If you want your whore back, you'll have to go in there and get her yourself. The woman at the desk is nice, and they have security around. I'm not risking that innocent lady, or myself."

I wished I could hear the other end of the call. Who the hell was S? Was he trying to get to the woman currently being treated?

"Fine. Whatever, S. You better pay up like you say you will."

She ended the call and I watched as she walked toward the street. I didn't know what was going on, but I had a feeling the woman at the clinic would need someone to see her home safely. I pulled out my phone and shot off a text to Steel. If anyone could keep the woman at ease, it would be him. Not only was he happily married, but he had a way with the ladies. Even terrified ones.

Need you at the clinic. Trouble came knocking.

It only took him a moment to respond. *Be there in ten.*

I went back toward the clinic and knocked on the door. "It's me, Glory."

The lock twisted and she pulled the door open, her face paler than usual. I hated that I'd scared her. If I hadn't said anything, or gone after the woman, Glory may have brushed it off and gone about her night. Just the same, I was glad I'd followed her. My instincts had been right. Whyever she'd come here, it hadn't been for medical help.

I stepped inside and shut the door behind me. "How much longer until the woman in the exam room can leave?"

"Maybe fifteen minutes? Could be a little longer. They were still treating her injuries when I was in there last. She needed stitches in multiple places. What did that lady want?"

"Nothing good. Sounds like she's working for someone, and I have a feeling she's after our patient. I called Steel to make sure she gets home okay. He can walk her to her car and follow her home. Best we can do. Anything happens after that, she'll need to call the cops."

"After she leaves, we can head home. She's the last appointment for today," Glory said.

Home. If only Glory and Sienna were coming to my house instead of the duplex. She'd made it clear she didn't plan to date anyone, so I'd tried to keep things as a friends-only relationship. I wanted more from her. So much more. With anyone else, I'd have gone after what I wanted. Glory was different. I didn't want to push her, make her feel cornered. She'd been through enough and had earned the right to have some space if that was what she wanted. There was also the age difference between us. I was sixteen years older than she was.

Of course, Glory was more mature for her age than most women I'd met. She'd graduated high school and finished a four-year degree in the time most women her age were still figuring shit out. I had a hard time picturing her with someone her age. For one, I didn't know too many nineteen-year-old men who wanted to be fathers, especially to a kid who wasn't from their own DNA. Most of us tended to be selfish assholes when we're younger. And some remain selfish assholes until they die.

Glory looked from Sienna to me. "Would you want to come over for a late dinner? I put chicken and dumplings in the crockpot earlier today. It will still be hot when we get back."

My stomach grumbled at the thought of food, especially food I didn't have to get from a drive-thru or cook myself. "You sure you have enough?"

She rolled her eyes. "Wolf, do you honestly think I can eat an entire crockpot of food by myself? If there's anything left, I'll set it aside for lunch tomorrow and the day after. If not, no worries."

"All right. Then I'd love to stop by for dinner." I smiled and reached out to run my finger over Sienna's cheek. "Any excuse to spend more time with my favorite girl."

"If you lived with her, you might feel differently. Her last ear infection about killed me. She was up at all hours because she was hurting, and only walking with her would keep her calm."

I moved a little closer, wishing I could take them both into my arms. "No. I wouldn't. I'd consider it an honor and a privilege to help her through the pain. Same for her mom."

Glory's cheeks went pink. *Shit.* I hadn't meant to say that last part. Before I could backpedal, she leaned closer and pressed her lips to my cheek.

"Thank you, Wolf. For everything, but mostly for showing me not all men are assholes. I've witnessed that same kindness with the Dixie Reapers, but it was Tank's wife who brought me into the fold, so to speak. But a single guy? There aren't too many of those like you. Some part of me knew that, even after what happened to me. Knowing it and experiencing it are two different things, and you continue to amaze me."

Now *my* cheeks were burning. I wasn't some saint or knight in shining armor. I was just a guy. One who was insanely attracted to the woman in front of me.

"I'm not anything special, Glory."

"I'd have to disagree," she said softly.

When the doc yelled out for her, she handed Sienna to me and went back into the exam room. By the time the woman left, with Steel following in her wake, I felt like I'd been tied in knots. I wanted Glory more than my next breath. Not just in my bed, either, but in my life, day in and day out. I wanted the entire package and not a one-night stand. What I wanted didn't matter, though. Glory had to want it too. Want *me*.

I followed them to Glory's duplex and parked my bike in the driveway. I knew my brothers would notice. They'd already given me hell the few times they'd seen me parked over here or Glory over at my place. Nothing had happened between us. She'd helped with my leg twice now when it had been overly irritated, and we'd shared a few meals. I'd even watched Sienna once while Glory ran some errands because the precious girl had been asleep. The rest of the time, the old ladies pitched in to watch the baby when Glory couldn't take her with her.

The smell hit me when I walked through the door and my stomach cramped from hunger. *Damn.* My mouth started to water as I made my way into the small kitchen. Sienna sat in her highchair, smacking her hands on the tray.

"Want me to feed her?" I asked.

Glory handed me a jar of bananas. "I'm going to make her a little rice cereal. It will fill her up more, so she'll hopefully sleep all night."

I cracked open the jar and started spooning the bananas into Sienna's mouth. She *hmmm'd* between bites, opening her mouth like a baby bird wanting more. God but I loved this kid! I used the rubber tip on the spoon to swipe some of the food from under her mouth and she latched onto it, eating that little bit too. She finished off the jar right as Glory put the bowl of baby cereal on the table. I reached for it and started feeding it to Sienna.

"You mentioned she's developmentally delayed. I know she doesn't walk or talk yet. And she's not feeding herself," I said.

"We tried some Cheerios a few weeks ago. She didn't chew them well enough and started to choke, so I went back to the baby food and cereal. If you watch her with the learning toys, she's not as advanced as she should be."

"Did the doctor say why?"

"It's a combination of things, or so they think. She was born a few weeks early. Even though she'd cooked long enough she didn't need to be put into NICU, they warned me she could have complications down the road. Those complications ended up being seizures by the time she was six weeks old. They got them under control, but they took a toll on her. Her motor functions aren't quite where they should be. There's a chance she could be autistic."

"That's... a lot."

Glory sighed. "There's so much they still don't know about seizures in infants and the long-term effects, and some of what they believe I think is mostly conjecture. Studies with rats aren't necessarily conclusive evidence, at least not to me. Sienna is just Sienna. If I find out later she's autistic, then I'll roll with it and do what I can for her. Right now, her motor skills are off, she's not speaking yet, and I honestly worry there may be other mental issues we'll be dealing with in the years to come."

Glory set a bowl of chicken and dumplings in front of me with a glass of sweet tea, then did the same for herself. I cleaned up Sienna's face and hands, then gave her some foam bath toys Glory kept in the kitchen for times like this. While we ate, I watched my two girls.

"You love your daughter unconditionally," I said.

Glory blinked at me. "Of course, I do."

"But the way you seem to frequently point out she's delayed, sometimes makes it seem like you think no one else could ever love her too. Even if she isn't their daughter by blood, she could still be their daughter by choice. Look at Steel and his family. He didn't contribute to Coral's DNA, but she's very much his daughter. Or Dagger and Guardian... they both adore their son, Luis, even though he was a toddler when they claimed his mother. Sometimes family isn't about what flows through your veins, Glory. Family comes in all shapes and sizes, and it doesn't always require matching DNA."

She dropped her gaze and worried at her bottom lip. "You're right. Maybe I'm doing her a disservice by avoiding men."

"Thanks," I muttered. "Do I need to start bra shopping with you?"

She'd just taken a drink of her tea and spewed it across the room. She coughed and patted at her chest. "No."

"You don't avoid me," I pointed out.

She wouldn't look at me. A pink tinged her cheeks. "You're different."

I could live with *different*. For now. It was a start at any rate.

Chapter Three

Glory

I couldn't stop thinking about what Wolf had said. He was very much a man, and I was certainly aware of the fact. When I'd said I avoided men, I hadn't even thought to include him in my statement. Because Wolf wasn't just any man. He'd been there for us, even when he'd thought I didn't notice. It's part of what had worn me down. I'd noticed him lurking in the shadows multiple times. I'd asked Slash about it when I'd gone to visit Shella. He'd barked out a laugh and looked rather gleeful when he'd told me Wolf was smitten. His word, not mine.

After that, I didn't mind having him shadow me. I felt safe, no matter what time of day I had to be out. The way he watched Sienna and played with her made me feel all warm and gooey inside. I'd often heard the way to a man's heart was through his stomach. Well, he'd apparently figured out the way to mine was through my daughter. I'd enjoyed spending time with him, which is why I'd offered to feed him on several occasions. Maybe subconsciously, I'd been testing the waters and seeing if not only I could handle dating someone, but if Wolf could also handle Sienna and me.

I'd already put Sienna to bed, and Wolf was pulling his keys from his pocket, ready to head home for the night. I swallowed hard, hoping he was going home and not over to the clubhouse. I didn't think for one minute he'd been faithful to a non-existent relationship between us. My stomach knotted at the thought of him being with the women at the clubhouse and bile rose in my throat. I pushed it down, my hands clenching and unclenching at my sides. Was I ready for what I was about to do?

Wouldn't know until I did it. Rip the bandage off, so to speak.

"Wolf."

He turned his head and waited, watching.

"Would you stay a little longer?" I asked. "Maybe... Maybe even for the night?"

Every muscle in his body visibly tensed and his hand tightened on his keys to the point I worried he'd draw blood. I wondered if I'd read the situation wrong. Had I just screwed it all up?

"Glory, you don't have to invite me into your bed. I enjoy spending time with the two of you. I wasn't trying to ask for..." He cleared his throat. "That wasn't the point of what I said in the kitchen."

"I'm not stupid. I know the men around here can have sex whenever they want with those women at the clubhouse."

He walked toward me. "And you what? Thought you'd offer up yourself to make sure I didn't go to them?"

He wasn't entirely wrong. And yet, he wasn't exactly right either. It was somewhere between the two. No, I didn't want him with those women, but the way he made me feel, I was curious what it would be like to be kissed by a man like Wolf. Held by him. Possibly more if I didn't lose my courage.

"I haven't been with anyone since the night Sienna was conceived," I said, my voice almost a whisper. "I can't promise I won't freeze or want to bolt if things get to a certain point, but I'd like to try. It's partially that I don't like the idea of you going to those women. And it's also because I think about you all the time."

He reached up, his touch light as he skimmed his fingers over my jaw, then slipped his hand behind my neck. He held me gently, easily enough I could break away if I wanted. "You think about me?"

I nodded. "I've noticed you watching me, making sure I get home at night. The way you are with Sienna, it's... you're a good man, Wolf. The way you reacted when I saw your leg, it's clear you've been damaged by other women, and I haven't been able to stand getting too close to men. We're quite the pair, but I thought..."

"You thought what?" he asked, his voice deep and gravelly.

"I thought we could heal each other. Sometimes two broken pieces fit together better than smooth ones, right? Like a jigsaw puzzle."

His lips tipped up on one corner. "Yeah, they do."

"Will you stay? Even if I can't give you... everything. At least, not tonight."

"Glory, I'd never ask for more than you were willing to give. If you just want to cuddle on the couch and watch movies, I'm all right with that. I'll let you set the pace. Not just tonight, but for every moment from this point forward."

I stepped closer, pressing my cheek to his chest and wrapping my arms around his waist. It was the first time I'd hugged a man like this, voluntarily. Since having Sienna anyway. It felt good. Right. I breathed him in, and my nipples went hard. I didn't know why someone hadn't snapped him up and begged him to marry them. They were all fools.

He ran a hand down my back and held me tighter. I waited, thinking panic would set in, but it didn't. Anyone else had tried this and I'd have been freaking out by now. With Wolf, I just wanted more.

"Would you kiss me?" I asked. "Please."

He tipped my chin up. "Sweetheart, it would be my pleasure. I've wanted to kiss you since that first week you were here. Then I felt guilty. You didn't need someone looking at you that way then, and Franny had left just me. My head wasn't in the right place, so I kept my distance. Or tried to."

"We're both single, Wolf. There's nothing standing in the way."

He leaned down, his breath fanning across my lips. "Call me Max."

Before I could question him, he pressed his lips to mine. It was a soft, coaxing kiss that made my toes curl and had me holding onto him. His arm tightened even more, molding me against his body. A soft whimper escaped me, and he took advantage, his lips ravaging mine.

It felt like lava flowed through my veins, the heat licking at me from the inside. My clit throbbed and I squeezed my thighs together, hoping to ease the ache. I rubbed against him like a cat in heat, the friction against my nipples nearly enough to make me come. It felt like everything was spinning.

He broke the kiss and attempted to pull away, but I didn't let him. Tugging him back down, *I* kissed *him*. Wolf groaned and stumbled back, taking me with him. I heard his back crash into the wall. The hand on my hip slid down until he was cupping my ass. I cried out, my panties getting more and more soaked by the minute.

"Max!"

"Tell me to stop." He kissed me again. "Tell me, Glory, or I may go too far."

I shook my head. No. I didn't want him to stop. I wanted him to keep going. I wanted... to come. How long had it been since I'd had an orgasm? Never.

That's how long. I hadn't been able to give myself one. I had a small vibrator, but I could never relax enough to enjoy it.

"I want to touch you," he murmured between kisses. "Taste you. Hear you scream in pleasure."

"Yes! Please, Max. I've never felt like this before. It's scary and thrilling at the same time." I panted and gripped the sides of his cut. "Don't stop."

"I'm not doing this in your front entry," he said.

Sienna was asleep in her bed, which was in the room we shared. I took his hand and led him over to the couch. "It's not a perfect solution, but would this work? Or... Wait!"

I let go and hurried to my room. I yanked the comforter off the bed and carried it to the living room, then I spread it on the floor. Not the greatest solution, but it was the best I could do. I glanced at him to see if Wolf was disappointed. He shrugged out of his cut before padding toward me. I'd already taken off my shoes and socks. Those were the first thing to go when I got home, and I'd changed out of my scrubs and into a tee and leggings.

He patted his thigh. "Can't take my shoes off because the boot on this leg is attached to my prosthesis."

I sank onto the blanket and waited for him to join me. "If you're trying to drive me away, it won't work. I've seen your leg already. But I want you to be comfortable, so..."

"This isn't about me right now," he said. "It's about you. I'll give you everything you want, and the moment it's too much, tell me."

"All right."

I stretched out and he lay down beside me, bracing himself on one arm so that he hovered over me a little. Wolf traced the contours of my face and brushed his fingers over my lips. "So beautiful."

He kissed me again, his lips devouring mine. I felt like I was drowning in pleasure. I squirmed on the blanket, needing more yet not knowing how to ask for it. He seemed to understand and slipped a hand under the edge of my shirt. He skimmed his fingers across my belly before slowly inching up toward my breasts. He cupped one hand over my bra and drew back, his brow furrowing.

"Is this okay?" he asked.

"More than." I licked my lips. "You can touch me any way you want, Max. If something makes me uncomfortable, I'll let you know. You don't have to ask permission every step of the way."

He'd trusted me enough to share his real name. The only thing I had to offer was myself. He'd never given me cause to think he'd go too far. He'd been a gentleman. Sweet, even. I didn't know what I'd done to be so lucky as to share this moment with him, but I didn't want it to end.

He nodded and edged my shirt up. My breath caught as he lifted it over my breasts, and I wriggled to help him pull it all the way off. My bra wasn't pretty, but it was comfortable. I wished I had something lacy, or at least silky, instead of plain cotton. The pink fabric had little gray dots spread across it, and I'd put on the matching panties. Not sexy. Not even a little. I tried not to think about what the women at the clubhouse worse. Or rather, how much they didn't wear.

He smiled as he ran his finger along the top of the cup.

"Cute and delicate. Like you."

Cute. Just what every woman wanted to hear in the middle of making out.

He tugged the cup down and my nipple tightened in the cool air. Wolf brushed his thumb over the tip, and I cried out, my back bowing off the floor. I kicked my feet and shifted my hips, my pussy pulsing with need. My lack of sexy undies was long forgotten as my body screamed for release.

"So fucking responsive, Glory. I'm one lucky bastard."

"Stop talking. More... just *more*."

He chuckled and leaned down. I felt his tongue flick across my nipple before he sucked it into his mouth. The light scrape of his teeth was enough to send me over the edge. I ground my teeth together so I wouldn't scream the place down and wake Sienna. My release soaked not only my panties, but I felt the wetness on my leggings too. My cheeks burned as I wiggled my hips on the blanket.

Wolf kissed me, then nibbled the column of my neck. "Want more?"

"You already made me come."

His lips curved against my neck as he smiled. "Sweetheart, you can come multiple times. If you want to."

If I wanted... was he crazy? Who wouldn't want more than one orgasm? Was that a trick question?

I felt his hand slide down my stomach and his fingers slip under the waistband of my leggings. He rubbed back and forth, each swipe sending his hand a little bit lower. My heart gave a kick when I realized he wasn't doing it to tease me. The tension in his body told me enough. Even though I'd said I'd let him touch me however he wanted, he still worried it would be too much.

Tears pricked my eyes at how wonderful he was. I only wished I'd found him sooner. Of course, too much sooner and being with me would have put him in jail. He slid his palm over my panties and between my legs. My breath hitched as I spread my thighs a little wider.

He growled as he stroked over the wet material. I felt the rumble straight through to my core. He rubbed against the swollen lips of my pussy before shoving the material aside. The first touch of his roughened skin sent a shock through me.

"Feel good, sweetheart?" he murmured, kissing my neck again.

"Yes. So good, Max."

He spread my pussy lips and circled a fingertip around my clit. It felt like my heart would pound out of my chest as he toyed with me. The first swipe of his finger and I had to clamp my mouth shut so I wouldn't yell out. He worked my clit in small, tight circles and I'd have sworn fireworks were going off over my head. My hips jerked. I felt like I needed something more.

Wolf rasped his whiskered chin against my shoulder and sank a finger inside me. He stroked it in and out, using his thumb to put pressure on my clit. I trembled and my thighs spread even farther. The world fell away when I came so hard I thought I might black out. I ground my teeth together, knowing I couldn't make any loud noises, but oh, how I wanted to!

"That's it, Glory. Come for me, beautiful."

"Max." I reached for him, fisting his shirt in my hand.

He devoured my lips and changed the angle of the finger inside me before adding a second one. He must have hit that special spot inside me, the one I'd thought was only a myth, because I soaked my leggings and the blanket with my next orgasm.

He removed his hand from my pants and sucked his fingers clean, and fuck if that wasn't hot. I slid my hand down from his chest to his belt, but he stopped me, gripping my wrist and prying me loose. "Told you. This isn't about me."

"I'm not letting you leave without you getting something out of this too." Besides, if he did walk out the door while he was hard as a rock, he might decide to wander over to the clubhouse for a little relief. And I knew it would gut me if I found out.

"You want me to come?" he asked, rubbing his nose against the shell of my ear.

"Y-yes." A shiver raked my spine, and I knew if he kept touching me I'd ask him to stay all night. I still might.

"No touching, pretty girl. You just lie there and let me look at you."

He rose to his knees, then shifted until he sat between my splayed legs. I watched in fascination as he unbuckled his belt and slid his zipper down. When he pulled out his cock, I licked my lips. I'd never wanted to suck a guy's cock before, but with Wolf? Yeah, I wanted to. I'd never been impressed with that particular part of a man's anatomy, until now.

He gave it a hard tug and pre-cum beaded on the tip. I wiggled on the blanket, wishing we were both naked. He was right to try and go slow, but my body was all lit up and ready for so much more. I wanted it all. Him inside me, his body over mine. I panted as he stroked himself. Was it getting warmer? My hands fisted the blanket and I looked up at his face. Wolf eyed my breasts like a starving man. I reached up and cupped one, rolling my nipple between my fingers.

He groaned, his hand moving faster. The hot spurts of his release splashed across my belly.

"Fuck," he muttered. "I had no intention of things going this far. You okay, Glory?"

I nodded. "More than."

"Stay right there. I'll get something to clean you up." He rose to his feet, fastened his pants, and rushed from the room. I heard the bathroom sink running and he returned a moment later with a warm, wet rag. He wiped his cum off my skin and left again with the rag in his hand.

"Will you stay?" I called out.

He returned to the living room and folded his arms, staring down at me. "Such a pretty picture. Know what would look even better?"

I couldn't bring myself to ask. What if he said a different woman would make the moment perfect? Yeah, I could admit I was a little insecure when it came to this particular man. Only because I'd never wanted another one before. Wolf was the only guy who'd sparked my interest. The few dates I'd been on in college had been more of an experiment than anything else. Always being younger than my peers hadn't made it easy to have a boyfriend.

He came closer and knelt next to me, brushing my hair off my face. "Only thing that could make this better would be having a bed we could share without Sienna an arm's length away, because if I go to bed with you, I can't promise I won't ask for more."

And if Sienna weren't in the same room, I'd gladly let him have whatever he wanted. I'd never been so turned on in my life.

He stretched out next to me again, helping me right my clothes. Wolf tugged me into his arms and held me. "Think we need to talk."

"No conversation ever turns out good when it starts with 'we need to talk.'"

He chuckled. "It's not a bad thing. At least, I'm hoping it won't be."

"Just spit it out, Max. You're killing me."

"You're not like the women at the clubhouse," he said. "I don't want you to think tonight didn't mean something. I want to see more of you, Glory, and I don't necessarily mean in the biblical sense. Although, I wouldn't say no to you taking your clothes off again."

"Like... dating?" I asked, hating the slight tremor in my voice.

"Would that be okay? Or do you need more time?"

Okay? Was he serious? "Max, I..."

He kissed me soft and slow. "Please say yes, Glory. As much as I enjoy the time we spend together, I need more of it. I fucking hate all the hours and days we're apart. If you were anyone else, tonight would end a lot differently."

I turned a little so I could look at him. "Different how?"

"I'd claim you. Both of you. You'd be my old lady and Sienna would be my daughter. I know what I want, Glory, and it's the two of you. Not just for tonight, or tomorrow. I want *all* your tomorrows."

My throat grew tight, and I felt tears mist my eyes again. He was killing me. So damn sweet and thoughtful. He really was the perfect man.

"You'd do all that if I were someone else?"

"Not exactly what I meant. I only want you, Glory. I just know you've had a rough time of it, and I don't want to send you running for the hills. Now that I've had a taste, I know I can't let you go."

Sweet, sweet man. I'd never met his equal. To think he wanted us, to be a family with me and Sienna.

It made me ache. I couldn't think of anything more wonderful than to be his.

I reached up and cupped his cheek. "I don't want you to let go. Hold onto me, Max. I've never wanted anything as much as I want you. Is that crazy?"

He smiled. "No. Not the least bit."

I decided to take a leap of faith. If anyone deserved my trust, it was Wolf. "Do it."

"Do it?" he asked.

"Claim us. I don't know what all that entails, and I don't care. I want all your tomorrows too."

His kiss was rough and demanding when his lips came down on mine. He growled and held me tight against him. It seemed I'd unleashed the beast. And I was loving it.

Right into the fire, Glory. I only hoped he didn't burn me.

Chapter Four

Wolf

I needed to do things the right way, except when it came to Glory, I found I didn't much give a fuck. There was no way in hell the club would deny my claim. They'd all vote her in as my old lady because if they didn't, I'd fight every last one of them. I'd waited long enough.

"You tired?" I asked.

"Not really." She cuddled closer. "What did you have in mind?"

I smacked her ass when she tugged at my shirt. "Not that. You're moving in with me. Both of you."

Maybe I should have prefaced it with how much they already meant to me. Glory had been around the club long enough to know most of us were domineering assholes, but I wanted to be a better man - - for her. She made life worth living. Gave me a reason to face each day with a smile.

She lifted her head, her lips parted like she might disagree, but she only shook her head, seeming bemused. "I'm going to have to get used to that, aren't I?"

"What?"

"You telling me how things are going to be. I've been on my own for a while now. I'm not used to having to think of anyone but myself and Sienna."

I cupped her cheek and brushed my lips against hers. "I tend to be a controlling man, Glory, but I would never do anything that would hurt you. I'm claiming you, so moving in is the next step. Sienna will have her own room. You can change anything you don't like about the house. It's going to be your home."

Even though Franny had come over somewhat frequently, a woman had never lived in my house. I'd never asked Franny to move in. Another sign I'd known in my gut she wasn't the right woman for me.

"I still have the boxes I brought with me. I just broke them down and stuck them at the top of the hall closet." She took a deep breath and released it. "We're really doing this, aren't we?"

"Yep. Any second thoughts?"

She shook her head. The soft look in her eyes made me want to wrap her in my arms and never let go. I didn't know what made her decide to be so brave tonight. I'd never thought she'd give me a chance, much less agree to be mine. I only hoped she didn't come to regret the decision later.

Glory stood and stretched, then disappeared into the hall. She came back a moment later with a stack of flattened boxes in her arms. I got up and took them from her, carrying them into the kitchen. She handed me a roll of tape and I got to work putting them together. I knew the kitchen stuff here had come with the place. When she'd arrived, all she'd had were clothes for her and Sienna, and of course Sienna's furniture and toys. It had broken my heart to see how little she had. I'd snuck in a few things when I could, left a few toys on the porch for Sienna when I knew Glory wasn't watching. It hadn't felt like nearly enough. I'd mostly given her things for Sienna because I knew she wouldn't refuse them.

"I can't pack the bedroom until the morning. I don't want to risk waking her up," Glory said.

"It's fine. We have the boxes ready so it shouldn't take us long. I'll load Sienna's bed and stuff into the truck in the morning after she's up and ready to face the day." I set my hand at her waist and steered her toward the hallway. "Come on, beautiful. We need to get some rest."

She balked a moment. "But Sienna…"

"Is asleep, and hopefully we will be too. Not going to try anything with our girl right there in the same room with us. I just want to hold you somewhere more comfortable than the floor." I tightened my hold on her hand. "Knowing you're mine, that you'll be in my bed from now on, there's no way I can walk away tonight."

Although, if she'd asked me to, I would have. I'd never force myself into her bed. Didn't matter if we were at her place or mine. When she moved in, if I ever made her uncomfortable, I'd gladly sleep on the couch.

She nodded and headed for the bedroom. Her cheeks were bright pink as she pulled a sleep shirt from a drawer in the dresser and started to remove her clothes. I watched as she stripped off her shirt and leggings, licked my lips as her bra hit the floor, and knew I was going to be hard all damn night. But it was worth it.

I set my cut on the top of her dresser and yanked my shirt over my head. I unfastened my belt and pants and shoved them down over my hips, then sat on the edge of her bed. I unlaced my boot and pulled it off. Tugging my pants leg up, I worked on unhooking my prosthetic leg and set it aside. I rolled the sleeve down and rubbed at the stump a moment. It took a bit of shifting, but I managed to get my pants the rest of the way off and left them on the floor.

I eased back against the pillows and reached for Glory. She curled against my side, her cheek on my chest and her arm over my waist. I felt her breath fan across my skin, and everything in me relaxed. I hadn't been able to lie down like this with Franny. We'd had

sex during our time together, but she wouldn't have
been comfortable lying in bed with me like this. My leg
would have bothered her. Glory took it in stride and
acted like it was no big deal. Maybe to her it wasn't.
She hadn't hesitated to touch it and had rubbed
ointment into the stump more than once.

Sienna fussed in her crib and Glory pulled away.
She lifted the baby from her crib and brought her to the
bed. I held out my arms for her.

"Let me see my precious girl."

Glory handed her over and crossed the room to a
small cart she'd gotten for Sienna's things. She grabbed
a diaper pad, fresh diaper, wipes, and some ointment,
then brought everything over to the bed. While she set
everything out, I kissed Sienna's forehead and
murmured to her.

"Does my beautiful girl need a dry diaper?"

Sienna pressed her face against me and made a
snuffling sound. The sweet angel had held my heart
from the moment I'd seen her.

"I can take her," Glory said.

I shook my head and waved her off. These two
were mine now, which meant I'd be changing my
daughter's diaper. I laid Sienna on the diaper pad and
removed her footie pajamas. The diaper was so full it
felt like it weighed several pounds when I pulled it off
her. Using the wipes, I cleaned her up, put a little
cream on her so she wouldn't get a rash, then wrapped
the new diaper around her.

"You're rather good at that," Glory said.

I wasn't about to admit I'd watched YouTube
videos to figure out how to take care of a baby. I'd held
quite a few of the kids around here, but no one asked
me to babysit. I'd offered, and I'd watched Luis a few
times, but he didn't exactly need to be changed.

Instead, I'd taught him to pee on a tree, which Zoe had
fumed over. The look on Dagger's face had told me
he'd already covered that lesson, even though his
woman didn't realize it. Apparently, Luis hadn't said
something since his mom had been so upset. But the
moment I realized I wanted Glory and Sienna to be
mine, I'd learned everything I could about babies.

"Think her pajamas are a little damp," I said.

Glory fetched a fresh pair and I changed Sienna
before cradling her against my chest again. I didn't
think Glory realized exactly what she'd given me. By
agreeing to be mine, she'd made me a father. Sienna
might not be my blood, but it didn't matter. She was
mine just the same.

"I think she's going back to sleep," Glory said
softly. "Want me to take her?"

I gently handed Sienna over, then settled back on
the bed again. Glory put our daughter to bed before
curling up against me. I ran my hand up and down her
arm, feeling more content than I'd ever been before.
When I'd gotten out of the military missing part of my
leg, I'd thought I'd never find a woman who would
accept me. I'd almost settled with Franny. Her moving
away had ended up being a good thing. It had given
both of us a fresh start.

"Thank you," I murmured.

"For what?"

"Being mine. Giving me a daughter. Best fucking
night ever."

"It is pretty fantastic," she said. "Multiple
orgasms, a guy who's almost too good to be true, and
Sienna gets a daddy."

My phone chimed in my pants pocket and I
groaned, not wanting to ruin the moment. Only the
club would be trying to reach me this late. I untangled

myself from Glory and yanked my phone from my pocket.

We have a problem. What the fuck? Of all the nights for something to go wrong, it figured it would be tonight. I often joked I wouldn't have any luck if I didn't have bad luck.

"Something wrong?" she asked.

"Steel texted me. Club business."

She sighed and rolled over, giving me some privacy. I liked that she didn't try to read the screen of my phone. She hadn't been here long, but she understood how things worked. Just another reason she was perfect for me.

What kind of problem? I hit send and waited to see if he'd respond.

My phone chimed. *Someone broke into the clinic. Trashed the place.*

Fuck! Glory would be devastated. I had to wonder if the break-in had anything to do with the strange woman who'd come in earlier, then quickly left. I ran a hand over my head, knowing Steel wouldn't have contacted me if I wasn't needed. At the same time, I wasn't ready to leave Glory.

I'm with Glory. I hesitated only a moment before hitting send.

The phone rang and I answered it quickly so it wouldn't wake up Sienna.

"You're with Glory?" Steel asked the second the line connected. "In what capacity?"

"In the way that means we need to call Church tomorrow because I need a property cut. I'm not asking. She's mine and that's the end of it."

Steel chuckled. "Won't get any arguments out of me. Think everyone knows how you feel about her. I'm glad to see you finally made a move. Don't worry about the clinic. We've got plenty of single brothers who can take this one."

"Thanks, Steel."

There was a tone to his voice that made me pause, but if he said they had it covered, I'd take him at his word. Just how bad was the clinic damaged? Had anything been stolen? As much as I wanted to ask more questions, I didn't want to get dragged into it tonight.

"Badger's blowing up my phone," he said. "I'll let him know about you and Glory. Save you a phone call."

"Can you ask everyone not to call me the rest of the night? I don't want the phone to wake up Sienna."

"Spoken like a true father." Steel cleared his throat. "Proud of you, brother. I'll let the club know you need some privacy tonight. Take care of your girls."

Before I could say anything else, he hung up. I tossed the phone onto my jeans and leaned back in the bed again. Glory curled against me once more, her fingers tracing a pattern on my abdomen.

"Does this mean you don't have to go right now?" she asked.

"I'm staying right here, sweetheart. Let's get some sleep. We'll have a busy day tomorrow." I ran my hand down her soft skin. "Close your eyes. Everything will be fine."

I would tell her tomorrow about the clinic. She didn't need all the details, but since she worked there, she needed to be aware there was a problem. I wouldn't keep her entirely in the dark. It would only put her at greater risk. I'd never agreed with my brothers who wouldn't tell their women when they could be in trouble. If Glory knew to keep an eye out, she might not get taken by surprise.

I lay awake until the sun started to creep through the window. My eyes felt gritty, and I rubbed at them. Even though I was tired, I hadn't been willing to miss a moment of my first night with Glory and Sienna. They may have been sleeping, but I'd lain here and just taken it all in. They were mine. My family. It hardly seemed possible.

When Sienna started shifting around in her crib, I pulled the sleeve back over my stump and pulled my jeans on before attaching my prosthesis. I picked my phone up off the floor and shoved it into my pocket. After I put on my boot, I took Sienna from her crib before she started to fuss. I knew Glory would need a little more sleep. I changed my girl, put her in clean clothes, and carried her to the kitchen. I'd need to learn how to make her baby cereal, but for now, she could eat a jar of fruit. I grabbed some peaches and one of her spoons before putting her into the high chair and making sure she was secure. Glory kept a stack of bibs on the counter, and I took the top one and fastened it around Sienna's neck.

"All right, my beautiful girl. You ready for some breakfast?"

She smacked her hands on the tray in excitement and kicked her feet. I scooped out some of the peaches and fed her a little at a time, wiping her face every few bites. She finished off the jar and wanted more, so I found a jar of pears. By the time she'd eaten both jars, she seemed content. I wet a cloth and cleaned her up before taking her out of the chair.

"Let's let your mommy sleep a little more," I said, kissing her temple.

I carried her into the living room and sank onto the couch. I flipped on the TV and put a cartoon on, even though I knew Sienna wouldn't pay much attention to it. Sometimes the colors or music would catch her attention. Mostly, she played with whatever was closest. I grabbed her stuffed bear off the floor and handed it to her. It made a slight rattle noise, making her giggle.

My stomach rumbled and I knew I'd need to eat before we got my girls moved into their new home, which meant Glory would want to eat too. I wasn't about to ask her to cook anything this morning. I pulled out my phone and shot off a text to Garrick, one of our newest Prospects. After Badger patched in all four of the ones we had before, we'd needed some fresh blood.

Pick up two ham and cheddar omelets from the diner and bring them to Glory's.

I got a thumbs-up emoji in response. With a shake of my head, I put my phone away and focused on Sienna. She had drool running down her chin and I cursed myself for not thinking about keeping a rag handy. I wiped her face with my thumb and rubbed it on my jeans.

"Most men don't voluntarily wear baby spit on their clothes."

I smiled and looked over at Glory, where she leaned against the doorframe. Her hair was tangled and sticking up a little on one side, and she had a pillow crease on her cheek. Fucking adorable.

"Morning, Sunshine. I ordered breakfast. Should be here before too long."

"You thought of everything. You got Sienna without waking me up, you're feeding me..." She stretched and padded over to the couch, sinking down next to me. "Guess I'd better keep you."

I leaned over and kissed her. "Yeah, you better. Because I'm certainly keeping you."

A knock at the door interrupted us. Either the Prospect had already been at the diner and had driven at the speed of light to get here, or someone needed my help. I knew Glory had made friends with the old ladies, but it was too early for any of them to come for a visit.

"Come in," I yelled out, hoping it was our breakfast.

Garrick strolled in with a sack hanging from his hand. He took one look at me, shirtless and holding a baby, then skimmed his gaze over Glory before he opened his mouth and promptly shut it. Looked like no one told him I was claiming Glory and Sienna. Why the fuck else did he think I was having breakfast delivered here? Apparently, my news hadn't yet reached the Prospects.

"Where do you want this?" he asked.

"Kitchen table is fine," I said. "If you can come back in about thirty minutes, I wouldn't mind some help getting the crib loaded into my truck."

He scratched the back of his head. "Um, okay."

"Glory and Sienna are moving in with me."

"This have anything to do with the incident at the clinic?" he asked.

I narrowed my eyes, wishing he hadn't said anything. I'd wanted to get Glory settled before I told her about the break-in. Thanks to his big mouth, I'd need to talk to her sooner rather than later. I'd hoped to keep her from worrying first thing this morning. "No. I'm claiming them."

He nodded and hesitated a moment. "If you want, I can grab the crib now, go ahead and load it while y'all eat. One less thing for you to do when you're done."

I knew he was thinking about my leg, and while I hated to admit I had any weaknesses, the truth was that my leg caused me problems from time to time. I could carry the crib to the truck by myself, but I'd pay the price later.

Glory smiled at him. "That would be really great. I still need to pack some stuff, and it would free up Wolf to watch over Sienna."

Leave it to my woman to make it sound like letting the Prospect load the crib was somehow a favor to her and not about me. I didn't know how I'd lucked out to land a woman like Glory. I knew she was out of my league. The woman was fucking incredible.

"On it," Garrick said.

I stood with Sienna in my arms and went into the kitchen with Glory. Even though Sienna had already eaten, Glory gave her some toys to play with in her high chair while we had our breakfast. Garrick loaded the crib and made himself scarce. There wasn't a lot left to pack, even though Glory made it sound like she needed hours to get things together. I knew we'd have her over to my place, and the truck unloaded, long before lunch. I'd also hoped to have more information before I spoke to her about it. Right now, there wasn't much I could say.

"About the clinic... We need to have a talk. I'd planned to wait until we were at the house and you'd unpacked, but I don't want you to sit here worrying about it. Someone broke into the clinic either late last night or early this morning. The place was trashed, but no one got hurt. We don't know what they were looking for, but I think it's related to the strange woman who came in last night."

Glory let out a sigh. "At least it happened while the place was empty. Did they take anything?"

"I don't know. Everyone's left me out of it so I could have this time with my two girls. We can find out more once we have your stuff unloaded at the house. If there was something to worry about, someone would have told me by now." At least, I hoped there wasn't anything to worry about. Since I'd asked everyone to leave me alone, there was a chance the situation was worse than it seemed. I wouldn't know until I either made some calls or dropped by the clinic. Either way, I wanted to hear it without Glory present. I'd keep her informed, if I thought she could be in danger, but that didn't mean she needed to hear every detail.

"All right." She reached over and took my hand. "I'll follow your lead, Max. I can't promise I'll always be the submissive little woman who asks how high when you say jump, but I'll try not to disrespect you in front of your club."

I smiled and leaned over to kiss her. "Don't want you all meek and submissive, Glory. I like your fire and determination. But if I give you an order, it's for your own safety. Disobey and I promise I'll spank your ass, and not in a fun, sexy way."

Her cheeks warmed and I knew I'd be finding out more of her likes and dislikes in the bedroom soon enough. The flush on her cheeks made me wonder if spanking might be something she liked or wanted to try at least once. I'd be willing to try most anything with her, as long as she didn't want anyone else in the bed with us. I drew the line at sharing. I was a selfish bastard and Glory was all mine!

Chapter Five

Glory

When Wolf had said the clinic had been broken into, I didn't know what I'd pictured. Anything glass had been shattered. The door lock had been busted along with the frame. My desk lay on its side and papers were strewn everywhere.

"It looked worse," Steel muttered from where he stood with Wolf a few feet away.

I had a hard time picturing *how* it could been worse. If they'd already been cleaning up, what exactly had happened in here? Paint had hastily been rolled over part of the wall. I wondered what they were covering up, but now wasn't the time to ask. For that matter, Wolf might decide I didn't need to know. He seemed the sort to want to protect me.

I stepped into the exam room and gasped. The padded table had been shredded. Deep grooves covered the walls, like someone had taken metal claws to them. Something sticky had splattered over the floors in different areas.

"Don't walk through there," Steel said. "Guy jacked off all over the damn place."

My nose wrinkled and I backed up. Great. I'd already stepped in some. Now I'd have to burn my shoes because there was no way I'd ever get them clean enough.

"We're out of commission for a little bit," Steel said. "Not only do we need to scrub the shit out of this place, but I want better security before we re-open. Those women shouldn't have to be scared someone will come after them. At least, not while they're here."

"What's Demon said about all this?" Wolf asked.

"He's asked Outlaw to pull up the footage from any nearby cameras. I almost pity the bastard once Demon finds out who did all this. There won't be anything left of them." Steel folded his arms and stared at the utter chaos surrounding us. "Asshole deserves whatever he gets. I just hope he didn't go after that woman."

"I understand why the clinic doesn't have any visible cameras, but I'd thought the club would install discreet ones. I think if it meant the women who came here were safe, they'd understand. You think it's someone looking for the rape victim we helped last night?" I asked.

"From what Wolf said, the lady who came in acting all twitchy was talking to someone who seemed to be searching for someone. My money is on the rapist trying to find his victim, make sure she keeps quiet. Dipshit didn't realize by coming here, she wasn't ready to admit who'd hurt her. If she had been, she'd have gone to the damn hospital instead." Steel shook his head. "I knew we'd run into trouble. I'd just hoped it wouldn't happen right away."

The look he shared with Wolf made me think there was more to it. If it was something I needed to know, I had no doubt Wolf would tell me. Until then, I'd try to keep my curiosity in check.

Wolf rubbed a hand across his jaw, eyeing me. I knew exactly what he was thinking, and he could just forget it.

"No," I said.

He smirked. "Didn't say anything, beautiful."

"You didn't have to. I know that look already. You don't like me being here now that trouble has come knocking, and you want to wrap me in cotton and tuck me away somewhere safe."

Steel snickered. "She's got you on that one."

I rolled my eyes. "Like you'd be any different if it were Rachel working here instead of me."

Steel sobered. "You're right. None of us like the idea of our women being in danger. And since Wolf just got you, he's not ready to lose you. Give him some slack, Glory. The boy worked hard to earn your trust."

I blinked at Wolf being referred to as a boy when he was so much older than me. Then again, Steel looked to be in his fifties or sixties, so to him, Wolf probably was still a kid. My brow furrowed as I studied Steel.

"Isn't your wife younger than Wolf? If you think he's a boy, what does that make Rachel?" I asked.

Steel narrowed his eyes at me and stomped out of the room, muttering under his breath. Wolf came closer, slinging his arm around my shoulders.

"You've done it now," he said. "He can be touchy about the age difference between him and Rachel."

I leaned against him. "Sorry. I just found it funny he called you a boy when his wife is younger than you. I couldn't resist. I'll apologize."

"Just leave it," Wolf said. "He'll get over it."

I looked around and winced at the destruction. So much hard work. Wrecked. Ruined. Much like the women who came here. We'd have to put in the time to resurrect this place. I'd healed from what happened the night Sienna was conceived, and this clinic -- as well as any women who came here -- could be healed as well. It just took patience and time.

"There's not much I can do here, is there?"

Wolf shook his head. "Sorry, baby. We'll get the Prospects in here to clean the place up. Until the security has been upgraded, we'll have to keep it shut down. I hate that those women and girls won't have anywhere like this to go, but we can't risk putting them or you in danger."

"I know. It just sucks. Now what am I going to do?"

He tipped my chin up. "I know you're the independent sort, which I admire, but you aren't in this alone. You don't have to work yourself to the bone. You want to volunteer here? Fine. Focus on your degree and don't worry about a paying job. I've got my girls covered, understood?"

I knew he wasn't trying to be bossy or keep me from working. The Wolf I'd come to know was kind and sweet. Of course, to be part of the Devil's Fury, I was certain he had a darker side. One I hadn't seen yet. But with me and Sienna, he'd been gentle and incredibly patient.

"I'm not used to someone else paying for things I need. Even when I lived with my parents, I still worked for most of what I wanted or needed. They covered the basics, but everything else came out of my pocket."

"And it made you a strong woman. Little did they realize they'd prepared you for the time they turned their backs on you. I'm sorry you went through that, but, Glory, I meant what I said. You're mine, and that means I get to take care of you. Whether it's buying diapers, paying for groceries, or footing the bill for anything else the two of you need or want. I consider it an honor."

I kissed him, letting my lips linger on his a moment. "Thank you, Wolf."

"I've wanted a family of my own for a while now, Glory. I should be thanking you. Having you and

Sienna in my life is the best thing that's ever happened to me."

I hugged him tight. "We should probably get her."

He ran a hand down my back. "We will. Soon. First, I need to take you somewhere, and no arguments. Not now and not when we get there. Elena wouldn't have offered to watch her if she couldn't handle it."

"Fine. I know she's watched her before, but that was a necessity while I went on my ride-alongs or searched for a job. This is different. But I reserve the right to call and check on her. Frequently."

He kissed my cheek. "You can call or text as much as you want. When you annoy the shit out of Elena and she refuses to share those enchiladas I know you love, you won't have anyone to blame but yourself."

Damn. He wasn't wrong about the enchiladas. I didn't know what she put in them, but they were like crack. The one time she'd brought an entire dish over to me I'd inhaled them in one night. Then paid the price when I thought I might explode. It had been my welcome gift the first week I'd been here.

"All right. I'll only check in once." No way I was going to ruin my chances of getting more enchiladas.

Wolf herded me out to his truck. Even though I'd have loved to ride on the back of his bike, we'd dropped Sienna off with Elena and Outlaw so the truck had been necessary. Although, I now had to wonder if he'd also brought it for whatever errands we were about to run.

As much as I hated surprises, getting to spend more time with Wolf wasn't a bad thing. He made butterflies flap in my stomach. I'd always loved watching romantic comedies, even though I'd never experienced any of those things for myself. Until Wolf. With him, I felt… everything. I wanted him to kiss me and never stop. To touch me. I wanted to hold his hand just because I liked having that small contact with him.

He parked at the mall and winked at me. "Ready to shop?"

"Shop?" I asked. "For what?"

"Everything." He got out and came around to my side, helping me down from the truck. "Let me spoil the two of you a little."

When he put it like that, I couldn't tell him no. I could tell it meant a lot to him. A flash of excitement lit his eyes when he took my hand and led me into the mall. It made me wonder if he'd gone shopping with Franny. Part of me wanted to ask, but I held back. What if I didn't like the answer? He'd known her before I'd ever moved to Blackwood Falls. It wasn't fair for me to feel jealous over the relationship they'd had. Clearly, she'd walked away and started a new life somewhere else. I couldn't imagine letting a guy like Wolf slip through my fingers.

"You're going to need the right clothes for riding on my bike," he said. "And boots, but we'll get those somewhere else."

He took me to a shop filled with casual clothes. The other shoppers looked to be near my age. More than one eyed Wolf in curiosity. I selected a few pairs of jeans, thinking it would be enough. Wolf had other ideas. By the time we left, I had six new outfits. I'd thought it would be the end of shopping for me. I should have known better. Wolf was a man on a mission.

"I don't really do the dressing up thing," Wolf said. "But there will be times you'll want something nicer to wear. Parties for the family at the clubhouse. Anniversary dinners. Holidays."

I dug in my heels as he tried to drag me into what I knew was an expensive department store. I'd been inside it a few times, just to browse, and I hadn't seen a single item under fifty dollars. He didn't relent and kept tugging until I fell into step beside him.

"Wolf, it's too much," I protested.

"Not nearly enough."

I eyed the tags of the dresses we passed and blanched. Most were several hundred dollars. Why would I ever need clothes like these? I had a hard time picturing the old ladies I'd met dressing in anything like this.

He took my hands and pulled me closer. "Look, Glory. I can more than afford this shopping trip today. I want you to have some nice things, and before you get all defensive, I'm not saying there's anything wrong with what you have now. I just want to add to it. Get one dress from here, and a pair of shoes to match. We can get stuff somewhere else after that."

I had to admit the dresses were beautiful. I'd never owned anything so nice before, not even when I'd lived at home with my parents. They'd led a comfortable life, but we'd never had a reason to wear things like these dresses.

"I've never seen a man so eager to open up his wallet," I muttered.

"Only with you." He winked.

"I didn't agree to be yours just so you'd buy me things," I said.

He stopped mid-step, his gaze narrowing on me. "You think I don't know that? Hell, I've been trying to sneak things to you from the first week you were here."

He'd been... "That was you?"

His cheeks flushed a little and he nodded. "I didn't think you'd accept them if I gave them to you outright, so I left them on the porch."

My heart melted a little more. I'd never realized it had been Wolf. He'd left so many things for Sienna, and even a few groceries from time to time. I'd been grateful to our guardian angel. Knowing it was Wolf somehow made it even more special.

"All right. But don't make a habit of this, Wolf. We don't need anything but you."

He kissed me, holding me close. "Promise."

"I only feel one hand at my waist. Did you just cross your fingers?"

"I'll never tell."

I shook my head as he made me try on multiple dresses until I found something I liked. After he paid for the dress and a matching pair of shoes, he dragged me to another store. By the time he'd finished convincing me we needed new wardrobes, new toys for Sienna, and things for the house, I felt like I might drop from exhaustion. I'd never been one to shop all day, and I wondered how people did it. No, how did they *enjoy* it? Because my feet hurt, my back ached, and I just wanted to go home.

"Ready to pick up our daughter?" he asked as he pulled through the gates of the compound.

"More than." I couldn't help but smile whenever he called Sienna his. She'd never had a daddy, and even if I'd known who her sperm donor was, I'd have never let him anywhere near her. Knowing she'd have Wolf to help guide her along and protect her made tears mist my eyes for a moment.

We pulled up out front of Outlaw's house and I laughed at the sight that greeted us. September in

Georgia was still hot and muggy, but they'd spread a large blanket on the ground. Their toddler, Valeria, was trying to play with Sienna, even though my poor girl didn't seem to know what was going on. Outlaw had stretched out on the blanket, his head propped on his hand, while Elena took pictures of the kids with her phone.

"Wishing I'd thought of this," Wolf said.

"I think Sienna will enjoy it more when she's a little older. Maybe in the spring we can have a picnic with her."

He flashed me a smile before getting out of the truck. I followed him over to the blanket and sank onto my knees beside Elena. I knew she was pregnant, but if she'd started to experience any morning sickness, or any other fun things, it didn't show. She glowed with health and happiness.

"I see the girls are having fun," I said.

"Valeria more than Sienna," Elena said. "But I thought the fresh air might be good for them. And for us. Outlaw was getting cranky looking at his computer so I made him take a break."

Outlaw grinned up at her. "Real hardship there. Spend time with you or stare at the computer. Besides, I'd given the club everything I could for now."

She reached for his hand, massaging it between hers. "If they need anything else, send them to Wire. You know how your hands get when you overdo it. You don't have to be Superman."

I wanted to ask what was wrong with his hands, but I figured it wasn't my place. If it was general knowledge, I'd ask Wolf when we got home. Even if I didn't have a medical degree, there might be something I could do to help. The way Elena talked, his hands caused him pain.

"Ready to go, my little angel?" Wolf asked, scooping Sienna up off the blanket. She latched onto him and started babbling.

I'd never considered having more kids since I'd thought it would just be me and Sienna forever. But seeing her with Wolf? Yeah, I kind of wanted another one. Maybe not right this second, but in the next few years. Which was a conversation we hadn't even had yet. What if Wolf wanted kids now?

My stomach cramped at the thought, but I tried to tell myself I was being ridiculous. He'd been so kind and understanding so far. There was no reason to think he'd demand I have another baby right now. Until I finished my degree, it was better to hold off. He might say I didn't need a job to help pay the bills, but being a nurse was my calling. I honestly didn't care if I worked at a private practice, hospital, or just helped at the clinic the club ran. I wanted to make a difference in someone's life. The how wasn't quite as important.

"Come on, girls," Wolf said, holding his hand out to me. I let him pull me to my feet and followed him to the truck.

"Thanks for watching her," I called out. Elena waved me off before focusing on her family again.

"Sienna didn't seem to know what to make of Valeria," Wolf said as we drove to our house.

"No, she didn't."

He glanced at me. "What are your thoughts of giving her a sibling or three?"

And it seemed we were having the discussion now instead of later. "I don't mind having more kids. In fact, I want to. Would you care if we waited a little bit, though? I'd like to finish my degree. I'm almost done, but dealing with a pregnancy while stressing over everything else going on isn't really the best idea."

He lifted my hand and kissed the back of it. "Then we'll do our best to make sure you don't get pregnant right now. Doesn't matter to me if we wait a day, a week, or even a year. All I need to know is if you're open to it at some point. If you aren't, then I could always get a vasectomy."

My jaw dropped. "What?"

"Why should you be the one responsible for the birth control? And sorry, baby, but condoms aren't foolproof. Even if that's what we use right now, there's still a chance you could end up pregnant."

"You'd do that, though? If I didn't want kids, you'd go get a vasectomy, which if it worked, would guarantee you never had any babies?"

His brow furrowed. "But I do have one. Sienna is mine, Glory, just like you are. Doesn't matter if I donated the sperm or not. I don't need a kid who's part of my DNA. The two of you are more than enough."

This man. He floored me at every turn. Sometimes I wondered how he could possibly be real. His kindness, gentle touch, and concern for myself and my daughter made him unique, at least as far as any men I'd ever known. Wolf was one of a kind, and for whatever reason, he'd decided I was his.

You are one lucky bitch, Glory. Don't fuck it up.

Chapter Six

Wolf

Whatever Glory was cooking for dinner smelled amazing. Sienna had gone down for a nap, and I was left to my own devices. My leg bounced up and down as I fought the urge to go help my woman in the kitchen. I knew she wouldn't run me out of there, but I would probably be more of a hindrance than a help. I reached down to rub at the area above my prosthesis. I'd changed into shorts when we'd gotten home and swapped out my prosthetic for the one I preferred when I was around the house. It wasn't pretty, but Glory didn't seem to mind.

Until I'd met a woman who seemed to accept me unconditionally, I'd never realized how freeing it could be. Going from being a competent soldier to a man with a missing limb had taken its toll. I'd not only had to learn to deal with the pain, and how to walk again, but psychologically I'd taken a beating. While I had trouble admitting I might have a few limitations, I'd always been tough and locked down the pain, pushing through to finish whatever task I'd started. I refused to let my missing leg keep me from doing the things I loved, like riding my bike, so I'd had to learn how to live with my new normal. Thankfully, my missing leg was on the right side and I hadn't had to modify my bike. It had taken Glory's acceptance for me to realize I'd been hiding. I'd thought I'd dealt with the fact I wasn't whole anymore, but I'd been wrong. I'd never let anyone see me like this -- less than perfect, at least physically -- until now. Until her.

I flipped through the stations on the TV, finally stopping on *Journey to the Center of the Earth*. I'd always been a Jules Verne fan. My middle school librarian had introduced me to his adventure books, and I'd been hooked on reading ever since. Not that anyone could tell by looking at my house. These days I kept everything digital and preferred to read on my phone. Being a geek didn't mesh with the tough biker persona I wore with pride. Or at least, I'd always thought it didn't. Maybe it was time to make a few adjustments in my life, and definitely to my perception of not only myself but others. I needed to stop hiding. From me.

I heard the clang of a pan hitting the counter or floor and got up to check on Glory. Sienna, thankfully, slept through the noise. I didn't hear a sound from her bedroom. My leg ached more than usual, and my steps were a little slower. Glory held her hand under the running faucet.

"Baby, what happened?" I asked, trying to hurry closer to her.

"I didn't pay attention and burned my hand. It's not bad."

I reached for her hand, inspecting the pale pink mark. Since she was the one studying nursing, I'd take her word for it on the severity. I reached up into the cabinet to the right and pulled down one of the med kits I kept in the house. I took out the burn ointment and a bandage, then helped Glory dry her hand and applied both. I lifted her hand, kissing it.

"Maybe you should let me finish dinner tonight."

She pushed her hair from her face and sighed. I could tell she felt like she'd disappointed me, or maybe she'd just let herself down. "I wanted to cook for you our first night in the house."

I gathered her in my arms. "Glory, you've made several meals for me already. Let me take care of you tonight. Go watch TV, read, or just close your eyes and relax."

She nodded, her shoulders slumping a bit. "Okay. I didn't get far with dinner anyway. I was warming the skillet to brown some meat when I accidentally burned my finger. I did make a pie that's already cooling."

"Spaghetti all right?" I asked. "Won't be gourmet, but I can cook the beef you set out, season it up a bit, and add it to a jar of sauce."

"I don't expect 'gourmet,'" she said. "Anything I don't have to cook sounds amazing. Are you sure you don't mind?"

"I'm positive. Now scoot." She turned and I swatted her ass. Glory gave a squeak and tossed a mock-glare over her shoulder. I found myself smiling as I picked the skillet up off the floor. I placed it in the sink and pulled a clean one from the cabinet by the stove. While it warmed, I opened the package of ground beef and dug through the meager spices I owned. Now that I had a family to care for, I needed to stock my kitchen better. And maybe look up healthier things for us to eat.

It wasn't long before I had the meat sizzling in the skillet, the noodles boiling on the back burner, and the sauce warming in a pot. I added a little minced garlic, oregano, and basil to the sauce since I'd opted for a plain marinara the last time I'd shopped. Thankfully, I liked garlic and always kept a few cloves on hand. It would come in handy tonight, otherwise dinner would have been rather bland. We certainly could use more spices. Hopefully Glory knew more about them than I did.

I drained the pasta, then the meat. I stirred the beef into the sauce and made sure I'd shut off all the burners. Before I could get the plates, I heard raised voices and the hair on my nape prickled. Glory's voice came through loud and clear, the tension putting me into motion. I cleared the doorway and froze.

"Franny, what the hell are you doing here?" I asked.

"I came home," she said, arms folded with a glare in Glory's direction. "What the hell is this *puta* doing here?"

I bristled and ground my teeth together. "Don't call her that! And for the record, this was never your home, Fran. Why the hell would you think you'd show up and suddenly move in?"

Sienna started crying down the hall and Glory rushed off to get her. She came back with our daughter clutched in her arms, tears streaming down Sienna's chubby cheeks. Glory pressed against my side and I placed my hand at her hip, tugging her even closer. I didn't know why my ex had dropped by out of the blue, especially when she was supposedly in another state and with another man, but I didn't like the way she was treating Glory. Still, I knew Franny had been on the fragile side and I didn't want to cause her pain.

Franny's eyes went wide. "What's going on, Wolf?"

"Why are you here, Fran? You left. Moved out of state. Last I heard from you, you'd picked up a new boyfriend."

She dropped her gaze, then grimaced when she saw my leg. She waved a hand at it. "Can't you put something else on?"

I felt Glory tense next to me. "Are you fucking kidding me?"

Franny jerked her gaze up to meet Glory's. "What?"

"You were dating Wolf, and you can't stand to look at him without his pants on? What the hell is

wrong with you?" Glory shoved Sienna into my arms
and advanced on my ex, fire in her eyes and fury
rolling off her in waves. God, but she was sexy as fuck
right now. Glory jammed her finger in Franny's chest.
"You have the audacity to show up unannounced,
question my presence in this house, *and* tell Wolf to go
put pants on? He's in his own damn home, and there's
not a fucking thing wrong with the way he's dressed."

"How can you look at it?" Franny asked, doing
her best to not drop her gaze to my missing limb.

"You're a bitch," Glory said.

Franny flinched, and I knew I should step in, but
honestly, I liked having my woman stand up for me.
Maybe some would consider it weak to let Glory fight
this battle, but I knew she needed to do this. My
brothers had my back, and I knew they'd die for me.
Having Glory face off with Franny was different. And
hot as fuck. I shifted as my cock started to stiffen.

"He lost his leg fighting for this country. Instead
of grimacing and making him feel like shit over
something he can't control, try thanking him for his
service! Why the hell were you with him if you can't
accept Wolf as he is?" Glory demanded.

I saw something flicker in Franny's eyes and it
made me wonder how much of her previous sweetness
had been an act. She'd never been an outright bitch
before. Had she played me and I'd overlooked it, or
made excuses for her? I didn't know if it was having
spent so much time with Glory that made me see
things differently, or if it was the space I'd had from
Franny.

"Can you honestly say it doesn't disgust you?"
Franny asked.

Glory's face flushed a deep red and I feared for
Franny's safety. My woman gripped Franny's arm and

hauled her over to the front door. Opening it, she shoved Franny out of the house and slammed the door in her face.

"That woman!" Glory growled and stared at the door.

"Easy there, tiger. She didn't mean anything by it." Glory whirled on me and looked like she might attack. I held up a hand to placate her. "You have no idea how much I appreciate you standing up for me, Glory. But Franny is... damaged. She was part of a human trafficking ring. They lured her here with promises of bringing her family over. She didn't mean to be offensive."

At least, I'd always thought she hadn't meant it. It was possible I'd been wrong. About a lot of things.

"Don't make excuses for her. She can either be a victim the rest of her life, or she can try to build something new. You coddled her, didn't you? That's why she's back. She wanted you to take care of her."

She wasn't entirely wrong. I'd thought Franny was independent, until I'd met Glory. The two were as different as night and day. To be honest, when Franny had left, I hadn't exactly been brokenhearted. More disappointed than anything. She wasn't the woman meant for me, and some part of me had known it. I'd tried to make things work with her, and we could have been happy. I just wouldn't have felt even half the passion I had with Glory.

A fist pounded on the door and I walked over to yank it open. Franny still stood there, arms crossed and looking fragile. Tears slipped down her cheeks, and she curled in on herself. Glory was right. She was playing the part of the victim. How had I never noticed? Dagger stood next to her, his eyes narrowed and his jaw tight.

"Why the fuck did you leave her out here on the porch?" Dagger asked. "She has nowhere to go. We all know you've been mooning after Glory, but shit, Wolf. What the hell are you thinking?"

Glory came up beside me. "She can't stay here."

Dagger's eyes widened a fraction as he took in Glory, then seemed to realize I was holding a baby. He rocked back on his heels. "What the hell is going on?"

Glory threw her hands up in the air. "Does no one around here communicate?"

"Apparently not," I said. "I told Steel I was claiming Glory. She and Sienna have moved in. He was supposed to spread the word. It's why I didn't stop by the clinic when we first found out about the break-in."

Dagger scratched at the beard along his jaw and looked from Glory to Franny, then to me. "So you didn't invite Franny back?"

"No." I glanced at Franny who was still crying. There was a part of me that wanted to help her. We'd been together for over a year. But I had to think about Glory and Sienna. I wouldn't ask my woman to accept my ex into our house, and I'd be damned if I let the club railroad me into it. Besides, now that Glory had brought it to my attention, I could see Franny was playing a part.

"I came back to be with Wolf," Franny said, another tear sliding down her cheek. "I should have never left him."

Glory rolled her eyes and huffed. "Oh, please. Are you suddenly madly in love with him?"

Franny nodded eagerly. She clearly didn't sense the trap Glory had just laid. I had a feeling my woman was about to shred her. While a part of me still felt inclined to shield Franny, I knew it would be the wrong move, and would likely drive a wedge between me and Glory.

"Really?" Glory asked, folding her arms. "So you'd not have any problem with him walking around the house just the way he is now? You'd help rub his leg when he overdoes it?"

Franny flinched and took a step back. Yep, and there was the answer plain as day. She'd never been able to handle my missing leg, and I knew she never would. The day she'd left had been a blessing. As much as I'd cared about her, I'd always felt like I couldn't relax in my own home when she was here. The blinders had come off. I no longer saw Franny as a sweet, helpless woman who needed me. She'd used me and I'd been a dumbass and let her.

"What the fuck is going on?" Dagger asked.

"Franny can't handle Wolf's leg not being whole. She told him to go put pants on to cover it up," Glory said. She pointed a finger at Franny and snarled like a rabid animal. "That bitch isn't coming in this house."

Dagger held up his hands. "I'll take her over to Slash's place. Maybe the VP can figure something out. I didn't have the entire story when I knocked on the door."

The tension eased from Glory and I pulled her against my side, wrapping my arm around her waist to anchor her just in case she decided to go after Franny. I only wanted the best for Fran, even though I knew we were wrong for each other. I hoped she found happiness and acceptance.

"I'm sorry, Fran," I said. "Even if you'd stayed, I don't think we'd have remained together. The moment I met Glory, I knew she was the one for me. And I'm not saying that to hurt you. There's a lucky guy out there who's perfect for you. But it's not me."

"Come on," Dagger said, reaching to gently take her arm. "Let's go see Slash. Maybe he'll let you stay in one of the duplexes until you get shit figured out."

Glory tried to take a step closer to the door, but I held on tight. "In case you didn't get the message, you aren't welcome in this house. Don't come back."

Before I could react, Glory slammed the door and twisted the lock.

"I can't believe her!" Glory tore herself from my grasp and stomped into the kitchen. I followed in her wake, a half-smile on my lips as I watched her bang things around and fix our plates. "The nerve! Showing up uninvited! Did she think you would just sit around pining for her?"

Knowing Franny, she'd probably never considered I wouldn't be sitting at home alone. Before her, I'd had my share of the club whores, but I'd been faithful to Franny, even when we weren't having sex. She hadn't seen the other side of me. Then again, Glory hadn't either, but she watched everyone around her, and she'd known the Dixie Reapers before coming here. She had to have some idea we were a bunch of horny bastards who had plenty of options.

I put Sienna in her high chair and buckled her in. Since she'd just woken up, I knew she'd be hungry. While Glory put the pasta into two large bowls, I got a few jars of baby food down from the cabinet and fed Sienna. I wondered when Glory had last taken her to the doctor and when she'd get to move on to something more solid. We hadn't really discussed it much.

"Does she have a pediatrician in the area?" I asked.

"No. I meant to ask Zoe and Elena who they use, but then I get sidetracked by something and forget."

"I'll get the name and number. Wouldn't hurt to set up an appointment and get another opinion on our girl here. Maybe things have changed since her last visit," I said.

Glory came over and ran her hand through Sienna's short hair. "I wish that were true. I haven't seen any difference in her, other than she smiles and laughs a lot now. She's happy here. Even though I knew the Dixie Reapers, I didn't hang around them much. I'd considered Tank's woman, Emmie, to be a friend, as well as a few of the other old ladies. I wouldn't have said we were close, though. Still, they were the only friends I'd had in a while. Sienna and I were largely on our own back in Alabama. To be surrounded by a community like this is different for both of us, and I think she's thriving with so much attention."

"Well, who wouldn't love our girl? She's pretty perfect, just like her mom." I winked at Glory, making her cheeks turn a rosy pink.

"We should eat before the food gets any colder." She sat and picked up her fork.

"Sorry about Franny," I said, feeling like I owed Glory an apology. Not just for Fran showing up unexpectedly, but… well, for everything the woman had said.

"Not entirely your fault." She eyed me. "You can't help being drawn to a damsel in distress, and she played the part perfectly."

She wasn't wrong. "Good thing I wised up and decided I needed a strong, independent woman."

Glory smiled and leaned over to kiss my cheek. A warmth spread through me, and I knew I'd made the right decision. Bringing Glory and Sienna here, claiming them, was exactly what we'd all needed. They were my family now, and I'd do everything I could to keep them safe and happy. No matter the cost.

Chapter Seven

Glory

Sienna had gone to bed an hour ago, and Wolf had dozed off on the couch. I'd crept from the living room and explored my new home, stopping in the master bedroom. My things were put away and I could see into the bathroom where my toothbrush shared the holder with Wolf's. It was intimate and should have scared the crap out of me. Moving in was a huge step. Instead, butterflies rioted in my stomach. I only hoped Wolf was everything he seemed and I didn't come to regret the choice I'd made. From what I'd learned, there was no going back.

Now that he'd claimed me, I was his.

Forever.

The butterflies swooped around some more and my hand trembled as I shoved my hair behind my ear. Seeing his ex earlier had scared me at first. She'd been stunning, and I'd worried he'd decide he wanted her back. But hearing the way she'd spoken to him, and seeing the revulsion on her face, had ignited a fire inside me. I'd wanted to punch her, drag her outside, and beat her ass. Somehow, I'd managed to hold back. How could she not see how wonderful he was? I'd known right away she'd been using him. I couldn't remember the last time I'd been so angry.

The fact his club hadn't noticed made me wonder if they just gave women a free pass. I'd heard Demon had once branded a club whore who'd endangered Dragon's woman, but I had a hard time picturing it. The men here might be rough around the edges, and perhaps they were rude and crude at times, just the same, they seemed to have good hearts and I had trouble imagining them harming a woman. Even if she had deserved it.

I moved farther into the room and ran my fingers over the quilt covering the bed. It didn't look like something a man would select and I wondered if Franny had bought it for him or helped pick it out. The thought of her being in his bed, *this* bed, made me want to burn the damn thing. It was stupid to feel so jealous over her. She clearly didn't have true feelings for him. But Wolf must have felt something for her to stay with her for so long, to let her bully him into hiding in his own home, unable to be comfortable or relax completely.

And she'd called me a *puta*. I'd Googled it because I'd never taken Spanish. If someone had said that to me right after I'd been raped, it would have hurt a lot more. I'd been a virgin until that night. Even though I didn't think more than two men had hurt me, since I'd passed out, I couldn't know for certain. It had bothered me for a while. Still did if I were being honest with myself. As much as I wanted to know who had done such a thing to me, not knowing was better. I could at least claim ignorance over the possible sperm donor for Sienna, which meant no one could try to take her from me.

I heard Wolf's steps behind me and eyed the room again. The walls were a soft blue-gray and the trim a bright white. The cherry-colored wood flooring was pretty and so was the throw rug with blues, grays, and a bit of teal. But the bed... I sighed. It was completely unreasonable to ask him to get a new bed. I wouldn't do it. I'd just have to pull up my big girl panties and deal with it. It wasn't like I'd ever imagined a guy like him would be a virgin. Franny had likely only been one of many to share his bed.

Wolf placed his hands on my shoulders, kneading the muscles. "You're too tense. Something wrong?"

"Only thinking."

"Must not be something good." He wrapped his arms around me, tugging me against his chest. "Want to talk about it?"

No, not really. I might be a bit insecure where he was concerned, but it didn't mean I wanted him to know about it. I was supposed to be a strong, independent woman. A single mom who could stand on her own two feet. Not mope because the guy I liked had been with other women. I wasn't in high school anymore and needed to grow the hell up. Then again, Franny was only a small part of my dark thoughts tonight, even if she'd been the catalyst.

"She called me a whore," I murmured, immediately wanting to call the words back.

"I'm sorry, Glory. You know damn well that isn't the case. You're the sweetest, most innocent woman I've ever known. She lashed out and went after you instead of me."

"After... the incident, I felt so dirty. I scrubbed my skin until I rubbed it raw. Several times a day, I'd shower in water so hot it hurt. People would whisper behind my back, saying I'd deserved what happened to me." I leaned against him, giving him more of my weight. "Sometimes I wish I knew who'd hurt me. Other times, I realize it's for the best I don't."

Wolf held me, giving me his support. I didn't spiral into dark thoughts often. Most of the time, I pushed forward, refusing to let one night ruin the rest of my life. Besides, I'd gotten Sienna out of it, and I loved her more than anything. My girl was amazing, and she made life worth living. If it hadn't been for her,

I might not have pulled myself from the darkness. And now I had Wolf...

"I guess hearing her call me that brought it all back," I said.

"Until you went toe to toe with Fran, I didn't realize how many excuses I'd made for her. She took me by surprise, but I promise I will never let someone speak to you like that again. I should have done something more than stand there."

I rubbed his arm where he still held it around my waist. "It's okay, Max. The two of you have history together. And I saw how manipulative she was with Dagger. I'd imagine she'd been the same with you."

He nodded, his five-o'clock shadow scraping my neck. "Yeah, she was. I guess with her past I made too many allowances for her. I didn't do either of us any favors."

"You saw a sweet woman in trouble," I said. "She played on that and used it to her advantage. Makes me wonder what happened with the man she was supposedly seeing."

"I'm not about to track her down to ask," Wolf said. "But I have a feeling Slash will have more than a few questions for her, especially if Dagger tells him the way she acted while she was here."

I turned to face him, his arm remaining around my waist. "No one seemed to know we were together. You said you'd told Steel, and I know you told the Prospect who brought us food. Do you think he forgot to let anyone know?"

"It's possible. He's probably been tied up with the mess at the clinic."

I ran my hands up and down his chest. "You know, it's my first night here. We should take advantage of Sienna being asleep. Especially since she'll probably wake up in a few hours needing to be changed."

Wolf cupped my cheek and leaned down. "Oh yeah? What exactly do you think we should do?"

I bit my lip so I wouldn't smile. "Well, you could make me scream your name. Isn't that what you bikers are supposed to be so good at? Making a woman beg for more?"

He growled softly and backed me toward the bed. "That what you want? To beg? I might like having you on your knees."

My breath caught and my nipples tightened. *Holy shit!* The image of me on my knees, dipping my hands into his pants, made me burn hot. I'd never sucked a guy off before and the idea of letting Wolf be my first and only? Yeah, big turn-on. I knew with him I was safe. There wasn't a single doubt in my mind he'd never hurt me. At least, not intentionally.

I slid down his body until my knees hit the floor, my hands dragging down his torso to rest on his hips. "You mean like this?"

His eyes darkened and I saw the muscle in his jaw tic. I reached up and ran my fingers back and forth just under the waist of his shorts. The rumble of his growl vibrated against my hand and I squeezed my thighs together. Licking my lips, I held his gaze as I tugged his shorts down. It didn't escape my notice he wasn't wearing underwear. Had I known he was going commando the entire time we'd been here tonight, I might have been tempted to try this sooner.

His cock bobbed in front of my face, pre-cum already beading on the tip. My heart pounded in my chest and anticipation raced through me.

"I've never done this before," I admitted. "If I do it wrong, tell me how to fix it."

He tangled his fingers in my hair. "It will be perfect because it's you."

His words warmed my heart, and I gently gripped his shaft. I lapped at the pre-cum, wondering how he'd taste. His flavor was surprising salty, but not horrible. I'd heard horror stories in high school about how bad it would taste, the girls in the locker room not caring who heard as they discussed their more intimate activities.

I ran my tongue along the length of his cock before flicking it across the head. He hissed in a breath and I felt his body tense. Feeling a bit bolder, I took him into my mouth.

Wolf groaned and his hold on my hair tightened. He gave it a slight tug but didn't try to control me. I took my time, exploring him, and figuring out what he liked. I'd always known I had a rather freakishly long tongue -- or at least longer than the average -- so I put it to good use. I took as much of him as I could, my lips nearly brushing the hair above his cock, before wrapping my tongue around his shaft and slowly dragging my lips up to the head again.

"Holy fuck!" His hold tightened even more and he panted a little. "Do that again. Please."

I smiled before repeating the stroke a few more times. I placed a hand on his thigh to brace myself and felt a slight tremor running through him. Working his cock, I let his scent wash over me. His body shuddered and he pulled free of my mouth, his cock dragging along my lips.

His breath sawed in and out of his lungs. "I don't want to come yet."

Wolf helped me stand and quickly removed my clothes before discarding his own. He sat on the edge of the bed to remove his prosthesis. As much as I wanted to help him, I didn't think he'd appreciate it. As it was, the fact he felt secure enough with me to take it off made me feel all warm and fuzzy inside. I liked that he wasn't trying to hide from me.

I crawled onto the bed and stretched out behind him, letting my fingers trail across his hip. I admired the ink on his back and traced a few of the lines. I saw the club logo, or whatever they called it, a script written in a foreign language, and a myriad of other images. One day I'd ask him what they meant.

When he'd finished with his prosthesis, he turned to face me. I reached for him, tugging him closer. Wolf flashed me a smile before leaning down to kiss me.

"I finally have you in my bed," he murmured against my lips.

I slid my hands up his chest and around his neck. "You make it sound like it's something you've wanted forever."

"Maybe not forever, but definitely for a while. I told you. The moment I saw you walk into Church, I wanted to know more about you. I don't think you realize the power you have over me, Glory."

I curled my hand around the back of his neck. "Max, I don't want power over you. All I need is for you to keep looking at me the way you are right now."

"Gladly."

He kissed me long and deep, his palm sliding up my ribs to cup my breast. The feel of his rough skin against me made my nipples harden even more. I whimpered as he stroked the peak, his touch driving me wild. Wolf threw his leg over mine and I felt the hard length of his cock press against me. He shifted, placing his knee against my pussy and put just enough pressure there I grew even wetter. With every brush of his knee, his cock rubbed against me, drawing a groan from him.

"Jesus, Glory. You make me feel like I'm a teenager again. Few more strokes against your soft skin and I think I'd come."

I didn't know many men who'd admit such a thing. From what I'd observed, they seemed to boast about how long they could last. But then, Wolf wasn't like other men. At least, with me he wasn't. I couldn't say what he'd been like with anyone else.

"Max, we need... condoms, or... something." It felt like my brain was short-circuiting. The tugging on my nipple and the pressure against my pussy made me feel like I'd come unraveled at any moment. I was so close to coming.

He nipped my jaw. "One of these days I'll get to fill you with my cum."

And why did he make it sound so sexy?

Wolf rolled away from me and opened his bedside table drawer. He pulled out a few condoms and dropped them onto the bed beside me. I tried really hard not to think about the fact he already had an open box of them in his bedroom. I knew they were likely from his time with Franny, and I didn't want that bitch in the room with us. Not even in spirit.

Wolf rolled to his back and my brow furrowed. "You aren't going to put one on?"

"Not yet." He patted his chest. "Come up here."

I tipped my head to the side, not quite certain what he meant. He grinned and reached for me, lifting me so that I straddled his chest, then he tugged on my hips until I got closer to his face. I felt my cheeks heat and grabbed onto the headboard.

"Max, what are you..."

He yanked me over his face and licked my pussy, making me squeak in surprise. "Oh, God. Max, I…"

He held me tight, not letting me get away. As if I'd want to! His wicked tongue was driving me crazy. Every flick against my clit made me want to grind against him. My fingers turned white from my grip on the headboard. Wolf slid his hand over the curve of my ass, and I felt his fingers dip inside my pussy.

A loud keening sound escaped me, and I couldn't hold back another moment. I rode him, alternating between pushing back on his fingers and thrusting forward toward his tongue. Ecstasy rolled over me and I nearly blacked out I came so hard. Even as my orgasm began to ebb, Wolf kept teasing me, pushing me for more. He didn't stop until I came twice more and my thighs were shaking so bad I worried I'd collapse and suffocate him.

Wolf released me and I toppled to my side, my lungs straining for air as the world spun. How could it get better than what we'd already shared? The man was beyond amazing. He leaned up on his elbow and ran his finger down my nose, across my collarbone, and down the slope of my breast.

"So fucking beautiful. I could make you come all night long and never get enough of you. I like the sounds you make. The way your cheeks flush. Your taste." He placed his hand over my pussy and shoved two fingers inside, pumping them in and out. "How hot and slick you are. The way you grip me when I hit just the right spot."

"Max, please…"

He drove his fingers into harder. Deeper. "Come for me again."

I lifted my hips, silently asking for more. He used his thumb to stroke my clit. It only took a few strokes before I was crying out his name and gripping the sheets so hard I worried I'd rip them. I felt my release soak the bed under me, but I didn't care right now.

Wolf reached for the condoms and tore one off. I watched as he rolled it down his cock. I'd expected him to take me right then and there, but he apparently wasn't done playing yet. He worked my pussy with his fingers again, wringing another orgasm from me. I was on the precipice of yet another when he covered my body with his and thrust inside me.

"Max!" I clutched at his shoulders. He stretched me wide, making me burn and yearn for more. He drove into me, each stroke making it feel as if he were claiming me, trying to brand me as his own. Sweat coated his skin and he leaned down, his lips near my ear.

"So tight. Wet. Fucking perfect." He growled. "Mine!"

"Yes! Yes, I'm yours, Max."

"Gonna ride this pussy hard, and one day you'll give me your ass too."

His words were enough to trigger another release and it felt like I was floating far above the earth. Pleasure zinged through me. Wolf slammed into me three more times, grunting with each thrust. When he stilled, buried inside me, I knew he'd just ruined me for anyone else. No one would ever be able to compare.

The fog cleared from my mind a little and I looked down the length of our bodies. I noticed he'd braced most of his weight on his good leg, and somehow managed to use the other one to balance. I'd wondered how things would work in the bedroom. I should have known nothing would deter him from taking what he wanted.

His cock twitched and throbbed inside me, and I clenched down on him. He groaned and reached down to grab the top of the condom as he pulled out. When I felt a rush of wetness between my legs, my heart skipped a beat. That felt like way too much to just be from me. The look on his face said it all.

"Fuck, Glory." His gaze held mine. "It broke."

He pulled back and I saw it hadn't just broken. The damn thing had popped like a balloon. I only hoped there weren't any pieces left behind. Wolf rolled what was left down his cock and palmed it.

"Looks like it ripped down the side. I'm so fucking sorry."

I ran my hand down his arm. "It's not your fault, Max. We both knew a condom wasn't a foolproof form of birth control. They fail all the time."

He set the broken latex on the opened wrapper and placed it on the bedside table. I curled against his side, placing my hand over his chest. His heart pounded against my palm.

"I promised to protect you, and I'm already failing," he said.

"No, you aren't." I kissed his shoulder, then his cheek. When he turned toward me, I placed my lips on his. "Things happen for a reason, Max. Maybe the universe is trying to say Sienna needs a sibling now rather than later."

"You really think you're pregnant after this one time?" he asked.

"I'm apparently as fertile as a rabbit. If we ever have unprotected sex, expect me to be knocked-up. I'd wanted to wait. Getting my degree was important to me, and it still is. But if I can't finish right now, then I'll try again later."

He cupped my cheek. "I'm not letting you put your dreams on hold, Glory. You've fought too hard to reach this point. Whatever it takes, I'll see you get all the way through to the end. You're amazing, and I know I'm fucking lucky as hell that you're mine. I don't want you to wake up one day and regret being with me."

I knew I could go get the morning-after pill, but the thought of doing such a thing, of getting rid of a baby we may have created, made me feel sick. I couldn't do it. I'd kept up with one semester of classes during my pregnancy with Sienna and then taken a break. There was no reason I couldn't finish the clinical part of my degree if I was pregnant again.

"I could never regret being with you. Max, you're one of the best things to ever happen to me. You think you're lucky I'm yours? You have it backward. *I'm* lucky to be *yours*. You're the most incredible, giving, sweet man I've ever met."

He audibly swallowed and the sheen of emotion in his eyes made me fall for him a little more. I'd meant every word I said. Wolf was... one in a million. Now that he'd decided I was his, I'd fight to keep him. If Franny tried to take him back, I'd claw her eyes out. Any other woman wanted in his pants or in his life? I'd stake my claim. Because I wasn't just Wolf's... he was mine.

Chapter Eight

Wolf

Leaving my girls at home hadn't been easy. After spending the night in Glory's arms and making her come so much she finally begged for sleep, I'd wanted to stay home with them. It seemed the club had other ideas. A text with *Church in ten* had made me haul ass into the shower and to the clubhouse while Glory and Sienna were still asleep. The sky was just starting to lighten as I rode through the compound.

I didn't know what the hell was going on, but I hoped it was over quickly. I didn't think I'd ever get my fill of Glory. Knowing Sienna would have to take a nap at some point made me want to hurry home. I planned on wearing my woman out. We'd talked quite a bit between rounds of making love -- and yeah, I could admit it was more than just sex -- and decided to roll the dice. After the condom broke, and Glory had decided maybe it was predestined or something, she'd decided to forgo birth control.

If she ended up pregnant before she finished her degree, I'd do what I could to help. Whether it was watching Sienna, making sure Glory had time to study, or anything else she needed, I'd take care of it. I wasn't getting any younger. Glory might have her entire life ahead of her, but I was quite a bit older than her. There were times I couldn't believe I was with someone so young but considering how many of my brothers had claimed younger women, I should have prepared myself for the inevitable.

Quite a few bikes were already parked outside the clubhouse. Looked like I was the last one to arrive, which meant I'd probably get my ass chewed by the Pres. A few club whores hung out in the main area, trying to sink their claws into the Prospects. I hoped those boys were wise enough to not get one of them pregnant.

I stepped into Church and took my seat, ignoring the glare Badger cast my way. I checked the clock on the wall. I might be late, but only by two minutes.

"Now that we're all here," Badger said, narrowing his gaze at me again, "let's get started."

Slash leaned forward, bracing his arms on the table. "As everyone knows, the clinic was broken into night before last. They destroyed the place. We aren't sure what they were looking for, or who is responsible."

"Wolf had a strange woman walk in while he was there with Glory," Steel said. "He followed her to the alley and overheard her on the phone. Sounded like she'd been there at the request of a patient's attacker. It's possible the two incidents are related."

"There's more," Demon said. "I painted over it so the ladies wouldn't freak the fuck out, but they left a message on the wall. I took some pictures."

Demon slid a file folder into the center of the table. I reached for it, flipping it open. Pulling out the images, I handed some down the table as I stared at the one still gripped in my hand. *What the fuck?* My gaze lifted and met Demon's.

"Why didn't someone tell me about this before now?" I asked.

"Why would you need to know?" Grizzly asked. "You already stalk the damn woman. If someone tried to take her, pretty sure you'd notice."

My jaw tightened as my gaze locked onto Steel farther down the table. The asshole had said he'd make sure everyone knew Glory was mine. I'd already figured out the Prospects didn't know, and obviously

Dagger hadn't either. Had he told *anyone*? He winced and looked sheepish, which meant he'd either forgotten or he'd been sidetracked.

"I'm claiming Glory," I said. "And no, I'm not asking. I've already moved her and Sienna into my house. It's why I didn't come to the clinic after the break-in. I was with Glory."

"So you're telling us she's yours?" Badger asked, drumming his fingers on the table. "She lived with Ripper first. What if he'd wanted to claim her? There's a reason we hold a vote for this sort of shit."

Ripper held up his hands. "Nope. Not me. Glory is sweet and all, but I'm not ready to be a daddy right now and she's a package deal with Sienna."

"Are you really going to fight me on this?" I asked Badger.

"You were with Franny not too long ago. Seems like you didn't wait long to move on to greener pastures. Maybe Glory is just a rebound," Badger said.

I half-lifted out of my seat, ready to go after him. Dragon sat next to me and placed a hand on my shoulder, holding me down.

"Franny is back," Slash said. "And causing trouble."

Badger sighed and rubbed his hands up and down his face. "What the fuck is going on now?"

"She showed up at my house. Got pissed Glory was there and said some shitty things to her. Then my woman kicked her ass out and shut the door in her face," I said, smiling as I remembered how fierce Glory had been. "She took exception to Franny's reaction to me wearing shorts around the house."

"I…" Badger shook his head. "I don't even know where to go with that. Why the fuck would your ex care if you wore shorts at home? Or anywhere else for that matter?"

"Because she can't stand to see his leg," Dagger said. "I found her on his doorstep, and she turned on the waterworks. She had me fooled, until Glory lit into her. She's something else."

"Right. Okay, so we'll table the discussion of Franny and what the hell to do with her. You want Glory, she's yours. I'll order a property cut. Now back to the clinic." Badger motioned to the pictures. "As you can see, they know who Glory is and she's been targeted, along with Dr. Amelia Abrams."

"Was anyone going to tell me Glory was in danger? We left the clinic and went to the damn mall. I wouldn't have done that if I'd known someone wanted to hurt her," I said. "How the fuck can I protect her if you don't tell me there's an asshole who wants her dead?"

I'd known something felt off when we'd gone to the clinic. Steel hadn't been acting right. He'd known I'd claimed Glory. Why the fuck hadn't he said something? If he didn't want Glory to hear, the ass could have at least texted me or called after I left.

"What the hell, Steel? You knew about me and Glory."

He held up a hand. "Sorry, Wolf. I'd planned to call Badger and pass the word along, but my fucking phone started blowing up with calls and texts about the break-in. By the time I had it all handled, I'd forgotten to tell anyone about you and Glory."

I growled and narrowed my eyes at him. How the fuck could he forget when Glory had been threatened? I'd let it go for now. Arguing over it wouldn't change anything. My relationship wouldn't have been high on his list of priorities. Knowing someone out there wanted to hurt Glory, and in the worst way possible, made my gut churn. I studied the image again.

The words were written with angry slashes in what looked like permanent marker. *I'll enjoy your little whores before I send them back to you in pieces.*

I knew exactly what he meant by "enjoy" and I'd be damned if Glory would ever go through that again. And send her to me in pieces? Over my dead fucking body! No one was going to hurt my woman. I'd find this fucker, and I'd make him pay for even daring to think such thoughts about Glory. I'd cut him up, maybe even make him choke on his own dick.

My hands fisted and a red haze settled over my vision. I didn't know who was after her, but I'd find out. Then the bastard was mine.

"I hacked into the cameras in the area," Outlaw said. "I found a possible lead, but I had to hand it off to someone else. Wire and Lavender were going to dig deeper and see if they could get us a name. There's no guarantee it's the person who trashed the clinic, but it gives us a start."

"Where do we go from here?" I asked. "If I leave Glory in the dark, she could leave the compound without protection. How much am I allowed to tell her?"

Badger leaned back in his seat. "Depends. What does she know?"

"She was with me when I went to the clinic yesterday morning. She saw the destruction. And she felt something was off with the woman who showed up, then took off. Glory isn't stupid."

"Never said she was," Badger said. "Let her know her life has been threatened. It will keep her cautious when she's not behind the gates, and since she usually has Sienna with her, she'll need to be extra vigilant. I don't know what the fucker would do to a baby."

I personally didn't want to find out. I gave Badger a nod and knew this was going to wreck the day I'd had planned with Glory. Still, I'd rather her know and be careful than keep it to myself even for another twelve to twenty-four hours. I'd just have to find ways to distract her when we were home.

"I need volunteers to patrol the compound, on the off chance the fucker knows Glory lives here. I also need someone to stay glued to her ass when she leaves, and someone else to watch the doctor," Slash said.

Ripper and Hound volunteered to patrol. Colorado offered to keep an eye on Glory when she left the compound, assuming I wasn't with her. And Bandit seemed eager to watch the doctor. It made me wonder if he didn't have a bit of a crush on her. It would be interesting to see how it played out. If the doctor did give him a chance, I had a feeling she'd lead him on a merry chase first. She'd been spunky the few times I'd spoken to her.

"Anything else?" I asked. "I kind of want to get back home. I left Glory and Sienna sleeping. What if they wake up while we're in Church and she decides to go somewhere?"

"Get out of here, Wolf," Badger said. "I'll text you with any updates. And congrats on getting the family you've been wanting."

Steel snorted. "That boy's been after Glory since she got here. You act surprised he finally coaxed her into his bed."

Badger grimaced. "Franny had us all fooled. I thought she was sweet and a great match for Wolf.

Seems I was wrong. I only hope Glory is the right one for him."

"She is," I said.

I stood and walked out, eager to get home to my girls. Before I got on my bike, I sent a message to every Prospect the club had, making sure they knew Glory wasn't to leave the compound alone. I didn't know what Badger would tell them, if anything, so there was a chance they'd think I was being a controlling asshole. Either way, I'd make sure Glory stayed safe. At least I could tell her what was going on. Past experience said it wouldn't guarantee she'd make good choices. The ladies of the Devil's Fury had a tendency to run headfirst into danger, usually in hopes of sparing everyone else. They were brave, if a bit foolish.

I pulled my bike into the driveway and noticed the club truck was still under the carport. At least I knew Glory hadn't woken up and left the house. I crept inside, trying to be quiet in case my girls were still sleeping. The door made a soft *click* as it shut. I checked on Sienna first. I smiled when I realized she'd rolled to her side and shoved her fist into her mouth. Too damn cute.

I made my way to the bedroom and admired Glory as she slept soundly in our bed. As quiet as I could, I removed my clothes and my prosthesis before climbing in next to her. She immediately sought me out, curling against me. Her breath fanned across my chest and my cock hardened, tenting the bedding. The woman was too sexy for her own good. Even sound asleep, I had a crazy need for her.

She wiggled closer and shifted her hand down to my abdomen, then slowly her fingers inched even lower. When she wrapped them around my dick, I stared at her, watching for any sign she was awake.

Her quick inhalation as she stroked me told me enough.

"You keep playing possum and you won't get to come," I said.

Her eyes opened and she gave me a smile. "Sounds like I need to be awake, then."

"I created a monster, didn't I?" I teased. "Greedy wench, wanting non-stop orgasms."

"Only because I'd never had one before you. Now I know how amazing they are, and I want tons of them." Her grip tightened and she twisted her hand on the next upstroke. "Are you complaining?"

"Not even a little. I love making you come." And I definitely loved what she was doing right now.

"Want to prove it?" she asked.

I slid my hand down her back to her ass, giving it a squeeze. "Depends. How adventurous are you feeling today?"

Her eyes went wide. "Not *that* adventurous."

I couldn't help but laugh. One day she'd let me play back there. Until then, I'd just have to give her lots of reasons to try new things with me. We had all the time in the world, so I wasn't in a hurry. The fact she'd let me get this far was a miracle.

"You ever played with toys?" I asked.

"I have a small vibrator, but it never really did much for me. Honestly, it's hard to use it when Sienna is so close. We've shared a room most of her life, and before that I was so busy studying I didn't really have time for self-pleasure."

"If I order a few things, are you willing to try them with me?"

"With you?" she asked. "How would that work?"

I rolled so she lay under me. "I'd use them on you, get you all worked up, maybe get you off a few times. They even have some you can wear all day."

Her mouth opened and closed a few times. I could tell I'd intrigued her, even if she didn't want to admit it. I'd save those sorts of toys for later. For now, I'd order a few basic things and see what she liked. I slid my hand between her legs and brushed my fingers over her wet slit before easing two inside her. I pumped them in and out, drawing a sexy moan from her lips.

"You need to come, sweetheart?" I asked.

She nodded. "So badly."

"Bad enough it hurts?"

"Yes! Max, please. I need it. Need you."

I smiled as I drove my fingers in deeper and harder. I curled them slightly on the next stroke and she cried out, her hips bucking. Fuck, but this woman drove me wild! She was... perfection. Sexy. Sweet. Naughty. Innocent. She was everything all rolled into one, and she was *mine*.

"Come for me, beautiful. I want to watch as you chase your pleasure. Move those hips. Show me you want it."

She whimpered and started jerking her hips to meet my thrusts. I ground the heel of my hand against her clit and felt her tighten as she grew even slicker. My cock throbbed, wanting to be buried inside her, but I knew it would all be over if I took her right now. And I wanted to play a little.

"You're amazing," I murmured. "I never thought you'd let me get this close to you, let alone be begging me to give you multiple orgasms."

"I never would have with anyone else." She panted and writhed under me. "Only with you, Max. I trust you."

And those were the most precious words she could ever say to me. I knew exactly how hard it was for her to trust anyone. After all she'd been through, I'd worried she'd never let me get close enough to even be her friend, much less have her in my bed. I'd been willing to take whatever crumbs she'd give me. Instead, I'd gotten the grand prize. Glory and Sienna. My woman and daughter.

"Now, angel. Come right the fuck now."

Her eyes went wide, and then she was coming, her release soaking my hand and the bed. I didn't slow the strokes of my fingers. One wasn't near enough. I'd make her come at least three more times before I gave in to the urge to slide deep inside her tight pussy.

After I'd worn her out and made her blissfully happy, I'd have to tell her about the threat lurking in the shadows, waiting to take her from me. Until then, I was going to make the most of our time before Sienna woke up.

Chapter Nine

Glory

After I'd spent an incredible night and morning in bed with Wolf, Sienna had woken with a scream and crocodile tears. I'd made breakfast for us while Wolf fed her, then she played for a bit. An hour later, she'd passed out on her blanket in the living room and Wolf had carried her to her room. Then he'd dropped a bomb on me that left me reeling. And angry. So incredibly angry.

I held up a hand. "Wait. You came home from Church, made me come so many times my legs feel like jelly, and you knew the entire time someone had threatened my life?"

Fury burned through my veins and my stomach felt like it had been engulfed in flames. He'd known yesterday morning. Why the hell hadn't he told me sooner? Logically, I knew the chances someone would get inside the compound and snatch me from the house were slim to none. I hadn't technically been in danger while I'd been in bed with Wolf, unless I counted the threat to my heart. I was falling for the man way too fast. Still, a part of me couldn't believe he hadn't shared the news with me immediately.

Wolf rubbed at the back of his neck. "I wanted to have some time with you, the two of us, enjoying one another's company and having an awesome start to the day before I had to tell you about the ugliness heading our way. When I left Church, I'd had every intention of telling you. I just… I didn't want to see the fear in your eyes. I knew I'd have to tell you, but I wasn't ready."

"*Our* way? They only threatened me and the doctor."

"You're mine, Glory. If someone's coming for you, it makes it my problem. The club's too. You aren't facing this alone, beautiful. And whatever asshole thinks he has a right to spew such nasty shit about you had better have his affairs in order, because when I get my hands on him, his death will be slow and painful."

The man looking back at me wasn't the sweet Wolf I'd come to know and care about. There was danger in his eyes. Death. Destruction. A darkness I had to admit I'd suspected was there, even if I hadn't seen it. A shiver raked down my spine when I realized he meant every word. If someone tried to hurt me, he'd kill them and in a brutal way. It should have scared the crap out of me. Maybe I'd been around the bikers too long. All I felt was relief that someone like Wolf had my back.

"I'm not used to relying on other people," I said, sinking onto the kitchen chair. "I'm sorry I got so upset. But, Max, you can't hide stuff like that from me."

"I wasn't hiding it," he said, dropping onto the chair beside me. He reached for my hand, rubbing his fingers across my skin. "I had every intention of telling you. After I'd given you a morning to remember."

"And Sienna?" I asked.

"He didn't mention her. Either he isn't aware of her existence, or he doesn't care about her. I'll keep her safe, Glory. Both of you. If you leave the compound and I can't go with you, make sure you take one of my brothers or at least a Prospect."

"I will. What does this mean for me right now? How much freedom do I have until he's caught?" I asked.

"Honestly, not a lot." He winced. "I know you're used to doing your own thing and not answering to anyone. I don't want to put a leash on you, Glory. You're my woman, my heart, and it would kill me if something happened to you. Whatever goodness I still have would be gone in the blink of an eye."

I smiled. "Max, you act like you're a monster. You are the kindest, sweetest man I've ever met. I know you're capable of violence. You wouldn't be part of this club if you weren't. It doesn't make you a bad man, or an evil one. Even the most innocent person out there has the potential to do harm to someone. It's called being human."

He sighed and closed his eyes, pressing his forehead to mine. "I don't deserve you."

"Maybe I'm the one who doesn't deserve *you*. Ever think of it that way?" It was on the tip of my tongue to tell him I loved him. I knew it was way too soon to say those words. Never having had a boyfriend, or been in love, it felt like I would burst if I didn't tell him how I felt. Excitement. Fear. Longing. It all filled me, and I didn't know what to do with it.

Wolf kissed me, his lips soft against mine. He threaded his fingers in my hair and I leaned into him a little more. I knew if I didn't pull away, things would go much further. When it came to Wolf, I seemed powerless to say no. Of course, I didn't usually *want* to say no to him. He might act like the sex between us wasn't different from before, but I knew we had something special. And it wasn't because he'd been the only man to give me an orgasm. The way he made every nerve in my body light up, the heat I felt from just a look, was the sort of thing books were written about. I wouldn't have felt like this with anyone else.

"I can't think when you do that," I murmured as I pulled back. "My body overrides my mind and I want to tear off my clothes."

Wolf laughed and lifted me, placing me on his lap. "You're too much, Glory. But in a really great way."

"It's your fault. Before you, I never would have given a guy half a chance. If they got close, I'd have run the other way. Somehow, you wormed your way past my defenses, and now I feel like a needy mess who constantly needs your touch. It's been two nights, Max! What the hell did you do to me?"

"Glory, you're nineteen. I'm pretty sure being horny is part of whatever hormone surges you have at that age. Maybe your body is trying to make up for lost time, so you want sex frequently." He leaned in closer, dropping his voice. "And you make me feel the same way. Until you, I could go weeks, even months without touching a woman. Now I want to bury my cock inside you and not leave our bed for days on end."

"Is this what they call the honeymoon phase?" I asked.

He went still, his gaze locked on mine. Had I said something wrong? I watched and waited, but the longer he went without saying anything, the more my anxiety tried to send me running the other direction.

"Honeymoon?" he asked softly. "Married people have those. Are you saying you want to be my wife?"

My heart leapt for a moment and I tried to analyze how those words made me feel. Did I want that? To be his wife? What sort of insane person married a guy after dating for two days? Were we even dating? I didn't know what to call our relationship. My somewhat organized life had been turned upside down by the biker holding me.

"You claimed me," I said slowly. "And it's forever."

He nodded. "Yeah, I did, and yes, it is. I'm not letting you go, Glory."

"Are the others married to their women?"

"In one fashion or another," he said. "Outlaw, or one of the other hackers, usually works some magic to make us legally married without the ceremony and paperwork. Unless a brother wants the romantic wedding for his woman's sake. Not all women want the white dress and preacher, though."

I turned his words over in my mind. Did I want to be married to him? And if I said yes, would I want an actual wedding? I'd never thought I'd have a husband or family, not after I found out I was pregnant with Sienna. Until Wolf, I'd thought I'd never trust anyone enough to get close to them, much less have a relationship. Perhaps I should have been asking what *he* wanted. Did Wolf want to get married?

"I would never force you to do something you don't want," I said.

"And you think I wouldn't want you as my wife?" He shook his head. "Sweetheart, if you want, I'll go get your name tattooed on me right fucking now. Marriage around here is just a piece of paper. What we have already is so much more. If you want the paper showing you're mine and I'm yours, if you want a ring, then I'll gladly do all that and more.

"I want you to be happy, Glory. This club may be my life, and they have my loyalty, but you're the reason I smile when I wake up in the morning. You're the reason I look forward to every damn day. Just say the word, Glory. I'll call Outlaw right now, or we can set up a real wedding."

I leaned into his side and rested my head on his shoulder. "You won't think less of me if I ask to have something showing I'm officially yours, not just in the club's eyes but to everyone outside this compound?"

"No, baby. I'll give you whatever you want."

I picked up my head and looked at him. "Let Outlaw know I want him to marry us. And yes, I want rings. They don't need to be fancy, but I want something to show the world I'm off-limits."

And I wanted all the damn women in town to know he was mine. I wasn't sure how he'd react to those words, so I held them back. I had a feeling he knew what I was thinking anyway. He smirked and ran his hand through my hair.

"Rings plural, huh? Staking your claim?"

"Would you rather I pee on you?" I asked.

Wolf burst out laughing and hugged me tight. "You're too much, Glory. To answer your question, I'm not into golden showers, so peeing on me is out of the question."

"But a ring isn't?"

"I'm not too crazy about taking you outside the compound right after I find out some asshole wants to torture and kill you. You want rings for us, I'll have someone bring them here."

I reached into his pocket and pulled out his phone, handing it to him. He'd planted the idea in my head of us being married, and now I wanted it to happen. Considering he'd already made me his, until death do us part, by club law, asking for Outlaw to make things official in the real world didn't seem quite so crazy. I'd already jumped in with both feet. If walking away wasn't an option, why not go all the way?

Wolf pulled up Outlaw's name in his contacts and hit the call button, then put it on speaker so I could hear too. When Elena answered, my stomach dropped, and I worried something bad had happened. Why else would she answer his phone?

"Outlaw's phone," Elena said.

Wolf's brow furrowed. "Why didn't he answer his own phone?"

Elena sighed. "Because he overdid it with his hands, and he can't grip the stupid thing. If you're calling to ask him for some computer magic, you're out of luck."

"Well, fuck," Wolf muttered. "I wanted him to marry me and Glory, but if he can't type…"

"I'll get Shield to do it," Outlaw yelled from the background. "Wire, Wizard, and Surge are all working on the other issue right now."

"Thanks," Wolf said. "Can you have him email something for me to print off when it's done? Just in case Glory decides she wants to frame it or put it in a scrapbook."

I eyed him. "What do you know about scrapbooking?"

"Not a fucking thing, except women seem to like using them for preserving memories."

Elena snorted on the other end of the line and I heard Outlaw laugh. "Congratulations, you two. I'll call Shield and put him on speaker for Outlaw to make your request. If you decide you want to celebrate and need some alone time, I'm happy to babysit that sweet girl of yours."

"Thanks, Elena," I said. "She's sleeping right now, but I may take you up on that in a little while. Maybe Wolf and I can have a romantic dinner here at home."

Wolf wagged his eyebrows at me and snickered. Yeah, he'd taken "romantic dinner" to mean he'd get laid again. And he was probably right, only because I couldn't seem to keep my hands off him.

Wolf ended the call and looked up some local jewelry shops on his phone's browser. He had to call three before anyone would agree to bring a selection of rings to the compound. I'd started to worry I'd be ringless until the psycho who'd torn up the clinic could be caught.

"While we wait, why don't we watch a movie?" Wolf suggested. "After you change. No one gets to see you in pajamas except me."

I looked down at his shirt and wrinkled my nose. "It's your shirt, Max. Not pajamas."

"Well, if it's mine, perhaps I should take it back." He reached for the hem, tugging it up my thighs and I smacked his hand.

"Behave! We don't have time for that."

"Not now, but later." He winked. "Definitely later."

I got up and hurried to the bedroom to take a quick shower and dress. I didn't know what the future would hold for us. The man who'd decided he wanted to hurt me could ruin everything. Snuff out my life before I'd really had a chance to live. Or I could have my happily-ever-after. For now, I'd take things one day at a time. It was hard to plan the future when you didn't know if you'd have one.

Enough morbid thoughts, Glory. Wolf will keep you safe.

It would be hard for the asshole who wanted me dead to get anywhere near me if Wolf never left my side, and so far, he didn't seem inclined to give me much space. I should have felt suffocated. Honestly, even though he'd known about the threat since yesterday, he hadn't treated me differently. Ever since

I'd agreed to be his, we'd been inseparable. His hovering and constant presence made me feel cared for. Loved, even. I didn't know if Wolf would ever actually love me, but it was clear he felt some sort of affection for me. It would have to do. Either way, it was more than I'd ever hoped to have. Wolf had given me so much, and I refused to let someone take it away.

I'd fight. And I'd win. Because I wanted a few decades, or more, with Wolf by my side, and I'd do anything to make it happen.

Chapter Ten

Wolf

One week of wedded bliss and the universe decided today everything would go to hell. Bandit had lost the doc while she'd been at her practice. Someone had smuggled her out the back of the clinic with none of us the wiser. She'd been gone three hours and I could only imagine the horrors she'd already faced at the hands of the monster who had her. We hadn't learned a damn thing about the fucker.

Wire had traced the plates on the car we'd seen leaving the scene after the clinic had been ripped apart. They'd come back stolen, which had left us with nothing. Whoever this guy was, he wasn't stupid. So far, he hadn't made a single mistake, which made fear snake its way through me. If he got Glory, I didn't know if I'd find her in time. Or at all.

We'd assumed it was the man who'd assaulted the patient at the clinic the night of the break-in. But after talking to her, we'd discovered her brother's best friend had hurt her. He'd checked out, which meant we'd been chasing ghosts. I still thought it was whoever the other woman had been speaking to, but she'd vanished, and I had no fucking clue who'd been on the other end of that call. Had the victim been in the sights of another psycho without knowing it?

I strode through the clubhouse, hoping someone would have a lead on the doc. The club whores were out in force, at least six on the dance floor and another half dozen trying to get into the pants of my brothers. I knew everyone needed to blow off steam right now, but it pissed me off to see so many lounging around, drinking, and screwing the club pussy. A woman's life was in danger, and my own woman would be next.

Bethany, a woman I'd fucked more than once, sauntered over. The intent in her eyes was clear for anyone to read, but I wasn't in the mood. Even if I didn't have a woman at home, I'd still have given her a pass tonight. Before she reached me, I held up a hand in hopes she'd get the hint and back off. Didn't hurt it was the one sporting a wedding band. I'd opted for a black rubber one so I didn't have to worry about catching on tools or weapons, and I'd bought Glory a platinum band with diamond chips scattered across it. It had taken some convincing before she'd relented on anything remotely sparkly.

"I bet I can make you smile, Wolf," Bethany said, moving in closer.

"Not in the mood. Now or ever. Leave me the fuck alone."

She frowned for a brief moment before plastering a smile on her face. "Not even for the best blowjob of your life?"

I snorted and kept walking. "Sorry, Bethany. You're not good enough to claim that title."

I heard her outraged shriek behind me and should have braced myself. Whatever she threw, hit the back of my knee and my leg buckled. I went down on the sticky floor, pain shooting through my stump and up through my knee and thigh. The noise around me came to a screeching halt.

"You fucking bitch," I growled as I pushed myself to my feet and turned to face her. I saw the empty bottle of whiskey on the floor and knew that was what she'd thrown.

Bethany backed up a step as I advanced on her. I didn't give her a chance to escape, closing my fingers around her throat and squeezing tight enough she knew I meant business.

"Wolf." She clawed at my hand and arm, trying to free herself.

"You're a convenience for the club, Bethany. Nothing more. A hole to fuck. A mouth that's okay at sucking cock but not overly great. I told you to back the fuck off and leave me alone." My hold on her tightened as I backed her to the wall and held her there, her toes scraping the floor as she tried to find purchase. "You have no power here. None. Whores spread their legs and do as they're told. If you can't even do that much, you're fucking worthless."

A hand landed on my shoulder and I cut my eyes that way, noting Demon had walked up. Another growl rumbled through me and I focused on Bethany again.

I heard more steps and soon Frost and Doolittle had joined us.

"She threw a bottle at him," Doolittle said. "At his bad leg."

Demon's eyebrows arched as he stared at Bethany. "You think it's okay to assault a brother?"

"S-sorry," she stammered. "C-can't b-breathe."

I narrowed my eyes and squeezed a little harder. Fury licked through me, making me want to destroy her. I'd never been so pissed at a woman before, and I didn't know why her behavior had set me off so bad now. Wasn't the first time a whore hadn't remembered her place. Wouldn't be the last.

I released her, letting her drop to the floor.

"You okay?" Frost asked, his head cocked to the side.

I ran my hands up and down my thighs. "No. I need a shower."

Demon rocked back on his heels. "This isn't about her throwing the bottle. What happened before that?"

"She wouldn't take no for an answer. Kept pushing to get in my pants," I said.

Demon climbed onto the nearest table and looked out over the small crowed. "Listen up, bitches. Wolf is off the market. Touch a brother who has an old lady, unless he invites you to do so, and the consequences will be severe. Fair warning, none of us will want you touching us. Why go slumming when we have perfection at home?"

I heard a few gasps from the women in the room as Demon got off the table. He eyed Bethany and I noticed I'd left fingermarks on her neck. I bit back the apology that rose to my lips. Anyone else and I'd have felt like shit for hurting them, but if she'd only listened and left me alone, I wouldn't have lost it. Besides, showing any weakness to these women would be a mistake.

"You're banned from the Devil's Fury clubhouse," Demon said, holding Bethany's gaze. "You come here again, and I will personally see to your punishment, and it won't be the kind you enjoy."

Bethany gave a jerky nod and stumbled her way to the door.

"Sorry, Demon." I shook my head. "I've never…"

"I know, brother. Come on. Steel, Dagger, and Blades are in Church trying to figure this shit out. I have a feeling that's why you're here. I know for damn sure it wasn't to get pussy since you have Glory at home."

"Why do these bitches have to cause so much drama?" Frost muttered. "They have to know the score. Since when has any of us taken one of them as an old lady? Never, that's when."

The clubhouse doors flew open, and Van rushed inside, looking seconds from puking. He shoved a small cooler into Demon's hands, then ran down the hall. I saw him slam his way through the bathroom door and heard the sound of retching a moment later. Something told me I wouldn't like whatever was in the chest.

"Let's take this elsewhere," Demon said.

Frost and Doolittle followed us into Church. Demon set the cooler on the table and opened the lid, his eyes hardening when he saw the contents. As much as I didn't want to know, I needed to find out how sick the bastard was who had taken the doc. That had to be where this had come from.

I peered inside and my knees felt a little weak. It wasn't one thing in there, but many. I saw at least four fingers. A few toes. Teeth. When I saw what the other bags held, I understood why the Prospect had thrown up. I was damn close to it myself.

"That sick son of a bitch," I muttered. "Demon, there's no way she's survived all that. And if she did, I don't think she'll want to live."

Demon frowned and reached into the chest, shoving the ice around. He pulled out a clear zipper bag with a flash drive inside. "Anyone have a computer handy?"

"Are we sure we want to see what's on there?" Doolittle asked. "Man, with the contents of that ice chest, I'm not sure I can handle seeing it in person. Cutting off a dude's fingers and other parts is one thing, but a woman as sweet as the doc? Fuck."

"I'll get a Prospect to find one and bring it here," I said, stepping into the hall. Too bad the one in the office was a desktop. I couldn't exactly pick it up and move it. I tracked down Garrick and sent him to retrieve one from Outlaw. I knew he always had extra ones lying around.

While we waited, I got all of us a beer, having a feeling we'd need it. Hell, I probably should have grabbed the Jack off the shelf instead. I downed mine in a few swallows and tried to sit still. I wanted to pace. Hit something. Scream the damn building down.

"The fucker is killing her while we sit here doing jack shit," I said. "Assuming she's not already dead. I only hope she didn't suffer. And Glory is next on his list."

"We'll find him," Steel said. "No one is getting to Glory. We'll put as many men on her as we have to. Even inside the compound."

"Fuck if I'm letting her go outside the gates until he's caught! I don't care if she gets pissed at me or not. The thought of opening one of those chests and finding *her* parts in there? No. I can't... I will lose my fucking shit." I closed my eyes and prayed for a damn miracle. We needed one. I couldn't lose Glory.

"Brother, we've got your back," Dagger said. "The club isn't going to let anything happen to Glory."

"I'll take a shift watching your house if you want extra security," Frost said. "Wouldn't hurt. I don't see the fucker getting inside the compound, but I won't completely discount it ever happening either."

He wasn't wrong. The compound wasn't perfect. If someone really wanted in, they could find a way. Over the years, we'd made it more difficult. However, difficult didn't translate into impossible.

A knock sounded at the door and Garrick popped his head inside. "Got the laptop you needed. Outlaw said it's not password protected."

Demon took it from him and booted it up. He plugged in the flash drive and pulled up the contents. The scream that blasted through the speakers made my hair stand on end. Demon's jaw tightened as he turned the computer so we could all see the screen, then he took a seat next to me.

"Holy shit," Doolittle mumbled.

The man on camera wore a mask covering the top part of his face. I couldn't see a tattoo or scar anywhere that might help identify him. Watching him rape and torture the doc broke something inside me. He'd filmed every second. Including her death.

He leaned in close, his eyes large on the screen. And that's when we finally got a small break. He had one green eye and one blue.

"Heterochromia," I said.

Demon nodded and turned up the volume since the asshole had lowered his voice, probably trying to disguise it.

"I'm coming for sweet little Glory next." He backed up and held the knife up, licking the doc's blood from the blade. "I bet she tastes even sweeter."

He licked the blood off his lips and grinned. "Is her cunt nice and tight? I bet you boys have ridden her ass good and hard. Does she scream as pretty as the doc did? I can't wait to find out."

He reached up and right before he ended the video, I caught a glimpse of something.

"Wait! Freeze that." Demon paused the video, and I dragged the laptop closer. I backed it up a few clicks and zoomed in. "Think we can clear this image up? That looks like a tattoo."

"Let me see it," Frost asked.

I slid the laptop over to him. After a few minutes, he turned it back around and we had a clear shot of the ink on the guy's arm. I leaned in closer, and the breath stalled in my lungs. This was a fucking nightmare.

"He's dead. It's not possible," I said. "His corpse is rotting in pieces on our property."

"Twister," Steel said, his eyes going hard. "No fucking way he came back from the dead. The ink says RIP under it. Anyone know about his family? Does he maybe have a brother? Can't see his face too clear, but the overall build and hair color are the same?"

Demon slammed his fist onto the table. "Fuck!"

"Is that a yes to the brother?" I asked.

"Yeah. Twister had a twin brother, but we'd heard he was long dead. POW or some shit who never came home," Demon said. "When Twister came here, he'd had no one. Grizzly brought him into the club as a Prospect to get him off the streets. Found out later, he had two siblings. A twin brother who'd gone missing overseas and an older sister."

"Why the hell are we just hearing about this?" Steel asked.

"Because Twister was dead and it didn't matter," Demon said. "The sister isn't a problem. She worked as a secretary in Atlanta until she passed away two years ago. Has a daughter who writes romances. I've kept tabs on her. Alora Danvers is the name she goes by. Twenty years old and lives outside Blackwood Falls out in the county."

"Got an address?" I asked. "Should we send someone to check on her?"

"Got a better idea," Demon said. He pulled out his phone and put the call on speaker. When it connected, I knew exactly who he'd called. "Beau, you ready to earn your club colors and name?"

"Name it and it's done," he said.

I eyed Demon, wondering if he had the authority to offer the kid his colors. He might be the Sergeant-at-Arms, but he knew damn well we'd have to take that shit to the table for a vote. And Badger or Slash should have been the one to offer it to Beau. I hoped this didn't blow up in our faces.

"Need you to head down the highway a bit. I'll send you an address. Find Alora Danvers and make sure she's safe. In fact, I want you to bring her here. Take her to your place if you need to. Her uncle is the one after Glory." Demon paused and cleared his throat. "The doc is dead. Fucker raped and murdered her on camera and sent us the video."

"Shit," Beau mumbled. "I'm on it. Get me the address and I can leave right now."

"Thanks, kid." Demon disconnected the call and sent off a text. As he leaned back in his chair, he looked tired. Hell, we all were feeling a bit worn down from this shit. "It would be nice if we could just have some peace and quiet around here."

"Think we'd have to go completely legit for that to happen," I said.

"Yeah, and that ain't happening." He sighed. "All right. We at least know who took the doc. As much as I don't want to see that footage again, we need to look for clues as to where he took her. I want this guy dead. I don't give a shit if he comes here and dies slowly, or if it's a quick bullet to the brain. Just make sure he isn't breathing."

"I have to ask," Blades said, speaking up for the first time. "Any other relatives of brothers we need to be worried about? Dead or alive. I know Badger, Dragon, and Slash all claimed Grizzly's daughters. Did Twister have more family? You sure the brother and sister are it? And some niece from the sister?"

Demon pinched the bridge of his nose. "Meredith."

"She's related to him?" Blades asked.

"His daughter. But she never knew him."

"Merry wouldn't hurt anyone," Doolittle said.

"And you would know," I said. He folded his arms over his chest and stared down his nose at me. Everyone knew he hung out with Meredith a little too much. Some of us had taken bets on when the two would become a couple. If it had happened, they were keeping it secret.

"What the fuck?" Doolittle stood. "What the hell does that mean?"

Demon sighed and pinned Doolittle with a glare. "You think no one notices the amount of time you spend with Meredith?"

"She's only eighteen," Doolittle said. "You think I've spent the last two years screwing a teenager? Is that what you're saying?"

"Glory is nineteen," I pointed out. "Meredith is of legal age so if you went there, no one's going to bust your balls over it except maybe Grizzly."

Doolittle retook his seat. "I haven't gone there. We're friends. She needed someone to talk to, and she likes coming over to hang out with the animals at my house. It's therapeutic for her."

I'd let him have his delusions a while longer. Even if he didn't look at Meredith in that particular way, she'd certainly been eyeing him. The girl lit up whenever Doolittle was around. Far more than she would if they were just friends as he claimed. If she made a pass at him and he walked away, I had a feeling it would crush her fragile heart. I hoped he knew what the hell he was doing.

Demon played the video over and over. Every time was worse than the previous, and it didn't get us any closer to discovering the dickhead's location. The walls were a plain white. The floor had what looked like cheap carpet. It could have been anywhere. Motel. Apartment. Hell, maybe he even used his own home. Sick bastard probably would get off walking through the room where he'd tortured her, remembering every twisted moment.

If it hadn't been for the cyclone tattoo on his forearm, peeking from under his shirt, with RIP written under it, I may not have ever pieced things together. As it was, assuming he was related to Twister was taking a bit of a leap.

Except, once the idea had lodged in my brain, I'd noticed a lot of similarities between the two. It made me question if this was personal. In which case, there likely wasn't a connection with the patient from the clinic.

So who the hell was the woman who'd come in? And was someone else after the patient who'd been there?

"Wait, back that up," Blades said, leaning closer. He pointed at the far corner of the screen. "Is that a shadow?"

I squinted and realized he was right. "There's someone else there."

The doors to Church swung open and Outlaw came in, taking a seat across from me. "You done trying to figure it out all out?"

"No, asshole. We just realized there's another person there." Demon slid the laptop over to Outlaw.

The broken hacker cracked his fingers, wincing, before he started typing. I didn't know what the hell he was doing, and I didn't much care as long as he could get us a lead. Well, more of one than we had so far.

"No one checked the drive to see if there was anything else on it?" Outlaw asked.

"The other file wouldn't open," Demon said. "I figured it wasn't important."

Outlaw smiled. "It's encrypted, but look…"

He spun the laptop so we could all see it. Two men were on the screen this time. I recognized the one who'd tortured the doc by his mismatched eyes. The other must have been the shadow we'd noticed in the corner.

"Didn't see that one coming," Dagger said as the sounds of sex filled the room.

"So it seems Twister's brother is bisexual. Or… maybe he doesn't like women at all. Could that be why he rapes and tortures them?" Frost asked. "He could despise women and that's how he deals with it. I mean, rape isn't about sex. It's not the fact he's going to fuck them that gets him hard. He gets off on the pain, the agony on their faces, the fear."

The two men finished, and Twister's brother flipped the other guy onto his back, placing his hand over the man's throat. We watched as he squeezed and pinned the man to the floor. They fucked again, and Twister's brother kept going, even after the other guy passed out.

My stomach knotted at how sick the bastard was. If I hadn't thought the shadow we'd noticed was the guy on the floor, I'd have worried he was dead.

"He's coming around," Dagger said.

Sure enough, the one who'd passed out shook it off, rubbing his throat as he stood. The depravity continued for another hour and included a third man and later two women. Seeing all the men tear those women apart nearly made me throw up. It seemed we weren't dealing with just one psycho.

"I think it's a club," Blades said.

"What?" I asked, turning to face him. "Why would you say that?"

"You saw the tattoo on the main guy's arm, but did you notice anything else? Look closely, along the hairline on their necks. Every last one has a tiny pitchfork inked right there. Same size, location, and color."

Blades ran a hand down his beard. "I've seen that before. Fucker in prison. Got arrested on three counts of rape, torture, and murder. Guy was untouchable inside. Kept saying something about the Sons would protect him. I didn't understand it and didn't care to. Now I have to wonder... is he part of a club that has Sons in the name, or refer to themselves as sons?"

"I have a feeling this is way bigger than we first thought," Demon said. "Wolf, go home to Glory. The rest of you with women do the same. I'm calling Badger and Slash. I'll fill them in on what we've learned so far. Outlaw, can you pass along all this info to Wire and see if it helps his search?"

"On it," Outlaw said.

"Don't let any of your women out of your sight," Demon said. "I know I damn sure won't be letting Farrah more than two feet away at any given time. Not until we've handled this shit."

I didn't know how to protect my family from an entire group of monsters. We had no idea who all these men were, where they were from, or if they were part of something so large it was global.

Until I had answers, I'd have to ask Glory to stay at the house. I didn't even want her wandering through the compound. It felt like there wasn't anywhere safe for her.

I only hoped she'd forgive me for keeping her under lock and key.

Chapter Eleven

Glory

I'd known something was bothering Wolf. Pain and worry flashed in his eyes off and on ever since he'd gone to the clubhouse two days ago. He'd said it wasn't safe for me to leave our home, and I'd trusted him to tell me the truth. Whatever he'd learned while he'd been gone, it must have been horrific. If I left the room for more than a few minutes, he came to find me. It was like he worried I'd vanish into thin air and he'd never see me again.

"Are you going to talk to me?" I asked as we lay in bed. "Or touch me?"

He'd gone from not being able to keep his hands off me, to giving me almost brotherly kisses. Not once had he reached for me or given in to my attempts at seduction. To be honest, he was scaring the crap out of me. If it weren't for all the hovering, I'd think he'd lost interest.

"I touch you all the time," he said.

"Not what I meant and you know it, Wolf."

He leaned up on an elbow and glowered at me. "Since when do you call me Wolf when we're in our own damn home?"

I reached up to cup his cheek. "You're scaring me. I know something's wrong. You barely leave my side, and at the same time you haven't done more than give me a quick kiss on the cheek in the last two days. Talk to me. Please."

"The doctor from the clinic is dead," he said. "The guy sent a video of him…"

He closed his eyes and shook his head, as if he couldn't handle seeing the images in his mind. I snuggled closer to him, breathed in his scent, and wished there was some way I could comfort him. But if he saw what happened to Amelia, then he knew what the man planned for me too. It occurred to me that was why he'd been hovering, why he'd been so worried when he didn't know where I was every second of the day. Whatever happened to her, it must have been horrific.

"He tortured her. Raped her. Then killed her on camera," Wolf said softly. "I can't handle losing you, Glory, especially in such a brutal way. I'm sorry if I haven't been myself. I didn't intend to pull away from you."

"I'm here, Max. By your side. Whoever the man is, he hasn't gotten to me yet, and as long as I stay in our house I should be safe. Right?"

He nodded. "It's Twister's brother. Apparently, he had a twin and an older sister. The club sent someone to fetch Twister's niece in case she's in danger too. Meredith is Twister's daughter, but we have no way of knowing if his brother knows about her."

He still seemed tense, and I ran my hand up and down his arm. "What else? I can tell you have something else weighing on you."

"They're part of a group. We don't know the name yet, but there's more than one, Glory. It's not just one man trying to get to you. It could be many more. We've seen two on camera. Twister's brother and someone we haven't identified yet. We don't know exactly how big this thing is yet. Blades said he remembered a man in prison who always referred to the Sons. The hackers are trying to get more information."

"So we don't know who the group is, what they want, or how many of them there are?" I asked.

"Right. And that's why I'm a bit obsessed with where you are every second of the day."

I could understand why he was so worried. It bothered me no one knew anything about the men who wanted to hurt me. Even worse, if they'd killed Amelia and filmed it, they'd probably hurt other women. Someone needed to stop them. I had no doubt the Devil's Fury would do their best to put an end to the monsters, but what if they couldn't?

"Is someone supposed to call you with an update?" I asked.

"Demon has sent a few texts out to everyone. I haven't heard anything since lunch."

I leaned over Wolf and picked up his phone from the bedside table. "Text or call him."

"It's almost midnight," Wolf pointed out. "If I wake up Farrah, or his daughter, Rebel, Demon will be pissed as hell. Trust me when I say you don't want to be on his bad side."

"You're stressing out and not sleeping well. Please, Max. Call him. Tell him I asked if there'd been any news. Make it sound like it's for me."

He sighed and placed the call, putting it on speaker.

"What the fuck do you want?" Demon asked when the line connected, not even bothering with a simple "hello" first.

"I have you on speaker and Glory is here. She's worried that we haven't found out anything new. I told her you'd been sending updates, but she asked me to call," Wolf said. "I told her what I could."

"Right." Demon sighed. "The group is called Sons of Vassago. From what Shield was able to determine, it's a group who worships a demon by the name of Vassago, a Prince of Hell. We believe the women, and the way they're killed, are intended to be some sort of sacrifice."

"Jesus," Wolf muttered.

"All the hackers, except Outlaw, are working on finding the names and faces of the members. At least the ones within a few hundred miles of here. It's possible some could have flown from other areas, but the Sons of Vassago appear to be global. I'm not sure we'll have a list of every single one no matter how long we work on this."

"Wait," I said, my chest feeling tight as anxiety crept through me. "If they're global, even if you get rid of whichever ones want to hurt me, won't more just try later? Or want revenge if you kill any of their members?"

"And that's why we haven't done anything yet," Demon said. "We need to determine how expendable these men are. The last thing we want to do is start a war."

"They already brought it to our doorstep," Wolf pointed out. "We didn't start shit."

"Any idea how this all ties in to the clinic?" I asked, hoping I wasn't overstepping. But since these assholes wanted me dead too? Yeah, it made it my problem.

"Wire helped out with that end," Demon said. "Twister's brother goes by the name Saul Sanders. We can't tell if that's his legal name or not, but everything Wire has dug up has that name on it. Wire and his wife went through camera footage in the area for days and finally found our man stalking the patient from the clinic. He may not have been the one to assault her, but she was on his radar. The fact we helped her, then made sure she got home safely, probably pissed him off. Add to that the fact his brother was part of this club, and is now lying in a shallow grave, and it put a target on you and the doc."

At least it wasn't something I'd done. And it wasn't directly related to the clinic and the work we'd been doing. I had to wonder if Saul hadn't discovered the club was affiliated with the clinic, if the doctor and I would have been safe. Or since his victim had managed to escape, would we still be considered a good alternative? I had a feeling we might never know.

"I'll call Church tomorrow and we can come up with a plan," Demon said. "Hopefully, we'll have more information on the men we're dealing with right now and who else might be close by. Each club helping us track down this information is also going to keep an eye on the Sons of Vassago."

"Thank you, Demon," I said. "I know you didn't have to let me hear all that, but it helps. Not knowing scares me more than having an idea of what I could face if those men get their hands on me."

"Not going to happen, Glory. You're Wolf's, which means you're club property, and we protect our own," Demon said.

I wasn't sure how I felt about being club property, but Wolf had mentioned something about a property cut for me. I hadn't gotten one yet. Something told me the club was too preoccupied with everything else going on.

Wolf ended the call and pulled me into his arms. "And now you know as much as I do."

"Except for the details of the video, and I don't need to know those. It's clear we're dealing with people who have no conscience. No soul. Do they really believe sacrificing women will gain them favors with a demon?" I asked. "Isn't that a little too…"

"Hollywood?" he asked. "Yeah, it is. There's a good chance they don't believe sacrifices will do anything. They may just enjoy the kill and use the demon Vassago as an excuse."

"What do we do now?" I asked.

"Get some sleep." He ran his fingers through my hair and kissed me softly. "You're too important for me to lose you, Glory. You're... everything. My heart. My soul. My reason for breathing. As much as I'd love to be up all night making love, I want to be sharp and focused. I can't let those assholes slip past me."

"I understand, Max." I bit my lip before kissing him. I couldn't hold back anymore. I needed to tell him. "I love you."

"I love you too, beautiful. I don't deserve an angel like you, but now that I have you, I'm holding on and never letting go."

I snuggled closer. "Good, because I'm not letting you go either."

He placed his hand over my belly. We hadn't been together very long, but I still knew what he was thinking. My big, sexy biker wondered if I could be pregnant. We hadn't been trying to conceive, even if we'd decided protection wasn't going to work for right now. Neither of us wanted to wait long enough for me to get on the pill, and since the first condom had broken, it hadn't seemed worth dealing with them. He was clean. I was clean. So we were leaving babies up to fate.

I pressed my hand to his. "I should start in about a week or a few days after. If I don't, I can take a pregnancy test and we'll see what it says."

"As much as I'd love to have another baby with you, I'd rather wait until the Sons of Vassago are out of the picture."

"Me too," I murmured.

"What about your degree? You haven't been working on your classes since you moved in here, not that I've seen. And you said something about needed to do a clinical or whatever it's called."

"I think I'm putting everything on hold for the moment. I want my degree, and I'll get it. The time just feels off right now. What seemed like the most important thing ever has taken a back seat to everything else. I have you and Sienna. That's what matters most. I'm only nineteen. I have the rest of my life to finish my nursing degree."

"Don't give up on your dream, Glory. Not for me or anyone else."

"I won't, Max. Nursing is still important to me, but my dreams are changing. I never counted on finding a guy like you. I'd thought it would be me and Sienna forever, or at least until she grew up and started her own life. Priorities change, and there's nothing wrong with that. It's why humans are so adaptive. Our lives are constantly shifting or turning upside down entirely. I still want to be a nurse, but it's not quite as important as before."

He pressed a kiss to my forehead. "My smart, beautiful, sexy wife."

I smiled and closed my eyes. With his arms around me, I felt safe and loved. As long as Wolf was by my side, I could face anything. Even some weird cult of psychotic murderers who sacrificed women. Nothing would take me from Wolf. I wouldn't let it.

I needed him as much as I needed air, and I knew he felt the same about me. He'd been lonely, even if he wouldn't have admitted as much. He might have been with Franny for a while, but it was clear she'd never really cared for him. She'd been selfish and hadn't accepted him. I loved Wolf with all my heart. I saw him. The real him, insecurities and all. Some might think tough, alpha bikers didn't have weaknesses, but I'd learned that was far from the truth. Everyone had a weakness. In Wolf's case, he'd wanted to be accepted. Loved. I would gladly give him that and so much more.

He might be protective of me, but I would defend him as well. Not just physically. No, I'd fight for all of Wolf -- his strengths, his weaknesses, his heart... his very soul. He was mine, just as I was his, and nothing would ever tear us apart.

If my parents were still part of my life, they'd be trying to pull me away from Wolf. They'd say it was too soon to claim I loved him. They'd say I was acting irrationally, and not doing the mature thing. They'd never really understood me. Yes, they'd pushed me to be the best I could be, and I appreciated all they'd done and sacrificed, but when I needed them the most, they'd tossed me out like unwanted trash. Me and my baby. I'd never forgive them for that. Hugs and kisses had been rare growing up. I wanted something different for my children.

One day I'd send them a letter and thank them. If they hadn't been so cruel, I'd have never met Wolf. I wouldn't have moved to Blackwood Falls, fallen in love, or met the incredible people here. Picking up and moving had been scary, but it had been the best decision I'd ever made. I wouldn't second-guess myself again. Whatever higher power had led me here had given me a gift. The best gift ever. Love.

"Love you," I mumbled softly.

A snore was Wolf's response and I smiled as I let sleep take me.

Chapter Twelve

Wolf

Church was getting crowded. I looked around the room and realized I wasn't the only one who'd brought my woman along. Because of the type of threat we were dealing with, the club officers had decided it was best if the women knew what was going on. Glory sat on my lap. Farrah stood behind Demon with her hand on his shoulder. Slash's woman, Shella, sat on a chair next to him. Badger's woman, Adalia, Dagger and Guardian's woman, Zoe, and Outlaw's woman, Elena, had opted to stay in the main part of the clubhouse with the kids. The other Fury ladies were propped against the wall near the door, each looking fierce and ready to tackle whatever evil dared to encroach on their territory.

And then there was our guest. Alora Danvers.

Badger eyed her before scanning the room. "You're probably wondering who this young woman is. Her name is Alora and she's Twister's niece."

I heard a gasp and my gaze landed on Meredith, Grizzly's adopted daughter. And Twister's daughter by blood. Apparently, no one had told her she had living family.

"We're cousins?" Meredith asked. "How is this possible?"

Doolittle stood and went to her, taking her hand. "Not right now, Merry. You'll get a chance to talk to her a little later, and I promise we'll explain everything."

Meredith nodded and gave him a slight smile.

"I have no idea who Twister is," Alora said. "Only family I ever had was my mother, and she died shortly after I turned eighteen."

"You don't look older than that now," Stitches said.

"I'm twenty." Alora folded her arms over her chest and tilted her chin up. "I also have a thriving business, own my house and car outright, and have no idea why you've dragged me here or what the hell is going on."

Slash coughed to cover a laugh. "Yeah, she'll fit right in."

"Business?" Frost asked.

"I'm a writer. A damn good one, too."

"Your business is writing?" Smuggler asked, as if it were a foreign concept. Since I'd never seen him with a book, that might not be far off.

"I write romances." Her cheeks flushed a little. "And before you make any snide remarks, you should know I've hit the bestseller lists multiple times and my net worth is somewhere around half a million dollars. So yeah, it's a business."

Bandit whistled. "Damn. Maybe I need to start writing."

I snorted. "Write what? I'm not sure the world is ready for the crap that goes through your mind."

Badger slammed his fist onto the table. "Enough! Alora is here because I wanted her under our protection. Her uncle, Saul Sanders, is not only part of the Sons of Vassago, but he seems to be the leader for this particular area. All the hackers have been working non-stop on this issue. What they've discovered is unsettling to say the least. The Sons of Vassago have been under our noses for years. Most of the unsolved murders within fifty miles can be contributed to their savagery."

Alora paled and looked like she might crumple at any moment. Doolittle was the closest and led her to a chair next to her cousin. He stood by the two, keeping an eye on them. The look he gave them wasn't of a romantic nature, so I believed him when he said he and Meredith were just friends. Although, now that she was of legal age, I wasn't so sure she'd let things remain on a friends-only footing for long.

"We need to drive them out of this area," Slash said. "I haven't figured out yet how we're going to do it, but if we take out Saul, it's only going to put our families at greater risk. They already want Glory. How long before they put a target on all our women and our daughters?"

"If he's my family, maybe I could reason with him?" Alora asked.

"Don't think that's a good idea," Steel said. "I'm not sure Saul would care if you were blood or not. If he didn't sacrifice you the way he's done so many other young women, he might very well try to marry you off to one of the members of his cult."

"So we're definitely calling it a cult now?" I asked.

Steel shrugged. "Can you think of a better word for it?"

No, not really. I saw the frustration on Badger's face and knew he wanted us to focus. He looked like he was seconds from erupting, and none of us wanted that to happen. He'd gotten his name for good reason. Ever met a badger? Those bastards were mean as fuck and would tear you up.

"They need a good reason to move out of this territory," Badger said. "The tricky part is making sure we aren't pawning them off on another club. Any ideas on where we could lead them?"

"And how are you going to 'lead' those men anywhere?" Guardian asked. "No offense, Pres, but we don't have anything to offer that they'd want other than Glory, and obviously we aren't handing her over."

Alora raised her hand and cleared her throat. I covered my mouth so I wouldn't laugh at how fucking cute she was.

Badger sighed and leaned back in his chair. "This isn't a classroom, Miss Danvers. You have something to say?"

She nodded and stood. "Not to state the obvious, but like I said, I'm a writer. If you need a creative way to get my... uncle to move out the area, why not give me some time to come up with something? Preferably a non-violent way where all of us stay alive and breathing?"

Badger opened and shut his mouth, clearly speechless. I was right there with him. My woman? Not so much. She leaned forward, excitement flashing in her eyes.

"You think you can write a scenario where your uncle would leave?" Glory asked.

Alora scratched her nose. "Well, in theory, yes. I mean, I write erotic romances mostly, but I've been known to throw in some danger. I don't see why I couldn't at least try. Unless someone already has a plan?"

The room was so quiet I could hear the clock on the wall ticking. Yeah, none of us had a damn idea as to what to do. We'd never been faced with anything quite like the Sons of Vassago. Even back when Slash's dad and his club had been raising hell in the southern part of the US, it hadn't been this level of horrifying. Not to mention, Abraxas and his brothers were only based in our country. The Sons of Vassago were worldwide.

"Right." Alora cleared her throat. "I just need my laptop or a pad and pen. A quiet place to think and write. Might take me a few hours."

"Find out which of the rooms aren't being used, make sure it's clean, and let her use the space," Demon said. "Assign a Prospect to make sure she has everything she needs, and make sure the fucker knows to keep his hands to himself."

Doolittle stepped closer to Alora. "I'll help her get set up. I need to go let the dogs out anyway."

Alora blinked at him stupidly. Then she snickered before doubling over and laughing until she cried. "Oh, God! Sorry! It's just... *Who Let the Dogs Out*?"

"I don't get it," I mumbled to Glory, whose shoulders had started shaking with silent laughter.

She pulled out her phone, tapped on the screen to pull up YouTube, and soon a song filled the room. The moment we heard the lyrics, everyone roared with laughter, and poor Doolittle just rolled his eyes.

"It wasn't that funny," he said. "And I really do need to let the dogs out if I don't want to clean up puddles."

"I think we needed that," Glory said after Alora followed Doolittle from the room. "Anyone else feel better? Cleansed?"

Most of the men at the table nodded, and the women too.

"Are we really letting a romance writer figure out how to get rid of a killer?" Dagger asked.

Outlaw leaned back and put his hands behind his head, stretching in his chair. "Anyone want to place a bet that her browser history includes multiple ways of killing a man or getting rid of a body? I wouldn't discount her just yet. We can at least hear what she comes up with -- unless someone here wants to give us some ideas."

We all looked at one another, none of us having a plan. If we could take Saul out of the picture, it would be easier. In this instance, killing him would only make more problems. He had too many men behind him, ones who would want revenge. None of us wanted to start a war, especially with such a large organization.

"What if she can't come up with anything?" I asked. "Shouldn't we still work on a plan?"

"We will," Badger said. "All right, ladies. Why don't you head to the main room? Not everyone saw the video from before, and it's not something you want to see."

Glory stood, bent to kiss my cheek, then followed the others from the room. I wished like hell I didn't have to watch the video again. Either of them. Outlaw played them for the entire club to see, and we spent the next several hours trying to find a way to get rid of the Sons of Vassago. It wasn't until Badger's phone rang that we had any hope at all.

"It's Wire," he said, as he answered the call. He placed it on speaker so we could all hear. "What have you got for us?"

"The Sons of Vassago have two enemies, and only two that I can find so far," Wire said. "Don't get me wrong. Lots of people hate these fuckers, but none are powerful enough to take them down or send them running for the hills."

"But there's someone who can? Or several someones?" Slash asked.

"Oh, yeah. And men we all know. Some of us more so than others," Wire said.

"Will you spit it the fuck out?" Badger asked, a growl to his voice belying his frustration.

"Casper VanHorne and the assassin we all know as Specter," Wire said.

The bomb he'd dropped made the room go silent. What. The. Fuck. Seriously? Why the hell had none of us thought to reach out to Casper before this? The man might be retired, but it didn't make him any less a badass.

"Did Torch already speak to Casper?" Badger asked.

"Just so happens, Casper is here visiting. He was going to head to Tennessee to see his granddaughter over at the Reckless Kings after he left here, but he said he can make a stop in Georgia. He's heading out within the hour," Wire said.

"And Specter?" I asked. "Anyone know how to reach him?"

"Casper does," Wire said. "He's already on it. Both men will be in your area later tonight. If they need any backup, do you have men who can help?"

"Yeah, but we don't exactly have a connection to Casper or Specter. Not sure us being there will do much of anything," Badger said. "Farrah might be with Demon, but she's Venom's daughter. Not Torch's. Which means she's not related to Casper. My club being present might escalate things instead of sending these fuckers running, not to mention they may decide to come back once Casper and Specter are gone."

Wire cleared his throat. "I have an idea about that, actually, but you may not like it."

"Hit me with it," Badger said. "At this point, I'm not afraid to say we're desperate. We're a bit out of our depth with these assholes."

"Mariah. Venom's youngest is... Well, she's got a crush on a cop and Venom caught her trying to elope with the guy. He's furious to say the least and has her on lockdown."

Badger scratched his beard. "I'm not sure what the hell that has to do with us. Besides, we already have Farrah. Isn't one of Venom's kids enough?"

"Venom wants to negotiate. Casper will guarantee your problem goes away -- permanently -- *if* one of your men will claim Mariah. I know it's not a connection to Casper himself, but it's more of a you do us a favor we do you one sort of deal. In this case, our favor is that Casper comes to help you out."

Badger's gaze shot over to Demon, who was shaking his head. "Wire, I'm sensing a trap. How old is Mariah?"

"Seventeen."

"Are you fucking kidding me?" Badger demanded. "She's still a kid! How the fuck was she going to elope anyway?"

"Age of consent in Georgia is sixteen. She's finished with high school, and you'll be taking her with Venom's blessing. Well, not *you* but one of your brothers. As to the other, we found a somewhat decent fake ID in her possession. Guess she thought she could get away with it if they went somewhere else, like Vegas or south of the border."

"Beau," Dingo said.

"Did you say Beau?" Wire asked. "Isn't he just a Prospect?"

"We're voting him in. Already promised him a patch. We were waiting until all this crap was over with, but to hell with it." Badger eyed all of us. "All in favor of Beau being patched in raise your hand."

Every hand around the table went up.

"Then it's official. Beau is now a member of the Devil's Fury. Now he just needs a road name, but we can deal with that after the Sons of Vassago are out of here," Badger said.

"I'll talk to Torch and Venom. They may want proof Beau can protect Mariah. Isn't he rather young?" Wire asked.

"Twenty-two," Dingo said. "He may be young, chronologically speaking, but the kid lived a hellish life and grew up fast. I'd trust him with any woman in this club."

Since Beau was the reason Dingo's woman had been repeatedly raped and abused, for him to say such a thing was really fucking huge. If Beau had told us about Meiling sooner, we could have saved her from the foster parents who'd pimped her out.

"I still need to clear it with Torch and Venom. Any other potential victims?" Wire asked.

The room was quiet. Long enough it started to feel awkward. I scanned the table, wondering if anyone would speak up. And if not, how long exactly were we going to wait? Because if Beau was agreeable, I didn't see the issue.

"I'll take her," Savage said.

Hadn't seen that one coming. I eyed Savage and wondered why he'd offer himself up on a platter like that. Far as I knew, he'd never met Mariah. What if he couldn't stand her? Hell, the fact she was being bartered away to another club meant she'd probably arrive here ready to lash out at everyone and run at the first opportunity.

"And who is I?" Wire asked.

"Savage," Badger answered. "Our Treasurer. He's more than a decade older than Mariah. That a problem?"

"No, and since he's an officer, the terms are acceptable. I'll let everyone know, and once your area is safe, Mariah will be hand delivered to her new home," Wire said. "And good luck. You'll need it."

Savage snorted, but he smiled faintly. "Think I can handle her. For the record, I'm not touching her until she's at least eighteen. And agreeable to being touched. She can have a separate room until then."

"Not my concern," Wire said. "She's yours now. You can handle her how you see fit. Just be warned. She'll try to escape and get back to the asshole cop she's crushing on. Venom's about to blow a gasket."

I didn't blame him. I'd heard the VP over at the Reckless Kings ended up claiming a cop's daughter, but since they lived in a different state, it wasn't a huge issue. Although, the dad had shown up to cause some trouble. Venom's kid shacking up with a cop in the same town? Yeah, that wouldn't fly. Even if the Dixie Reapers ran a much cleaner ship these days, I knew their hands were still a bit dirty. None of ours were clean.

"Casper and Specter will need a place to crash. I don't imagine they'll stay longer than one night," Wire said.

"We'll have something for them," Badger said. "And tell them thanks."

He ended the call and leaned back in his chair, looking like he'd just aged ten years. I didn't envy him his position right now. Being the President of a club facing something like an entire group of murderers and rapists? Yeah, not something I'd want to deal with.

"Think that's all we can do for now," Badger said. "Someone get two of the small apartments cleaned up and stocked for our guests. Everyone else, go be with your families, or blow off some steam in some other way. No club whores inside the compound until this is finished, and I don't want anyone outside the gates unless it's a life-or-death reason. If you're single and need to fuck, I suggest you get reacquainted with your hand. Now get the fuck out!"

I stood and made my way to the main area, looking for Glory. I hoped someone informed Alora we didn't need her services after all. With some luck, this would all be over soon, and she'd be safely back in her home. If nothing else, maybe this would give her something new to write about.

Or it could just give her nightmares.

I knew I'd have them for a while, to add to the ones already plaguing me some nights. I had to admit, since Glory had moved in, I hadn't had any episodes. No PTSD flare-ups, no nightmares about what happened over there. I'd slept peacefully, except for the times I'd woken in a cold sweat the past two nights -- since I'd discovered Saul had put a target on her.

"Already done?" Glory asked.

"Yeah. Wire came up with a solution, but we can't implement it just yet. Badger ordered everyone back to their homes. You and Sienna ready?" I looked for our daughter and found her in Doolittle's arms. Considering he had a monkey on his shoulder, I could see why she seemed so happy. Our little girl stared at the monkey with wide eyes while she sucked on her fist. Not once did she reach for the creature, but it was clear she adored the little furry thing. It kept leaning down to inspect her, making noises that had Sienna squealing in delight.

"No," I said, eyeing Glory. "We aren't getting a monkey."

She snorted. "I wasn't going to ask for one. They throw poop."

I stifled a laugh as I watched the monkey and our daughter for another minute. If she liked animals, maybe Doolittle had something more domestic we could adopt. Like a cat or dog. I didn't think we were up for anything exotic.

Glory retrieved Sienna, who put up a fuss over leaving her new furry friend, and we headed out to my truck. I didn't know if I'd be called to back up Casper and Specter later, so I wanted to enjoy what time I had with my girls this afternoon. No one had said whether Casper and Specter would want to strike tonight or wait until morning. Either way, I was thankful we had backup coming our way.

It also made me realize something... our club wasn't quite as fierce as we'd once been. I knew back in the day when Blades had been young, and Grizzly had been newly patched in, the Devil's Fury had been far different than we were now. Good changes, from what I'd heard, but we were weaker. Settling down with families had made us softer. Or perhaps it was the fact we were all getting old enough to want to slow down a bit. I knew our fingers weren't in quite so many pies, as far as the illegal shit went. We had some legit businesses around town, and we'd been discussing opening yet another one.

I couldn't complain. I enjoyed life with the club, and now I had a family. There wasn't much else I could ever want or need. Except to guarantee their safety. We needed to bulk up our security, or possibly patch in more ex-military guys. There was a reason I'd been medically discharged. I wasn't as quick on my feet as I'd once been. I knew men who ran marathons on two prosthetic legs, and I only had one. But kneeling down for long periods, and being stealthy, wasn't as easy as it had been before.

I slowed as I neared the house, noticing Outlaw's truck was pulled up out front. He got out and leaned against the front fender while he waited. I parked in the driveway and leaned over to kiss Glory on the cheek.

"Head inside with Sienna? I need to see what Outlaw wants," I said. In case it was something bad, I didn't want Glory to hear it. Not until I'd decided the best way to tell her. And that was assuming it was anything to do with her.

After she'd gone inside with our daughter, I walked down to meet Outlaw at the street. "Should I be worried you're here when I just saw you in Church? And how the fuck did you beat me to my own damn house?"

"You were too busy watching your daughter try to enchant a monkey." He smiled. Then I noticed the folder in his hand. "Thought you might want this. What you do with it is entirely up to you."

I opened the file and my heart nearly stopped. "Is this what I think it is?"

He nodded. "Lavender decided to work on this while everyone else focused on the Sons of Vassago. There weren't two men that night. There were three. Their names and locations are all there, as well as the footage Lavender was able to unbury. The school saw what happened and conveniently lost the video, claiming the cameras weren't working in that area on the night your woman was attacked. They lied to cover their asses and did a fairly good job of hiding the evidence."

I eyed the men and realized Sienna had the same shaped eyes as one of them. Parker Waite. That was the fucker who'd created Sienna. Fury rolled through me as I eyed the men in the pictures. Boys, really. Men didn't rape women. Only sick fucks would do something so horrific.

"Elena saw what I had," Outlaw said softly. "She got pissed as hell."

I looked up at him. "Why are you telling me that? Is your woman going to track them down and slit their throats or something?"

He gave a short bark of laughter. "Elena? Not likely. No, but she did ask me to make them suffer at least a little. So I drained all their accounts. Bounced the funds a few dozen times to make it impossible to trace, even went through a few offshore banks, and the money is now all pooled together in one safe place. An account under your name."

My eyebrows rose. "My name? Why not Glory's?"

He shrugged. "I didn't know if you'd want to tell her about the men or not. She's suffered so much already. She may not want to know the details. There's an SD card taped to the back of the file. You can insert it into your laptop if you want to see the footage, or you can burn it and throw it away.

"They weren't rich men, so it's not a ton of money. Between their checking and savings, the total came to around thirty thousand. I put it into a money market account so it will hopefully increase over the next eighteen years. With some luck, it will double, possibly more than double by the time Sienna is of age. She can use it to do whatever she wants. College. Buy a car. Start her life wherever she wants."

I folded my arms. "You think I'm letting my little girl go traipsing off far from home? Knowing sick fucks like these three and the Sons of Vassago are out there? Just waiting to get their hands on someone sweet like her? Fuck no!"

Outlaw smiled. "I feel you, brother. I'm not too keen on my daughter running off to start a life either. But it will happen sooner or later."

"Thanks for this," I said, lifting the file. "I'll wait until this other shit is handled and then decide what to do. Glory once said she didn't think she'd want to know what happened that night. I'll leave it up to her. Until then, I'll put this in my safe."

Outlaw got into his truck and pulled away, leaving me holding a small handful of papers that felt like they weighed a ton. One day at a time. Right now, we had other things to take care of. These fuckers could wait.

Chapter Thirteen

Glory

I put Sienna down for a nap and went to the kitchen. I didn't know about Wolf, but I was starving. The meeting had gone longer than I'd expected. A Prospect had made some burgers and fries for everyone, but I'd been too anxious to eat anything. My stomach had been in knots. I still didn't feel settled. I didn't know what was going on, or how the club was going to get rid of the Sons of Vassago. What if Wolf got hurt? What if their plan didn't work and those men still came for me?

I blinked when I realized I'd been staring into the freezer. I shut it and foraged through the cabinets and small pantry, not having any idea what I wanted but I knew we needed to eat. I found a can of chili and some macaroni noodles and decided chili mac would be filling. I boiled the pasta and warmed the can of chili on the stove.

I heard Wolf's steps behind me before his arms circled my waist. He pressed a kiss to the side of my neck, and I leaned back against him.

"I hope chili mac is okay," I said.

"I'll eat whatever you cook. We should probably go to the store again soon. Get some steaks, pork chops, and chicken breasts. Last time most of the fresh stuff at the store was close to expiring, so I couldn't grab much."

"I keep waiting for this nightmare to be over, but part of me worries it never will be," I said. "What if they don't leave? Will I be trapped in the house forever?"

His hold on me tightened. "No, you won't be. The club has ties to the Dixie Reapers. It's part of why

Tank knew what we were doing with the clinic. Demon's woman is the daughter of the Dixie Reapers VP."

"What do the Dixie Reapers have do with any of this?" I asked, turning to face him.

"Their President is married to an assassin's daughter. Casper VanHorne is feared by a lot of men around the globe," Wolf said. "And he's coming here to help us, as well as another man who goes by Specter."

"And they're going to help just because Demon is married to Venom's daughter?"

He shrugged and his gaze darted away. Okay, so maybe Demon wasn't married to her. I knew being an old lady was enough for some of the women I'd met both here and at the Dixie Reapers. Not all of them required a wedding ring.

"Not exactly," he said. "Venom's other daughter will be coming here. And moving in with Savage."

I couldn't recall which one was Savage, but I hadn't been around the men of the club very much. Only those who had old ladies, which meant Savage was probably single. I narrowed my eyes at Wolf. "Why is she moving in with Savage? And why will they only help if she does?"

"Dammit, Glory. The club doesn't work the same way as the world out there," he said, waving a hand in the general direction of town. "Venom needs her protected and tied to a club far enough away from his own that she'll stay away from temptation. A cop. She's chasing after a badge, and the VP isn't pleased. Just stay out of it, please. It's not our business. It's between Savage and Mariah. They'll work it out."

I backed up, pulling away from him. "It's not okay, Wolf. If she doesn't want to be with him and she's forced to --"

I didn't get to finish my words before he'd growled and advanced on me, backing me to the counter. Fury lit his eyes and anger rolled off him in waves. All right, so I'd said the wrong thing. My pulse pounded, but I knew he wouldn't hurt me. Not physically anyway. I had a feeling I was about to receive a verbal lashing, though.

"You think anyone in this club would rape a woman? You think Savage would hold her down and force himself on her?" Wolf snarled. "Is that what you think of me too?"

"What?" My eyes went wide, and I reached for him. "Wolf, no! I didn't... I don't know what I meant. It just hit me wrong that she's being forced to move in with him."

"He won't touch her, Glory. Not until she's ready and wants him to, but she'll be his either way. It's what Venom wants. Mariah grew up with the Dixie Reapers. It's the only life she's ever known. It won't come as shock to her when her dad arranges for her to belong to someone else. She had to know it was coming when she defied him and tried to elope with a cop."

"I'm sorry." I reached up to cup his cheek. "I didn't mean to offend you, Wolf, or anyone else. I didn't understand what you meant. I'm still learning, and I'll make mistakes along the way."

He closed his eyes and blew out a breath. "I know. I didn't mean to scare you or come at you like that. I'm an asshole. You called me Wolf. I hate it when you do that."

I couldn't help but smile. "Sometimes you can be an asshole, but you're mine and I'm yours. We're going to disagree and fight from time to time, Max. And calling you Wolf seemed appropriate at that moment because you weren't my Max just then. You were every inch the predator."

"You're never my prey, Glory. You're my woman. My wife. My equal." He kissed me, soft and slow. "I think you're burning the chili."

I gasped and faced the stove, hurrying to stir both pots. It looked done so I drained the noodles, then plated them and smothered them with chili. Wolf handed me a bag of shredded cheese to top it with. We'd just started eating when I heard a giggle outside the kitchen window. I glanced that way, wondering if we were about to have company, and nearly choked on my bite of food.

"Um, Max. Is that… Alora?" I asked.

He looked out the kitchen window and started laughing. "Looks like she's decided to have some fun."

"There are kids in the compound," I murmured, watching as she streaked from yard to the next, losing clothes as she went. "Who is that chasing her?"

"That would be Colorado. Good for him." Wolf went back to eating, ignoring the two as they ran through the compound, now nearly naked, like they hadn't a care in the world.

"Think they'll end up together?" I asked.

"I guess it's possible, but Colorado doesn't seem ready to settle. And I'm not sure she's the type who could hold him for long. They're probably just enjoying each other's company."

I couldn't wrap my mind around being with some random guy like that. She hadn't met Colorado until today and they were going to sleep together? Being so much younger than my peers all through school, and then being raped, had skewed my view of things. I knew if it weren't for Wolf, it would still be me and Sienna with no man in our lives. If Alora could be with Colorado for a one-night stand, or short fling, then I envied her. It wasn't something I could have ever done. I'd told myself it was what I'd settle for with Wolf, but I'd been wrong. If he'd walked away from me, especially after we'd been intimate, it would have shattered me.

Wolf reached over and took my hand. "Hey, she'll be okay. He won't hurt her."

"I know. I was thinking I'd never been like that. So carefree and open. I envy her a bit. Even though I did end up right where I belong." I smiled at him. "With you."

"Love you, Glory."

"I love you too. So much."

"Our girl is sleeping," he pointed out. "How about we go wash off the ugliness of the day? I'll wash your back if you wash mine."

I set my fork down. "Together? How…"

"There's a bench in the shower for a reason. I usually hop into the shower, literally, and wash quickly. Sometimes I sit on the bench and let the water soothe any aches when I can't manage to get in and out of the tub. There's a prosthetic leg you can wear in the shower. I've looked into it, but I haven't decided to cough up the money for it yet. The one I'd need is around twenty thousand, and since it's considered non-essential, I'd have to pay out of pocket for it."

"We'll start a fund for it," I said. "Might take a while, but we'll save the money, Max. If it will make things easier for you, then I want you to have it."

"Come on, beautiful. Let's go shower. We can talk about finances later. Much later."

I let him lead me to the bathroom and I started the shower. I let him get in first, watching as he hopped over to the bench and sat down. I didn't know how he didn't slip and fall. His heated gaze watched every move I made as I stripped out of my clothes and got into the shower with him. After I soaked my hair and body, I reached for his shower gel and worked up a lather in my hands. I spread the soap over his chest and shoulders, making my way down his body. His cock jerked in my grasp as I gave it a stroke.

"Playing with fire," he said.

"I know, but it's fun." I kissed him as my hands explored. When I'd washed all of him I could reach, I took down the detachable shower nozzle and rinsed him off.

"My turn." He picked up my shower gel and motioned for me to come closer. I stopped between his splayed thighs and shivered as his fingers ran over my skin. By the time he'd soaped every inch of me, I was ready to beg him to fuck me.

I rinsed the soap from my body and let him tug me closer still. Wolf lifted me and settled me across his lap so that I straddled him. When he lowered me, I felt his cock brush against my pussy, and I held onto his shoulders. We hadn't done it this way yet. What if I was terrible at it?

"Easy, baby," Wolf murmured. "Just do what feels good."

I nodded and lowered myself onto his cock. He stroked my clit as I slid down his length, moaning at how full I felt. "Max. I…"

"I've got you." He leaned forward and took my nipple into his mouth, sucking on the peak. I cried out and my hips jerked. The sensation was overwhelming and soon I was riding him without even realizing it.

My body seemed to know exactly what to do. "That's it. Come for me, Glory."

I moved faster, my hips having a mind of their own as I rode Wolf. It didn't take long for me to come. I cried out his name as he gripped my hips and thrust up into me, hard and deep. He growled and I felt the heat of his release.

"I think we both needed that," Wolf said.

"I'm not the one who pulled away," I pointed out.

He kissed me, holding me closer. "I know. I promise I'll make it up to you."

I trailed my finger down his chest. "Right now?"

"Mmm. I think I created a monster. What does my beautiful wife have in mind?"

"Sienna will sleep a while longer. Why don't we take this to the bedroom?" I suggested, knowing it would be more comfortable for Wolf.

"Then you better clean yourself up because I got you dirty." He grinned. "Then get your ass on the bed. When I get in there, I expect to find you on your knees. Ass in the air. Thighs spread."

My clit pulsed and my nipples got even harder. I climbed off Wolf's lap, cleaned our mingled release off me, and hurried to the bedroom. When he joined me, I was in exactly the position he'd demanded, eagerly waiting.

"You'd mentioned having a small vibrator," he said. "So I ordered a few things online the next morning. They arrived yesterday. Feeling adventurous?"

"With you?" I glanced at him over my shoulder. "Of course."

He tossed a small bag onto the bed beside me and a bottle of lube. I felt the mattress dip under his weight and the heat of his body curve over mine. Wolf placed his lips by my ear and lowered his voice to a sexy growl. "Can't have you screaming and waking Sienna. You going to be good and muffle all that yelling you do when you come?"

"I-I-I… Max, I don't know how to do that. What if I can't?"

He reached into the bag and dropped something in front of me. I stared, not quite comprehending what it was. What did he intend to do with a length of cloth? Until… "Is that… a gag?"

"A nice, soft material to make sure you keep quiet," he said. "You scream and we'll be trying it out."

My pussy clenched and I wondered what sort of beast he'd unleashed inside me. Before Wolf, I'd have never contemplated such a thing. Not even when I'd lain in bed at night, alone and a virgin, had I ever thought I'd let a man do something like gag me. What else did he have planned?

A length of white, silky rope landed on the bed next to the gag. "How much do you trust me?"

"With my life," I admitted.

"I'm going to tie you up, Glory." His nose traced the shell of my ear. "You okay with that?"

"We can try," I said, not knowing how I'd react since I'd never done anything like that before.

He kissed my neck, then my shoulder. "That's all I ask, baby. Try it and see. If you can't handle it or don't like it, we'll stop, and I won't tie you up ever again. I like the thought of you helpless. Unable to do anything but take all the pleasure I'm going to give you."

His words lit a fire inside me and I felt my pussy get so slick the wetness slid down my thighs. He wound the rope around the headboard, then wrapped the length around my wrists, binding them together and stretching them over my head. I tugged and realized I couldn't break free.

I heard a soft buzzing and tried to see what he'd picked up next, but I couldn't. Not with the way he'd positioned himself. "What's that?"

"You'll find out in a moment."

He worked his hand under my body, and I felt something vibrate against my nipple. I arched my back as pleasure shot through me. "Max!"

"Ah-ah. Remember what I said? You make a bunch of noise and I'll have to gag you."

I knew I was about to lose the battle of keeping quiet. He rubbed the vibrator over one nipple, then the other. It set off a small orgasm that made me cry out again and he took the toy away. He sighed, sounding aggrieved, even though I could feel the excitement in the air. He'd hoped I wouldn't be able to stay silent!

"Open up, Glory," he said, holding the cloth in front of me. I parted my lips, and he slipped the material between them before tying it behind my head. "Not too tight?"

I shook my head, unable to answer him verbally.

Wolf ran his hand down my spine, then I felt the vibrator against my clit. I thrashed and screamed against the gag, coming immediately and so hard I nearly saw stars. Wolf didn't let up. It felt like my orgasm was never-ending, and my body still cried out for more. He slid the toy away from my clit and plunged it inside me, thrusting it in and out.

"Got to get it nice and wet," he said.

I heard a *snick* and felt something cold slip down the crack of my ass, making me jolt. Wolf soothed me, running his hand over me while he teased me with the toy. When he pulled it free and worked it between my ass cheeks, it felt like my heart stopped a moment. Was he about to do what I thought he was? He teased me with the vibrator before slowly easing it inside me.

My thighs shook and I lifted my ass higher. God, it felt... strange but good.

"That's it. So pretty. You like that, don't you?" he asked.

I nodded.

He thrust the toy in and out, slow and deep until I thought I'd lose my mind. My pussy felt empty, and I wanted to come again. I whimpered and wiggled, wanting to beg for more. He plunged the toy deep and leaned over me, his body trapping the toy so it wouldn't slide out. I felt his cock press against me and soon he was filling my pussy. I threw my head back, nearly sobbing with how incredible I felt. Between the toy and his cock, I was so full, and the buzzing sensation was almost too much.

Wolf fucked me. Slow. Deep. He took his time, teasing me. Bringing me close to the edge only to back off again. All it took was one swipe of his finger over my clit and it felt like I broke into a million pieces. Stars burst across my vision and I couldn't breathe, the pleasure was so intense. Wolf pounded into me and I felt the hot splashes of his release as he drove his cock into me again and again.

"Fuck!" He roared as he slammed into me three more times, then held still, filling me up and panting for breath. He worked the gag free and pressed his head to my shoulder. "Damn, Glory. That was... incredible. You okay?"

I nodded. "Yeah."

My pussy clenched on him and my clit felt like my heartbeat had moved down there. He groaned and thrust into me a few more times before pulling out.

"We didn't even get to the other toys I'd bought. We'll have to try them soon. If you react the way you did to these, then we'll need someone to watch Sienna for the night because I'm going to make you come for hours."

I groaned. "Max, you're going to break me. Is death by orgasm a thing?"

He chuckled. "No. You'll survive, but you may be walking funny the next day. Your pussy and ass will be sore, but it will be the good kind."

I sighed. "I think we need another shower."

He kissed my shoulder, my cheek, then claimed my lips. "No. I want my cum on you the rest of the night. Besides, I plan on fucking you again later."

He pulled the toy from my ass and tossed it aside. After he untied me, he pulled me into his arms and held me. It wasn't long before I managed to fall asleep, even though sunlight still streamed through the windows.

Chapter Fourteen

Wolf

Casper and Specter had arrived two hours ago and had already managed to set up a meeting with the Sons of Vassago. We'd agreed to meet in a clearing down the highway after nightfall. Away from town and prying eyes. I stood behind the two men, along with Badger, Savage, Beau, and Demon. Saul Sanders came into view with three other men. I recognized one from the videos. The man he'd been fucking.

"What's this about, Mr. VanHorne?" Saul asked as he stopped a few feet away. His gaze scanned over our group, lingering a moment on Specter. Was it my imagination or had he paled a little? "This isn't your territory."

Casper gave a humorless laugh. "My territory? Boy, who the fuck do you think you're speaking to?"

Saul lifted his chin, but I noticed his hand trembled a little at his side. This fucker was seriously scared of Casper VanHorne. If the assassin weren't on our side, I'd probably be the one ready to piss myself.

"The Sons of Vassago have had a foothold in this area for years," Saul said.

"About that." Casper took a step closer to him. "Do you see the men behind me? The Devil's Fury?"

Saul nodded. "What of them? They're a bunch of pussies."

Savage laughed. It was a dark sound that made chills run down my spine as he stepped up beside Casper. "You think I'm a pussy?"

Saul straightened to his full height, which was still shorter than Casper and Savage by a few inches. "Yes. We've been here for years and you've done nothing."

"You targeted one of their women," Casper said. "Trashed their clinic. Killed the doctor helping them. I'm afraid I can't look the other way."

"Why do you care?" Saul asked.

Casper tipped his head to the side. "The man beside me is Savage. He's an officer in the Devil's Fury club, but more importantly, he's claimed my granddaughter's friend. One of the men behind me has ties to me as well. His woman is my granddaughter's best friend. Both women are the daughters of the Dixie Reapers VP, and as most people know, my daughter is their President's wife. So you see, the Devil's Fury are my family."

Saul glanced at us, his gaze lingering on Specter. "And him?"

Specter smile. "I'm just here for some fun. You like playing, right? I saw your video. Sloppy work. Don't worry. I'll be happy to show you how it's done. Seems only fair since the Sons raped, tortured, and murdered my daughter."

Saul definitely lost some color and motioned for his men to back up. "We didn't realize our presence was a threat to your family, Mr. VanHorne. We will stop looking for the woman from the clinic."

Specter moved closer, not making a fucking sound even as he stepped on leaves and twigs. "You'll do more than that. You'll move your pansy-ass cult. We don't want you in this state. In fact, we don't want you anywhere in the south, east, or mid-west. If we hear you've set up shop anywhere near any club we consider family or allies, we'll both be coming for you."

Saul's hands shook and he looked ready to piss himself. "Mr. Specter, with all due respect, I was unaware your daughter had been taken by my brothers."

Specter snarled. "I don't give a shit if you knew. The result was the same."

Saul turned to his men, only to discover they'd backed up so far he was left facing our group alone. And it seemed the big, bad man who could torture women wasn't so tough when faced with a bunch of men.

"And if we don't agree to your terms?" Saul asked.

Now that took some balls. He'd just told Specter and Casper to fuck off, just not in so many words. I grinned, pulling a knife from where I'd strapped it to my thigh. I had a gun with me, but I wanted to get up close and personal for this one. I wanted these fuckers to suffer. Looked like I'd get to blow off some steam after all. I heard each of my brothers arming themselves and knew we were going to have a bit of fun with these fuckers. And since they'd been given an out and not taken it, even the sick fucks they called family and friends wouldn't be coming to settle the score. Not after they found out what we'd done to these assholes. I had no idea how Casper and Specter planned to make sure no other Sons came this way, but I knew they'd have something up their sleeves. Some way to guarantee this town, and our women, would be safe.

Casper let out a whistle and that was all it took. We advanced on the men, with Casper and Specter going for Saul. As much as I'd wanted him for myself, I focused on the others who were trying to escape. Beau had run around behind them and worked on herding them back toward us. Savage took the right flank and ran at them, ready to do some damage. Demon and I took the one in the middle. I sank my knife into the fucker's gut as Demon slammed a set of brass knuckles into his jaw. Once we had him on the ground, Demon pounded the little shit, breaking as many bones as he could. The video I'd seen still fresh in my mind, I worked on exacting the same savagery on the asshole in front of me. I took his fingers. His ears. And any other parts I had access to.

Blood soaked the ground as all got justice for the sweet doc who'd lost her life, and all the others these bastards had tortured and killed. We made the men scream. Beg. It didn't matter. We weren't granting them any mercy. I watch as Beau pounded a guy so hard his face looked like raw hamburger, and his swings weren't slowing even a little.

Casper and Specter had Saul on the ground. I noticed the glow of a phone screen and heard the little bitch sobbing as he spoke to someone on the other end of the line. The man on the ground in front of me had stopped breathing. Demon had moved on to get revenge on the others, and I stood to make my way over to Casper and Specter. I held back, not want to overstep. Instead, I decided to enjoy the show.

My blood pounded and adrenaline raced through me as I watched how brutal the two assassins were. I saw Badger filming the two of them and knew it would be a message to any other Sons of Vassago. They weren't welcome here, and the same fate would befall any who dared step foot in our territory, or any other areas now under the protection of Casper and Specter.

When Saul had given his last gurgled breath, and the life had drained from his eyes, the other men were no longer recognizable as human, we all gathered in the center of the field.

"I'll take care of the cleanup and delivery," Specter said.

"Delivery?" Badger asked.

Specter nodded to the phone. "I'll need that video footage, but I'll also be sending a few pieces to some key figures in the Sons of Vassago. Not just stateside, but around the globe. It's time to send a message. One they won't forget."

"Why are you doing this?" I asked. "I mean, helping us. You don't have any connection to our club, and as far I know, you aren't connected to Casper."

"Like I told the asshole earlier, the Sons of Vassago are responsible for the murder of my daughter. She was thirteen, and I'd thought I'd hidden her well. Maybe too well. No one knew she was mine. I've been biding my time. When Casper told me what was going on here and that he needed help with the Sons, I knew it was my chance to get my revenge." Specter stared at the remains of Saul Sanders. "This fucker wasn't the one who hurt her, but I know who did. I'll be paying them a visit in person."

Casper eyed our small group. "Everyone go clean up and head home. I'll stay with Specter until the cleanup is handled. Then we'll crash at the compound tonight and head out first thing in the morning."

Specter shook his head. "I'll sleep on the plane. I have a jet on standby. I'm done waiting."

Casper clapped him on the back and Badger motioned for us to head out. I wasn't about to go home covered in blood and gore. Thankfully, we'd all stashed a set of clothes at the clubhouse in case things ended up getting a bit gruesome. Each of us showered and changed, had a beer to unwind after the massacre, and then went home.

I knew Glory would ask what had happened tonight. I'd made sure my shirt was identical to the one I'd left in. The blood-soaked one would be burned, along with the other clothes we'd removed. Nothing would be left but ash, and even that would be disposed of. Nothing would tie us to the night's bloodshed. Our cuts had been soaked in blood so many times before. A little more wouldn't change anything. They'd be cleaned by professionals. Hell, as good as Casper and Specter were, I doubted anyone would know those men had been killed in that field.

The lights were on when I pulled up outside the house. I'd known Glory would wait up for me. I took a breath and went inside, hoping she wouldn't take one look and know what I'd done tonight. I should have known better.

She opened the door before I could even grip the knob, staring up at me with worry and relief. She threw her arms around me and breathed in deep, then stepped back, her brow furrowed. She looked up at my hair, touching the wet strands, and I cursed myself for not thinking to make sure it was dry first.

"What did you do?" she asked.

I went inside, shutting and locking the door behind me. "You really want to know?"

"Yes, I think I do." She led me to the couch and sat, tugging me down next to her. "Are they gone? Did you kill them?"

"I took a shower, Glory. What do you think?"

She leaned against me. "I think you had to wash the blood off you. Thank you."

I jerked my gaze toward her in surprise. "What?"

"Thank. You. Did I suddenly start speaking in tongues?"

"Smart-ass," I muttered. "No, but why are you thanking me? I killed a man tonight, Glory, and watched as the others were slaughtered. Those men didn't go easy. They suffered. We made sure of it."

"Good." She gave a slight nod. "Maybe they hurt as much as Amelia did. At any rate, you made sure they won't be raping or killing anyone ever again. That doesn't make you a bad man, Max. It makes you a hero."

I kissed the top of her head and held her close. "You're an odd one, Glory. But you're mine."

"Is it wrong I'm glad you killed them?" she asked.

"No. A little bloodthirsty maybe, but that just makes you perfect. A Devil's Fury old lady should have some fire in her veins. You're strong. Beautiful." I paused and looked down at her. "Perfect. I didn't think you'd be able to handle the darkness I hide inside me. Glory, I didn't just slaughter that man. I liked it."

I took a breath and looked away, trying to gather my thoughts. She reached up, her fingers brushing my chin, bringing my focus back to her. "Max, you don't have to hide any part of yourself from me. I accept all of you."

"Even the ugliness? There's a monster locked down tight, Glory. I don't let him out often, but tonight... he got a free pass. I liked the smell of the blood in the air. Got a thrill over hearing their screams as they begged for mercy. I... I'm a killer."

She shook her head. "No, you're a protector, Max. Sometimes that means getting your hands dirty, to make sure other people stay safe. You aren't going to go off and kill a bunch of innocents. There's a difference. Those men deserved what they got, and so much more. I'm not scared of you, or ashamed. I'm *proud* of you."

I swallowed hard and held her tight. I didn't know what I'd ever done to warrant having the love of a woman like Glory, but I'd thank the fates every day for sending her to me. She was the light to my darkness. An angel. I smiled faintly. Maybe an avenging angel since she'd been okay with me slaughtering that man. Although, could I really consider him a man with all the evil he'd done? I wasn't sure he'd even had a soul.

That sobered me a moment. The men we'd killed tonight weren't the only bastards out there who hurt women. And I needed to tell Glory I knew who'd hurt her. I'd let the decision be hers. I could burn the file, show it to her, or hold onto it for safekeeping. Whatever she decided, I'd stand by her.

"There's something I need to tell you," I said.

"What?"

"It's about the night you were attacked on campus." She lifted her head to hold my gaze. "Lavender, Wire's woman, is a hacker like her old man. She found the video the campus had hidden of what happened that night. I have the faces, names, and addresses of the men who hurt you. And I'm pretty sure I know which one is Sienna's sperm donor."

She pulled away and ran a hand through her hair. "Why are you telling me this? And why now? You had to know before tonight."

"Outlaw gave me the file earlier. I'd planned to sit on it for a bit, but I decided after everything that happened tonight, we need a fresh start. How can we begin our lives with one more ominous cloud hanging over us?" I asked. "But I won't do anything you don't want me to do."

"Are you asking if you can kill them?" she asked.

"Not exactly, but I'll do it if you want me to." I didn't reach for her, even though I wanted to. I could tell she was sorting through her feelings and weighing her options.

"How many?" she asked softly.

"Three." My throat felt tight as I watched the pain flicker in her eyes. "The school hid the evidence, which means someone there knew. All this time. It's why they paid you off. They knew once you signed something and took the money, they'd be in the clear."

Her hands fisted and her lips thinned. "I want them to pay. All of them. The school. The three boys who raped me."

"Outlaw drained the three rapists' accounts. He put the money into a money market under my name with the intention of Sienna having it later when she's old enough for college or whatever she wants to do. Travel. Buy a place of her own." I did reach for her then, pulling her into my arms. "Tell me what you want, beautiful, and I'll make it happen. But after tonight, this is done. We don't have to ever speak of it again. I'll burn the damn file and we'll move on."

She nodded. "Make their lives hell. And if you find evidence they've hurt other women, I want them in jail."

"Jail?"

Her eyes went dark as she stared at me. "Bad things happen in jail, right? I don't care how it happens. I want them to suffer the way they've made me and other girls suffer. I doubt I was their only victim."

"Consider it done," I said. I pulled out my phone and messaged Outlaw with Glory's wishes.

I'll take care of it.

That was all I needed to know. I showed her the message from Outlaw and some of the fight drained from her. "The school... they need to pay too."

"We'll use the footage to make them toe the line. They don't have to know it's from you. It can be a concerned citizen who stumbled across it. We'll figure it out. Or rather, the club will. Your only job from this point forward is to live a full and happy life."

She kissed me, her lips soft against mine. "I found my happily-ever-after the night you claimed me. Anything else will just be a bonus."

I stood and lifted Glory into my arms. I was done with the ugliness of the world tonight. I planned to spend the rest of my waking hours making love to the beautiful woman who'd captured my heart. An angel had been dropped in my lap, and I'd gladly spend the rest of my life making sure she, and our daughter, were happy and knew they were loved. Because they were my entire world. As long as I had them, I didn't need anything or anyone else.

Epilogue

Glory
One Month Later

I stared at the stick in my hand and felt like my stomach was doing flips. Moment of truth. Wolf had said he would be fine either way, but I could tell he really wanted another baby. He adored Sienna, but he'd missed the first year of her life. I clutched the pregnancy test in my hand and went to find my husband. He'd stretched out on the living room floor with our daughter, smiling as they rolled a ball back and forth.

"Max." He didn't look up immediately, but when he did, he struggled to get to his feet and came to me.

"What's wrong?" he asked.

"Nothing. I think." I held up the stick. "Unless you don't want to be a daddy again. Because this says we're pregnant."

He stared at me, then the test before letting out a *whoop* and lifting me into his arms. He spun me before he stumbled, and we nearly went down. Sienna giggled at us and threw the ball. It bounced off Wolf's head, making him laugh.

"I think the doctors didn't know what they were talking about. Clearly our girl is going to be a softball or basketball star. Delayed development, my ass!" He smiled at me tenderly. "And now she's going to be a big sister. You okay with all this?"

I nodded. "Yeah, I am. The clinic on Main Street called this morning. They said I can get my hours in there. I'll be done before I'm so far along I won't be comfortable standing for long."

"Then everything is working out, baby." He kissed me. "Our family is growing, and you're realizing your dream of becoming a nurse. I'm so fucking proud of you."

"There's just one other thing. I have a question. I know we said we'd never speak of it again but… a large amount of cash appeared in our account today. Know anything about it?" I asked.

He rubbed the short beard that he'd started growing a week ago. "Maybe. I'd hoped you wouldn't notice."

I rolled my eyes. "Max, over half a million dollars just appeared overnight. You thought I'd miss that? I'm not blind. Or stupid."

"Never said you were. In fact, you're a little too observant and smart." He led me to the couch and sat, tugging me down onto his lap. "Outlaw convinced your school to cough up more money, and he's making them put in better security around campus. He gave them a plan to follow, and if they take one step out of line, then he leaks the story to the media. The college covering up a rape isn't going to help their bottom line any. So they're meeting every demand. The money was his way of making them admit they'd done wrong by you."

"As much as I want to throw it in their faces, I'm not going to pass up that kind of money. We could do so much with it, but the first thing we're buying is that prosthetic you need for taking a shower. And no arguments!"

He kissed me, his hand wandering down to smack my ass. "Love you, Glory. You're always taking care of me."

I leaned in closer and dropped my voice to a whisper. "Oh, I plan on taking care of you. Just as soon as Sienna takes a nap. And Max? I've heard pregnant women get really horny. Be prepared for me to want your cock all the time. I may not have felt the urges last time because of what I'd been through, but now that I know about toe-curling orgasms, all bets are off. I'll constantly be reaching for your zipper."

His eyes sparkled with mirth. "It's yours for the taking. Any time. Any day. Anywhere."

My life had been far from easy, but somehow it had put me on the right path. Because I had no doubt that I was meant to be here with Wolf. He was charming, sweet, an amazing father to Sienna, gave me mind-blowing orgasms, and had a protective streak a mile wide. I couldn't imagine spending my life with anyone else.

Thank you! Whoever brought us together, thank you a million times over.

I cuddled in his arms and soaked up all the love and warmth. Our house would never be like the one I'd grown up in. We'd give Sienna a life of love and happiness. Acceptance. And no matter what happened, we'd always be there for her. I placed a hand over my belly. For both of them.

My Prince Charming rode a Harley and liked to get his hands bloody from time to time, but he was mine and that was all that mattered. I only hoped one day my sweet Sienna would find someone who would accept her, flaws and all, and only see perfection when he looked at her. As long as she had love, she'd never need anything else. With Wolf's love, I knew I could face anything life threw our way, and I wanted that for my children. Happiness, love, and acceptance. Those were the tools they needed. Everything else was just… extra.

Harley Wylde

Harley Wylde is the International Bestselling Author of the Dixie Reapers MC, Devil's Boneyard MC, and Hades Abyss MC series. When Harley's writing, her motto is the hotter the better -- off the charts sex, commanding men, and the women who can't deny them. If you want men who talk dirty, are sexy as hell, and take what they want, then you've come to the right place. She doesn't shy away from the dangers and nastiness in the world, bringing those realities to the pages of her books, but always gives her characters a happily-ever-after and makes sure the bad guys get what they deserve.

The times Harley isn't writing, she's thinking up naughty things to do to her husband, drinking copious amounts of Starbucks, and reading. She loves to read and devours a book a day, sometimes more. She's also fond of TV shows and movies from the 1980's, as well as paranormal shows from the 1990's to today, even though she'd much rather be reading or writing. You can find out more about Harley or enter her monthly giveaway on her website. Be sure to join her newsletter while you're there to learn more about discounts, signing events, and other goodies!

Harley at Changeling: changelingpress.com/harley-wylde-a-196

Changeling Press E-Books

More Sci-Fi, Fantasy, Paranormal, and BDSM adventures available in e-book format for immediate download at ChangelingPress.com -- Werewolves, Vampires, Dragons, Shapeshifters and more -- Erotic Tales from the edge of your imagination.

What are E-Books?

E-books, or electronic books, are books designed to be read in digital format -- on your desktop or laptop computer, notebook, tablet, Smart Phone, or any electronic e-book reader.

Where can I get Changeling Press E-Books?

Changeling Press e-books are available at ChangelingPress.com, Amazon, Apple Books, Barnes & Noble, and Kobo/Walmart.

ChangelingPress.com

Printed in Great Britain
by Amazon

34875115R00145